Get E. M. Aguilar's Starter Library for FREE
Sign up for the no spam newsletter and get an introductory novel
and lots more content, for free.
Details can be found at the end of the novel.

THE CALL]

Authors N

The Calling is a work of fiction : Some of the events do occur in real places, but — tain artistic license to have them fit into the plot of the book. I hope you, dear Reader, will forgive me in advance. I hope I would not offend anybody in my pursuit of story-telling and the fictional dream life of this book.

❦

E. M. AGUILAR

Part 1

The Ways Are Open

Hello, dear reader, come with me into a world which is like ours, but it is not ours. A place where, if you came, you would say it is exactly how you remember your dreams to be – those half forgotten truths and fantasies floating in our brain. The moon and the sun will float above us while our life blood spills into the heaven and we will stare into the darkness and proclaim we are alive and we fight the nothingness. Listen.

Interlude 1: the Report

Report 1
From the Desk of the Head Historian of Magical Studies in New California, Jacob Reynolds.

Introduction:

This is a secret informal history of the two year reign of terror after the breaking of the Bastion seals which held the Earth's magic for eons. At this moment in history, nobody had named the time preceding the spilling of magic and I, Professor Jacobs, have gathered historical accounts and important data from the many interviews people have given during that time. I would want to call it the time of the Calling or the Breaking of the Earth, but I don't have a suitable way to express those times except by laying out my research. The next page is an excerpt from a top secret document given to all the Presidents and World Leaders of each country when they take the mantle of Power. My hope for this small report is to clear the time of upheaval and create a lasting record of the events that followed the Great Catastrophe.

** TOP SECRET: FOR YOUR eyes only **

Project Guardian:

To all new government heads of each nation. We, the secret society of the Illuminati, have been the guardians to the Bastions. (See photos in the attached folder).

In the beginning of time, there was real magic. Not the kind magicians use for mere illusions, but the kind where powerful individuals used to manipulate and control the forces of nature, time and space. In each of your lands and the lands of the other countries, Bastions held these magics underground in a controlled area, away from the general public and from prying eyes. It was necessary to guard these magics because the powers held by the Bastions could enslave or destroy our world and peace would never have reigned (See history section attached in a separate folio) for example, the Dark Ages.

We, the Illuminati, were given the task to guard the Bastions by the true magical beings of our world, the elves. Yes, elves are real, but they do not live among us (see the Great Purge). You will understand this information is Top Secret and can never be divulged to anybody, including your spouse, parents or other relatives...

⁌⁌⁌

THE EXCERPT ABOVE WAS added to this file to show the absolute secrecy Project Guardian had before the breaking of the seals and how these Bastions that are now merely relics were part of our history. The next series of works are interviews gathered by individuals, found in the archives of the Historical College in New California.

Breaking of the Seals: Survivors

Interview 1

Survivor: Marla Helms.

Interviewer: John Haskins.

Digital Audio: Recorded two years after the Breaking of the Bastions

John: How did you survive the Breaking of the Bastions? It is fine to talk here. Nobody will come after you.

Marla: Are you sure? An agent of the new government came to me and threatened me if I talk.

John: That was the old regime. We now want to record the stories of the survivors. This will be confidential. (The sounds of rustling paper.) Marla, you were a nurse at Los Angeles Memorial Hospital.

Marla: Yes, I was covering the morning shift when he came in.

John: Please state what you are doing now.

Marla: I am now the principal teacher at Water Dynamics and Magics at the Magical Studies Center.

John: Thank you. Describe the Alpha.

Marla: He didn't look like much. The police brought him in and placed him in the mental ward for violent individuals. That was my station. He was sedated and was malnourished. We gave him fluids and medicine for schizophrenia, clozapine. I administered the medicine.

John: Did you know he was the Alpha when you saw him?

Marla: No, the Alpha didn't look like much. He was a bum, a man living on the streets. He was also going through a schizophrenic episode. He was shouting about his quest and such.

John: This was on Day Zero, the day of devastation.

Marla: Yes, I remember while I was working, watching on TV the giant wave that came toward us. We thought, I mean the hospital staff, the giant wave would not reach us since we were inland. But it did. I was checking on the patients and making my rounds when the wave hit. I was one of the lucky ones.

John: Because your magic manifested at that moment.

Marla: Yes, but it didn't happen at first. I was thrown by the first wave. But there was another wave behind it. The first wave hit the hospital and everything went black. I found myself floating in a pocket of water. People and things were all around me.

John: We have read that magics manifest after a tragic event.

Marla: Yes, I thought I was dying and then something changed. I felt strong and powerful. I awoke on the ground far away from the hospital. John: (Sounds of rustling paper) You saw your first Grog around that same time.

Marla: Yes, but I must have been unconscious for several hours because it was dusk. I remember the taste of the seawater in my mouth. I couldn't describe how I felt. Too many things have happened.

John: Your magic manifested with the death of your colleagues and friends.

Marla: I believe in God and have been a practicing Catholic since I was a child, but at that moment I felt betrayed. God existed. I was sure about that. Yet he was laughing at me and my plight. So when I saw the bodies I almost cried.

John: So your belief system was questioned? This is where you saw your first transformation.

Marla: Yes, the man was a few feet away from me. He was still breathing. I quickly went over to him to try CPR. But when I pushed him over he suddenly stood up and contorted violently. I thought he was in shock and I tried to make him sit, but the man trembled all over and transformed. The man said over and over the word, Grog. This is when I knew I was in hell. The man turned into a large hideous beast. Heck, all the bodies around me started to change. Some of the people changed into large wolves and others changed into insects. They attacked me and I merely reacted. My powers came forth. I destroyed the creatures with water magic.

John: Did you know the Alpha was near you?

Marla: No. I was trying to survive. If I knew he was close, I would have gone to him. He would have saved me like he saved the others.

John: What do you miss of the old world?

Marla: Technology, air conditioning, cell phones. You name it. Soda.

Chapter 1

Lazarus stood at the office window gazing at the brightness of the morning sun. On his wrist was a silver bracelet that featured a large black opal gemstone. His coworkers sat in their cubicles, focused on the keyboards and not noticing how long he stood there.

Lazarus could hear the sweetest tune in his head, playing over and over. He touched the gemstone, remembering finding the box waiting for him when he got home from work yesterday. It didn't have a return address or a note and when he opened it he found a black leather box. Inside the box, nestled in black satin, was the bracelet he was now wearing.

A sunbeam dazzled him and for a brief second he sensed something calling him. It was the sweet tune of a thousand bells, each twinkling in unison, creating a cascade of music that played endlessly in his mind.

"Lazarus? Are you ok?"

He turned to see his manager looking at him. "I'm fine. It's been really hot the last few days."

"Yes, are you coming down with something?" She made a move toward him.

"No, I'll be fine."

He almost asked her if she heard the sweet music, but instead tore his eyes away from the sun and walked over to his desk. His computer screen saver was on, showing bubbles floating over the screen. He sank onto his chair, ignoring the squeak of protest it gave.

Lazarus was fast approaching middle age. His once black hair was now peppered with gray. He had been with this pharmaceutical company for several years now, working in the accounting department. He was in charge of the accounts and vendors, making sure shipments and payments were in order. It was more bookkeeping than accounting.

He started working on his spreadsheets checking and rechecking his figures and invoices but was distracted by the opal on the bracelet that had started to glow and pulsate. He took it off and placed it on his desk, looking around to make sure his coworkers hadn't noticed anything.

He couldn't stop thinking about the opal, it had become a beacon to his memories. He tried to concentrate on his work, but his mind drifted to his life and why he ended up here. He thought about high school and the girl he was madly in love with. Her name was Yvonne, a haughty Latin girl with light skin and long wavy brown hair.

Lazarus was too shy to talk to her, much less ask her out on a date. He was a short, gawky kid, who always talked to his best friends, George and Cindy. He never ventured out and talked to other people. He graduated high school never talking to Yvonne. The last thing he remembered, Yvonne was having her second baby and was happily married to a man she met in college.

He had a few girlfriends, of course, when he attended the California State Long Beach College. He got a degree in accounting, but never took the CPA test. He felt it was a waste of time. Now, he wished he had done things differently and taken that CPA test, and got married.

He felt his life was a series of moments that went nowhere, like his current job. Lazarus was adrift. He never wanted to push himself to make his situation better by getting that promotion, trying to get his CPA or talk to the girl he loved.

He couldn't breathe and was beginning to shake. Jumping up, he walked towards the break room. As he walked down the hallway his vision blurred, as though he had rubbed his eyes. He lifted his arm and saw the bracelet on his wrist. The opal was no longer glowing but he barely noticed. He was trying to remember putting that bracelet back on, and could not.

Lazarus saw the door to the break room in front of him. He shook his head. What was happening to him? He had never felt or done things like this. He walked into the room. Black chairs and round tables were organized in the interior and several large windows showed the patio where people either smoked or sat in the sun. It was empty at this time of day. It was nearly 8:30 am, the beginning of the work day.

He walked over to the automated coffee machines. He calmed his breathing and decided it was only his nervousness getting the best of him.

Lately, as he slept, he had odd dreams of a place dark underground and a cavernous area where he saw large round cylinders like the oil storage tanks he saw off the freeway.

A stack of styrofoam cups sat on a counter with tea, creamer and sugar for coffee. He reached for the cup when everything blew away as if caught in a large wind. Stirring straws, cups and napkins, sugar packets and creamers flew around the room, lazily coming to rest on the tables and white tiled floor.

"What happened here?"

Lazarus turned and saw Peggy, the manager of HR, walking through the break room door. Her face was a mask of anger and bewilderment.

"I don't know. I found it like this," he said.

Peggy said, "It's those guys in IT. They are always doing pranks, but they've gone too far this time." She stormed off.

Lazarus grabbed a few of the cups and napkins and threw them into the trash, stopping when he felt something strange. It was not the music, but a rumbling noise deep within the ground. He looked around, but nothing was moving or falling. He closed his eyes, sensing it through his fingers.

Stop, he thought. This was crazy. None of this was real. He took a clean cup and pushed the button for black coffee, watching as the liquid fell into the cup. It pooled and swirled. He felt like he was falling into a deep chasm.

Chapter 2

The elevator dinged as the doors slid open. Cindy walked inside, her high heels clicking against the floor. Men, who she knew by sight, flanked her, all dressed in suits. She flipped her hair with her fingers and walked forward as somebody pressed the button for number twenty-five, her floor. She held her dark leather briefcase and stared at the backs of the men and women in front of her.

Around her neck was a new necklace. A box had been delivered to her office and was lying on her desk when she came back from lunch yesterday. Cindy asked her secretary who delivered it, but she didn't know. The necklace was gorgeous. She held it up to the light and the stone sparkled. It was neither dark nor colored, nor was it an opal or diamond.

The elevator opened and the people around her walked out. She was alone and forgot about the necklace as the elevator traveled up to her floor, the numbers glowing as it moved up. She thought of Southern California, where she came from. She was still trying to adapt to living here in New York. Outside, it was snowing and cold, and she couldn't get used to the weather.

Cindy recalled the warm climate and beautiful skies of California. Yet, her job, and her promotion were centered in New York. In fact, her rise to the prestigious Ames and Zucker Financial services was mesmerizing. She wished her friend, Lazarus, could see her. They were friends in high school and college. She had a major crush on him way back in Junior year in high school but he was always looking at the cheerleader, Yvonne. The elevator opened and she walked out toward the hallway.

Her office was at the end of this corridor. She opened the double glass doors and her secretary, Charlotte, greeted her.

"Hello, Cindy, do you want some coffee?"

"Yes, please. What time is the meeting?"

Charlotte said, "At 8:30, Mr. Ramble wants an update on the Langers account."

Cindy nodded and went into her office, placing her briefcase on the desk. Today was a big day. The Langers account was one of the large hedge funds that she managed. She was brought in to check on the last manager's figures and investments. Something had gone wrong. Half the money in this hedge fund had gone missing. She and her staff had been trying to piece together the problem.

She took out several large files from her briefcase. Cindy had many meetings before, but this one, for some reason, was making her nervous. Charlotte came into her office and placed the coffee on her desk.

Cindy said, "Thank you. Can you remind me about my boyfriend's birthday dinner tonight?"

"Yes, I got the present you told me to get."

"Thanks, I have been so busy with this meeting."

Charlotte smiled. "It's fine. I got what you picked out. It will be great."

"Thank you again. You are my life saver. Where is the gift?"

"It will be delivered today."

"Thanks."

Her secretary went to her desk. Cindy was thinking that her secretaries had been getting younger of late. She was on her third one this year.

CINDY WAS SEATED IN the meeting room. Everything was set up. Her boss was stationed in Seattle and would patch in a call. Today, it was an audio and video conference.

"Terry," she said, "is everything ready."

A skinny man typed into a computer, standing rather than sitting. Terry was the IT man, who oversaw everything from fixing downed computers to printer jams. He looked at her, his large glasses making him appear almost comical.

"Yes," he said absently.

Cindy knew that something was wrong. She could tell from Terry's posture and uncommunicative shrugs. She had been through many of these video conference calls and knew it didn't take this long to set-up. She even prided herself that she could have set this up herself in an emergency if needed.

She edged closer to him, sensing something was amiss. The laptop was on, yet the screen had wavy and curly lines on it as if somebody was spinning and moving on the screen. The closer she got to the computer, the more the screen became agitated, branches of white snow falling on the moving pixels. She thought about the course she had taken in the computer program, Photoshop, when she took a picture of herself and used some of the filters to change it to something scary and hideous.

Terry cursed, and said, "We need a new computer."

"We have no time. They are waiting for us."

She heard a noise, rumbling close to her, a sound so sweet, like twinkling bells and starry skies. Cindy turned, looking for the sound. It made her feel the wonder of the world, as though it had become larger.

The phone before her rang in a shrill tone, constant and berating. She tore herself from the sweet song, turning toward Terry, but he was not there anymore, nor was she in the room.

She stood upon a large dark cavern. Before her were gigantic round cylinders. The darkness spread around her like a lurking beast. A humming noise vibrated from the cylinders.

"Cindy?" Terry said.

Terry's voice sounded far away from her.

"Yes, I'm here."

Cindy was back sitting in the board room.

"There is something wrong with the computers here. Can you reschedule the meeting, or call it in?"

Cindy's mind was confused. She still saw the large containers and the darkness swirling, calling her.

"Right," she said and reached for the phone. "I will call Mr. Ramble. When will this be ready?"

"Tomorrow, I have to check on all the wires and get another laptop."

"Fine, whatever it takes."

Cindy wished tomorrow would never come. She was not to know that the beginning of the end was near.

Chapter 3

"**M**atthew, wake up. The cops are here."
Matthew looked at his friend through the opening of his large box. Matthew wore an assortment of clothes: a black t-shirt with a large smiley face on it, an oversized blue jacket now the color of charcoal, faded blue jeans and black tennis shoes. He received these clothes from the homeless shelter a block away.

Matthew grabbed all his belongings from his hiding place, and a large red sack filled with an assortment of odd items. He couldn't recall the man speaking to him.

Matthew said, "Are you also on a quest?"

"No, man. The cops will kick us out. Let's split."

Matthew didn't understand what this man wanted. He was a knight on a grand quest to kill the evil wizard. He grabbed his long stick, a weapon of formidable power, and held it against the man talking to him.

"Don't do this, Matthew. Get out of it. You're not acting like yourself."

Matthew sensed he knew this man and these cops he was talking about. It was like staring at a wide, long corridor, seeing himself as another person. Matthew crawled out of his box. The first thing he noticed was the alley he slept in and the reeking scent of dirt and excrement. He held up his stick before him.

"You are in league with the evil wizard. You shall die."

Matthew swung the staff over his head. The man who spoke to him ran down the alley and onto the street, disappearing into the daylight.

Aha, Matthew thought. The man was one of the evil wizard's minions, sent to distract him.

A commanding voice said, "Place the stick down!"

He turned and saw several men dressed in black shirts and pants, pointing weapons at him.

"I am a knight on a quest. You cannot stop me," Matthew said.

"Sir, we have told you to put the stick down!"

"No, I shall not."

He swung the staff a few times and saw the magic Merlin had given him. He could destroy the Evil Wizard's minions. The men stayed away from him. He was ready to get out of this trap.

Then something shot at him. Several small projectiles attached to his clothes. Matthew was about to laugh when he felt a cold shower encase his body and he went rigid. He fell to the ground, writhing in pain. Black boots were in his sights. The last thing he remembered before waking in a hospital bed was the sound of sweet music twinkling, like many bells.

THE LIGHT WAS BRIGHT, almost as bright as the sun. Matthew tried to move, but he was held down on a bed by several straps over his arms and shoulders. His stench assailed his nose. He smelt like the streets, of urine and dirt and something else. A bright light shone on his face.

"Matthew, can you hear me?"

He nodded.

"My name is Dr. Johnson. Are you hurt?"

"No."

"Do you know who you are?"

Matthew looked at the IV stuck in his arm. He felt clear and knew the answer.

"My name is Matthew Carlson."

"And you know where you are?"

"A hospital."

"Which hospital?"

"Los Angeles."

"Right," the doctor said.

Somebody was behind him and he recognized her. He didn't say anything about his quest to kill the Evil Wizard. Merlin told him he had to complete this quest with the aid of his knights. Dr. Johnson inspected his arms and body and nodded to the lady behind him. He walked out.

The woman walked up to him. She said, "Matthew, we have been looking for you for months. And you have not taken your medications. You know what happens."

"I don't need the medication. It makes me think wrong."

"I read the police report. You are not a Knight of a Quest. You are Matthew Carlson, a teacher of Medieval Literature."

He knew she was right. But his mind refused to acknowledge that she was correct.

"I cannot be your case worker anymore. You will be assigned a new one."

She shook her head and stalked out of the hospital room. Matthew looked around the austere interior. The walls were bright white with no pictures and the window was affixed with large bars. From his bed, he could see a police officer standing at the door. He realized two things. He had done something wrong and he had been on the run. He wondered if he had hurt somebody this time. His medication was clearing his mind, making him recall things he did not want to remember.

Matthew heard the soft twinkling sound of mellifluous music. The sound was something he had never heard before. It was so sweet and melancholy. Something flashed in his hand. He tried to stare at it but the straps held his right arm down.

He wriggled to try to look at the glowing object. It was on his finger. He thought the evil wizard had given him a poison charm. But when he was finally able to see it, he realized it was a harmless gold ring with a dark crystal attached to it. The crystal was not glowing as he thought, but twinkling in the light of the lamps. And then he realized he only had a day left before darkness would come to his lands. Matthew needed to get out.

The policeman looked into his room and Matthew stopped struggling. He sensed they were waiting for somebody to come and take him away. Matthew couldn't let that happen. He kept trying to get out of his straps but to no avail. He had to await his destiny.

Less than an hour later, several men came in, dressed in white clothes. Behind them was the doctor who talked to him before.

"Hello, Matthew, we are transporting you another facility. These men will escort you out."

The men dressed in white clothes started to unstrap his arms, wrist, and legs. They grabbed him and pulled him upwards. As they moved, Matthew sensed a tremor under his feet. The world shook. A large noise rose from the depths of the magical Bastions, just like Merlin told him. He knew this for sure. The men holding him let him go and Matthew rushed out of the room.

Matthew's feet slapped on the floor. The walls rumbled and spat and water flowed through the cracks.

One man said, "Hey, get back here!"

He ran through the hallway. The floor shook so hard he lurched to the sides, back and forth. People around him scrabbled under doorways and desks.

He ran until he saw an exit sign. Bursting out into the daylight, he saw a large wave taller than the tallest building pounding toward him. His ring glowed an incandescent white so bright he could not see his hand.

Chapter 4

Royce drove his truck through the desert. He didn't like his post in Arizona, but he went where the Army told him. He reminded himself that he was the son of the famous Colonel John Daggers, respected soldier and leader, who did several tours in Desert Storm and was now fighting in Afghanistan. Yet Royce could never measure up to his dad. He barely finished boot camp with the lowest scores any person could get and still pass. He thought he was allowed to stay in the Army because of his dad.

Plumes of dirt flew behind his car as the truck bounced down the dirt street. Royce didn't care that he was stationed in this remote area. He was glad he was not sent to a hotbed of fighting like his buddy, John, who was knee deep in sand trying not to be killed by insurgents of Isis or the Taliban.

His army issue truck turned toward a group of buildings, drab and nondescript, painted the color of gray mud. He parked his car at the entrance. The building was attached to the side of a large mountain that overshadowed it. The base was honey-combed into the mountain and extended, he supposed, hundreds of feet below. Royce didn't care. He was getting paid for this shit job. The only time this place was interesting was when they came. Royce didn't believe in aliens, but these people who dressed in black and white suits looked like aliens. They were tall for one thing, and unusually thin and they had visited once since he had been here.

He walked up a small flight of steps to a brown door. Royce touched a small scanner to the left of the doorway. He placed his right eye next to it. The door clicked and he opened it. Royce always like this new tech. He felt like James Bond going into his headquarters at MI6. The soldier greeted him from his seat at the table. The man was looking at several monitors showing the surrounding area in front of the building.

"Hello, Royce," the soldier said.

"Hi, Dale, anything new?"

"Same shit. Same sand."

Royce nodded. "Have the tall Thinners visited?"

"No," Dale said. "And don't call them that. If they knew, they'd fire you."

"Whatever."

He walked to the next set of doors. A swirl of sand lay on the floor. Sand was everywhere on the top floor but not on the lower floors. The door clicked.

"Thanks. See you after your shift."

"Sure."

"Yo," the soldier said, "do you want to go to the titty bar after work?"

"Nah."

He grabbed the handle and walked into a long corridor that ended at a set of elevators. Royce glanced at the security camera mounted on the wall. He was going to give Dale an obscene finger as his dad, the Colonel, always called it, but he didn't want the other guards stationed below to see him.

The elevator opened as if by magic and he entered. The silent machinery moved him into the belly of the beast. Every time he went to work here he felt as if he was going into a different world, a place where a poor schmuck with a worthless job and a crazy father could do something important. He recalled his dad waking him up every morning at the crack of dawn to exercise and clean the house. The Colonel always told him he had to be a good soldier and learn discipline. His mother was a forgettable figure in the kitchen, who never talked. She looked downwards when his dad spoke to her.

The therapist the Army made him see told him that he was raised by an abusive dad who had anger issues. He also had anger issues, the therapist pointed out. Royce smirked. *Hey*, he thought, *it was not my fault I had to beat a man because he told me I was a sissy.* It was his right to show this man he was not a fairy. His father, the Colonel, would never let that remark slide. The therapist said he had wounded child syndrome. He told her that was bullshit. He didn't need his parent's attention.

The elevator stopped and he stepped out into the hallway. The temperature was climate controlled, but he always felt warm.

Royce's station was located at the end of the adjoining hallway. He took a left and saw a room with bullet-proof glass. Soldiers dressed in army fatigues like him stared at several consoles showing the corridor he came from and the other rooms of the underground structure. He nodded to the soldiers and they barely looked at him.

He walked until he was at the very end of the path. A dark gray door greeted him. Royce knocked. The door clicked. Moving inside, he saw a soldier sitting behind the desk with his boots up on the polished surface.

"Hey, Royce, you're late."

"No, I'm not."

The soldier stood and moved toward the exit.

"I'll see you in a week. I got some R&R."

"Lucky bastard. I will see you later. Don't drink yourself silly like last time," Royce said.

"Haha, see ya."

The soldier opened the door and left. Royce turned to the rows of monitors before him, feeling like God before his followers. He thought, *I know all and watch all and don't call my name in vain because I can see and hear everything.* He shook his head and saw the broad expanse of Bastions on the monitor sitting silent against the black background, like sentinels at rest waiting for something. He had been watching these Bastions, as they were called, for almost five years.

Today's and yesterday's newspapers were strewn on the table next to the screens. The sports page was open and he scanned it and saw the Lakers were in the championship again. He saw movement at the corner of his eye and reached for his handgun. On the monitor before him, he saw shadows roving along the Bastions.

"What the hell?" he said.

The shadows melted and shimmered, casting doubt on what he saw. Royce stood and moved closer to the monitor. He saw it again. Suddenly, as if in premonition, a sound he had never heard before blasted along the room and the hallways beyond.

A buzzing noise sounded and then a mechanical voice said, "Security breach in sectors 4, 6, and 8!"

Royce knew sector 6 was his area. He grabbed the M16 rifle along the wall and ran.

Chapter 5

"The world ended within the slightest, smallest vibration as if it was held by a silk web and a powerful force broke the glue and string which held everything together." Lazarus didn't realize he was speaking aloud these words. It came out of him in a rush. Luckily, he was in his car eating his sandwich. The voice was coming from inside his head, making him see and say things.

"We need," he said, "to find the nexus, the beginning where the mage began his work."

Lazarus shook his head and he stopped taking. Clamping his mouth for fear of speaking again he touched his head, thinking that he felt feverish. He recalled a time when he was young and had the flu. His brother, Dustin, the comedian and tormentor, decided to play a trick on him. He strung several of his army toy men on the windowsill in his room. He lay in his bed staring at his toys. Lazarus, in his delirium, didn't see toy army men, but giant gargoyles flying from the burning, erupting sky to take him to Hades. He yelled and fell on the ground screaming about demons from the pit of hell ready to devour him.

He said to himself, "What is happening to me? I don't speak in riddles."

From his vantage point in his car, he could see the small, two story brick building where he worked and he thought he saw something odd and dark glinting from the many square windows on the first floor. Was it a trick of the light? He moved his head from side to side, when a syrupy thickness pervaded his sight. He saw an inky blackness with large round cylindrical structures hanging from the ceiling while people ran next to him. People he had a kinship with and history, but he had never seen them before. Yet there was a woman who looked familiar. Her face was determined.

"Where am I?" he said.

"Be quiet. The soldiers are close."

"WHAT DID YOU SAY?"

Lazarus was standing with his co-workers looking at a table with a birthday cake on it. Candles were lit on top of a chocolate cake.

"Nothing."

"You don't look good."

"Ok, everybody, we need to start singing for Lacy."

As they started to sing the first few bars of Happy Birthday, Lazarus felt odd, like a cold shower flowing over him. His eyes dimmed again and he didn't see an office where his co-workers sang a cheerful song for Lacy, but a bright light coming alive before his eyes. And he realized nothing would be the same again.

He was back in his office standing with his co-workers. He held a piece of cake up to his face. A fork was impaled into it. Lazarus wanted to laugh and then cry. He sensed the impending doom had started and he could not do anything about it.

Somebody looked out the window and said, "What's that?"

Lazarus suddenly grabbed the bracelet on his wrist. The stone was glowing an intense cool blue hue. He looked outside through the large windows. Against the horizon was a wall of water higher than the tallest buildings. A roar screamed through his brain and sent him reeling backwards. He dropped his plate and food.

The first echoes of people screaming filled the office. His back hit his cubicle and he laughed, a mirthless sound. Before the glass panes broke under the pressure of the giant wave and before the lady who had sat next to him for the last five years yelled a horrified screech, he felt an exhalation of sadness tinged with joy and he sensed something he would understand later as arcane power, surging in his blood.

The ground shook with the monstrous tidal wave encroaching upon his building and he understood why his mom named him Lazarus. He would be reborn in this new world. Lifting his hand, the light of his bracelet started to reform around him in a spherical barrier. The giant wave hit the windows, shattering glass, stone and cement. It was the giant hand of God pulverizing everything around him.

Lazarus was flung backwards in a cocoon of watery darkness and he knew the way had been opened and he was instrumental in opening the Bastions. Yet, he was not sure what he was thinking about. He started to speed as his force field hit the broken walls of his old building, his old life.

Broken bodies floated around him in a concert of dance, swimming along the ripples of the current of the tidal wave. He spun faster, traveling to a place he didn't know. He forgot his whole world had changed. A wonder bloomed in his mind. He could control this sphere. Lazarus held up his hand and ceased spinning and moving. The water receded almost as fast as it came and his mind and body sensed this tidal wave storm was more than water and millions of gallons of the deep blue sea. It was imbued with the power of the earth's lifeblood.

He was gently placed on a jagged piece of ground filled with the debris of buildings, cars, and people. The barrier around him disappeared and the stone in his bracelet stopped glowing. He heard people moaning and he realized he was not the only survivor. He ran to the man who was stretched out on the ground.

The man looked remarkably well, even though he had been caught in a tsunami. His eyes opened and glared at him.

"Hey," Lazarus said and kneeled close to him. He repeated, "Do you hear me? Are you hurt in any way?"

The man opened his mouth and said, "Grog, grog!"

"What is that you are saying?"

"Grog, grog!"

The man must be delirious, he thought and placed his hand on the prone man's shoulder, but the man stared at him with hateful eyes. The stranger stood up and melted and shimmered. Lazarus shook his head and moved back a few paces. The stranger started to shake all over. Long brown hair sprung over the man's skin and large talons sprouted from his hands.

Lazarus stood mute and could not move. The transformation, as he thought of it, was almost complete. The man's face changed into a hideous mask of a wolf and bat. The eyes were the worst. They shone with intelligence and hatred. The creature saw him and started to move forward on all four legs, growling. Lazarus looked for any weapon or stick to defend himself with, but all he saw was rocks and debris.

The monster was a mutation between a large gorilla and a canine. The creature started forward, sniffing the air, and its mouth salivated with wet slops of spray. And in one smooth motion, it lifted its muzzle and howled toward the sky. The creature called Grog was answered by other Grogs far in the distance. It was a blood curling sound which caused Lazarus to fall backward, hitting his head on a jutting piece of concrete. His eyesight blurred and misted for several seconds. He saw the creature turn to the side and howl again. The call was answered and the Grog bounded away.

Chapter 6

Royce's breathing was ragged. His orders were clear and he didn't want to perform them because, well, he knew he was a coward. He took this job because there was absolutely no way anybody could breach these security protocols and stroll around the large round structures and why would they, he thought. There was nothing here. He was not guarding gold or diamonds but these stupid Bastions.

Royce had been instructed from day one to capture or even kill any invaders. The ratchet thunder sounds of gunfire were heard from his hiding place inside the men's restroom. Royce's M16 gun was still in his hand. The safety was on. More screaming voices were clearly audible. He wiped his brow with his free hand. It was surprising how much he was sweating.

Then a thought bloomed in his mind and he wondered what his dad, the famous Colonel John Daggers, would do in this situation. And Royce decided that he had to do something. He had been a coward since he was a little boy and only stood up to his dad once, when Colonel Daggers decided to hit his mom because she didn't want to clean up his plate. The little Royce stood between the Colonel and his mother and he said, "No, dad. You are a bully!"

The Colonel's eyes were livid but he smiled a toothy grin. "Ah, I admire your courage. So, you will take your mom's punishment."

His dad beat him until he passed out. Royce felt exalted and joyful when he stood up to his dad, even though he ended up in the hospital with several broken ribs and a fractured skull. His parents lied, saying he fell down the stairs.

Royce opened the stall he was in and clicked off the safety on his gun. He pointed it forward and crouched as he was trained, but the barrel of the M16 trembled.

He positioned himself at the front door and took a deep breath before exiting in a rush, looking at both sides of the corridor. He moved fast along the hallway and passed the now empty guard station. The door to the Bastions stood open and he apprehensively strode into the apex of the opening. More sounds of gun battle were heard coming from the inner sanctum and he saw the first large, round structure. It sat like all the Bastions, dead and silent. Without thinking, he rushed out into the large room which went for miles underground. The intruders were in his quadrant, moving steadily toward the largest of the Bastions. His other comrades jokingly called this Bastion, Big Ben or Gigantaur because this Bastion was twice the size of the others.

He moved deeper into the chamber, looking against the wall as the alarm shrilled. He wondered how these interlopers passed the guards on the surface. He guessed it was some spy shit. Before him in a heap on the floor were several dead soldiers shredded by gun shots. Royce braced himself and almost had a bout of nausea but he controlled his stomach and nerves. The first series of Bastions were humming and glowing an amber color.

Royce was so surprised at the sudden glowing structure that he touched it with his outstretched hand. He was vulnerable here. Anybody, especially the invaders, could see him standing looking stupid and touching the Bastion. When his fingers touched the rough surface he felt a feeling of rightness, of things being correct. He almost wept until he heard something behind him. It was a group of four people, but they were not normal people. They moved like liquid, staying close to the ground.

Royce pointed his gun and shot a spray of bullets at the intruders. The people scattered and disappeared into the dark. Royce crept forward, pointing his gun back and forth. He saw something moving in the far corner of his sight. He shot at the thing. Suddenly, he was pushed to the ground. His gun was still in his hands and he sprayed upwards and then to the side but missed. Then Royce saw something standing in front of him.

It was two tall creatures. They looked like giant insects. He heard their voices in his head, saying, "You cannot defeat those people until you have power, real power."

"What did you say?"

His fingers tingled and then his torso vibrated. Royce was rooted to the spot and could not move. Pain exploded through his mind and his body. His body twisted downward and his hands started to change. Long claws grew from his fingers. He squirmed and writhed on the ground. A screamed erupted from his mouth. His voice sounded odd. Fur sprouted from his skin and his clothes burst from him. He looked at the creatures for some explanation, but they were gone.

The torture ceased.

His M16 gun was on the ground next to his clothes. He tried to speak but all he said was, "Grog, grog!" Royce felt powerful and strong. He bounded toward the four enemies running around the area. He knew by instinct. These four interlopers were opening the pathway. He needed to stop them and with his new powers, he could defeat these enemies. He jumped between the Bastions, seeing the four people moving fast. Royce roared and attacked the first person.

One of the four interlopers turned and faced him. It was a man. Yet, this person was more. The man shot at him, kicking at his face. Royce swiped at him with his claws. He missed him by inches. He snarled and attacked the man. Catching him by his paws, he cut into him, but the man disappeared.

Royce scanned around and was giving a glancing blow to his ribs. He kicked out and hit the man's shoulder. Royce howled. He could defeat this man who tried to shoot him with a rifle. Bullets erupted toward him and Royce jumped out of the way. He saw with his animalistic eyesight. The man came running at him and bullets rained forth, but Royce understood what his new feral body could do. Royce attacked, pushing his claws at the man, cutting into his torso, shredding bones, gut and tissue. The man screamed.

Royce was elated. He killed one and could kill the others, but then he saw and knew he was too late. All the Bastions lit up in brilliant white-blue light. Royce was blinded for a second. The rumbling of the ground told him he needed to leave now.

Royce scrambled out of the large chamber and leaped up and out toward the hall leading out. Dark fissures grew on the ground, stretching in all directions. Royce jumped and made it to the hallway. Debris started to rain down on him. Royce's mind was confused. He was heading toward the staircase, but his body was too big to squeeze through the doorway. He smashed his way through it and ran up the many stairs ahead. Another set of tremors shook the structure.

He smashed his way to the exit and leaped out onto the sandy surface of the outside. The heat of the sun burnt him, but he kept on running. The ground shook and started to implode into the Bastion's chambers below. Royce ran, it seemed, for miles. The ground stopped shaking and he ceased his maddened escape. He turned and saw a large hole where the military structure once stood.

Royce howled into the sky. He would find the other interlopers and kill them.

Chapter 7

Lazarus walked along the broken ground, being careful not to fall through the small fissures and large pits. The floor and buildings were wet and glistened in the sunlight. He thought he was in a dream.

This was not happening. He should be eating cake and talking to his co-workers about the upcoming basketball finals. His shoes sucked into the muddy ground and he realized he had to find new clothes. He stood in a parking lot, or a place that was once a parking lot. The black asphalt was bunched together like kid's legos and mud, roots and grass were jumbled together in exposed areas like a mad cook's recipe.

He turned, looking for anybody who could be alive. The typhoon or tsunami took them by surprise. He hoped help was going to be here soon. The firemen or police would be coming at any moment. He didn't see any more people besides the guy who changed into a beast and ran off. Picking his way along the broken ground, he saw a collapsed structure. Most of the walls were gone, but he saw clothing, boxes and other merchandise strewn along the ground and asphalt.

He wondered why there was no early warning detection or even news coverage before the storm. This was the informational age when anything could be found online from phones. He laughed. Phones. He felt in his pockets and found his cell phone still intact. Opening it with a swipe of his finger he saw the normal glowing screen and was elated until he noticed on the top left of the screen the words, no service. He tried it anyway by pressing the phone button and dialing 911. No connection, nada, zip. He stared at the device for several seconds, maybe a minute, because he had never felt so disconnected and alone. Finally, he threw his phone and watched it as it hit a brick wall, then turned away and quickly approached the building. He would need some supplies and new stuff. He remembered how after Hurricane Katrina the inhabitants of New Orleans waited for several days for help and assistance. A fishy smell rose from the wet ground. He was surprised as there were no fish or aquatic life dying on the ground.

He found a backpack, clothes, shoes and bottled water among the wreckage. Lazarus saw his first dead body. It was a young blond woman, wearing a red shirt and no pants. Her eyes stared up to the air. She was beautiful or was beautiful. She would never become the woman she might have been. A name tag was still affixed to her wet shirt. It read, "Darla. How can I help you?"

Seeing the name tag, Lazarus started to cry. He couldn't help it. He bent down and wept like a baby. He thought, *This should not be happening.* His watched showed the time as being 3:00 pm and he should be having a break right now. He looked away from Darla, grabbed a few pieces of clothing and placed it over her.

The sun was high above and he needed to get out of this area and dry his new found clothes and backpack. He grabbed his stuff and moved out. Scanning around, he saw a tree still rooted to the ground. The leaves had fallen off and it tilted oddly to the side, but there was a clean area of asphalt where he could put his things. Before he left, he found a set of boots in size nine. It took him almost fifteen minutes to find both boots because everything was thrown all over the ground.

Lazarus sat near the tree, trying to get his bearings. The landmarks he was used to seeing were gone or destroyed. He scanned the ground and the building and noticed there weren't any cars or even any metal objects on the floor. A creaking noise came from the structure. He saw one of the standing metal beams start to move toward the right and then vibrate.

His metal belt started to force him upwards. Lazarus grabbed his belt and release the clasp. He was being dragged forward. Pulling the belt out of his pant loops, he saw the belt fly into the air and out of his sight. His keys also flew out of his pocket.

A loud scream pierced the broken structures. Lazarus was not sure if he heard it correctly. Another screech came. He jumped toward the noise and picked his way through the devastation, ducking when he saw a metal siding almost knock him down. Slipping, he fell on the muddy ground, face-planting on the dirt.

Turning the corner, Lazarus saw something which at first he couldn't comprehend. A man floated several feet above the ground while metal objects of all kinds floated around him. Several rods pierced through him like a pin cushion, keeping him aloft. The man stared at him. He had sandy brown hair and wore khaki pants and a button-down white striped blue shirt. It was obvious that pain wracked his body.

Lazarus tried to find a way to navigate the metal objects levitating around the man. Another metal object passed close by him and Lazarus sprang. He moved so fast he was not sure if he even touched the ground. He was fifty yards away. He shook his head and wondered how he was able to run so quickly. The metal object was a long rod and it was floating around and then it bolted and struck the man on his leg. He screeched.

Through his pain, the man said, "Help me!"

Lazarus glanced around. None of this made sense. He wondered why these metal objects were attracted to the man like a magnet.

He yelled, "Why are you magnetized?"

Lazarus felt it was a stupid question because the man clearly was not sure why he was attracting these metals. He was thinking that a magnet could repel these objects. He recalled that by turning a magnet over he could reverse its polarity and have it repel the metal objects, but he couldn't understand how he would do this with a man.

Lazarus said, "You need to repel the objects. You're acting like a magnet."

The man shook his head, not understanding what he needed to do. He tried to speak but a long metal siding flew from behind him and beheaded him. Bright red blood squirted upwards in a small mist and all the metal objects fell to the ground. Lazarus began to move further away and transported himself several feet. He found himself next to a broken brick wall. He braced his back against it and stopped the tears flowing. Nothing would be the same again.

Chapter 8

Matthew scanned the scene of devastation. He had a crazy ride inside a magical bubble. Waves of water pummeled him as he rode. He looked at the ring on his finger. It started to pulsate with a white luminescence and he realized he had to find somebody. From his vantage point, he saw a group of large feral wolves roaming around broken and now dead buildings. The creatures spoke an odd word over and over, "Grog, grog!"

The animals didn't bother him because there were plenty of dead people to devour. Matthew had to find a weapon. He walked down a broken ramp, picking his way across the ripped and torn ground. Waves of evaporating water were seen in the air. The scent of salt water, dead people and something else, a predatory musk, was strong in his nose.

Matthew bent low to the ground, sticking close to any high debris or brick walls. All the buildings were smashed as if the hand of God had come trumpeting along the city, smashing and thrashing. He was looking for a sporting goods store for weapons and supplies.

Matthew still wore his hospital gown and even though he was half dressed the sun gave him warmth. Living on the streets gave him tough skin and rough hands. Luckily, he found a pair of sneakers that fit him from a dead man a few streets back. He kept moving, roving between the large chunks of ripped and torn asphalt and cement. Stopping, he saw several dead people with blood seeping on the ground. It was a family - a mom, dad and child. They must have been caught in the typhoon. They were wet and had their arms, legs and bodies contorted at odd angles. The child was still holding her mom's hand. He looked at them for several seconds. Matthew knew he should leave before the Grogs came here to feast, but the look of sudden terror on their face made him wonder why he was spared. The earth's magical lifeblood and essence were finally spilled and released into the world. He should be dead.

He had been receiving dreams from the Druids about the arcane Bastions, the storehouse of magic, for several years now. Matthew never liked taking his medicine because it blocked his visions and dreams. Nobody believed him, but now it was all coming true. Matthew tore his eyes away from the dead people.

He roamed along a street he thought he recognized, but was not sure. Matthew thought he was in the downtown Los Angeles garment district. The tall buildings were all half broken with high metal spires jutting into the sky. His robe whipped in the wind. He thought that if he was alive and saved by the magical sphere, he must be one of the chosen. Matthew felt the calling tugging him to find the man who would be their Leader. He was far away, but he would find him. This man was in danger and did not know his true potential. He had seen him in his visions. An older man with peppered hair.

Matthew also felt the magic flowing in his body. He needed to learn his powers. Lifting his hands, he held out his palm, focusing his mind. Nothing happened at first, then a small ball of fire appeared. He held onto the flame until his mind hurt. He stopped and the ball of fire disappeared. It was a start.

⸎

AFTER SEARCHING A FEW blocks Matthew found a street filled with clothes spilled all over the ground. Everything was wet and drying in the sun. Also, among the clothes was money and coins. He laughed. In this new world, money didn't amount to anything. He begged strangers for these scraps of paper money and coins for years and now he could have filled bags of them. Matthew shook his head. He recalled a writer had said, "All that glitters is not gold." He mused, thinking he was not always a knight errant, but a teacher. Yet he was not sure what he taught.

He found several pairs of jeans, shirts and shoes. Sitting on an overturned table he checked his drying supplies. His stomach started to rumble. He needed to eat. Everything was inedible because the water spoiled all the food he found. He almost entered a destroyed fast food restaurant with a big M in the front, but he was scared of gas. Also, he remembered being run off by the manager of an establishment such as this because he begged for food in the front. Yet his hunger pains made him search for this place again, but he was turned around and found a small liquor store with windows covered in metal grating that was now all broken and bent. He entered and found the owner, dead, behind the ripped and broken counter.

He grabbed a potato-chip bag and opened it. The food was not spoiled and he ate it by shoveling the chips into his food. He felt for his beard, but the nurses at the hospital must have shaved it.

The store had the stink of the ocean and water pooled along the ground. Food and drinks were strewn on the floor and Matthew grabbed a soda and drank it. The drink was lukewarm but it tasted good. He finished it off and was about to grab a candy bar when he saw a handgun among the debris. It must have been the shop owners. He grabbed the weapon and held it close to him although he knew the dangers of using it. It was cold in his hands and water dripped from its muzzle and grip. It was small and fit well in the palm of his hand. He would only use it if needed, and only to scare the Grogs away.

He went toward the back of the cash register and looked around. The paper bags were useless, drenched with water and falling apart, but he found a bunch of white plastic bags in a corner. He grabbed them and fanned one open. Beads of waters splashed all around. *This will do,* he thought.

Grabbing all the food he could find, he stuffed it into the bag, before turning toward the dead man. He thought he heard the man yelling for him to leave. Many angry store owners had chased him out of their back alleys and front doors, but this man was mute.

Being a bum made him a pariah, a non-person in front of everybody. A girl who could have been his daughter saw him once when he was lying in the park. She wanted to give him some change, but her mom grabbed her and took her away from him. Matthew was used to people reacting like that to him. Those people were right, after all. He was a dangerous person.

Matthew grabbed his goods and went back to retrieve his clothes, still drying in the sun.

Chapter 9

Lazarus grabbed his still damp supplies and walked away from the decapitated dead man hanging with all the rods sticking out from him. He needed some space away from that display of carnage. He was not in a dreamland anymore, but a nightmarish land of creatures and magic. He tried to understand what was happening. He needed some water because he thought he was dehydrated or coming down with a fever. None of this could be happening. He should be at his desk, in his cubicle, looking at his spreadsheets.

He thought about his parents. His dad was a retired bookkeeper who loved reading mysteries and his mom was a school teacher who still taught her adolescent seventh-grade class. She never wanted to retire. But she was being forced to next year, by the principal of her school. Then he realized they were not here anymore. If the tidal wave came this far inland, their house would have been engulfed by water and his parents would have drowned. His dad would have been in his large reclining chair in his house and his mom would have been teaching down the street at her school. Tears sprang to his eyes. If he had known this was going to happen maybe he could have saved them. He shook his head.

He had no destination and was walking around listlessly. He noticed the bracelet was still attached to his right wrist, sparkling in the sun. Looking at the opal stone he relaxed as if everything was going to be fine. The local police or firemen would be here and save him. Then something leaped in front of him, but there was nothing there, at least nothing physical. It was a picture, similar to that on a TV screen. He saw a large man dressed in a hospital gown walking toward him. The vision disappeared. There was another survivor and he needed to find this person. The opal glowed faintly. He turned to the side and it shone brighter. Lazarus needed to go in that direction.

He wondered who this man was, and why he looked like he had been on the streets for a long time. Lazarus also felt he needed some type of weapon but didn't know what or where to find one. He started to move quickly out of the area, picking his way to an area that looked like a road. He couldn't find any street names or landmarks. Everything was smashed. He wished he could find a jeep or a truck. It would take a long time to find this man on foot. He placed his hand on his head and a thought came to him. The man's name was Matthew and he needed to reach him. This man, Matthew, knew things.

Another vision came to him, showing two women. He knew one of them. It was Cindy, his old friend from high school, but the other was a stranger like Matthew. Her name was Grace. They had to do something important. It was The Calling and he was not sure what that meant.

He stopped walking as doubts formed in his mind. He was not a man of action. He should wait in a safe area for the proper authorities to come to rescue him. Behind him, he heard something moving in the debris and wet, broken interiors. The sound of howling pierced the area and another animal howled back. A large creature covered in brown and black fur walked in front of him. It stood on four legs and was as tall as he was. The creature padded closer to him. Before it growled, the creature said, "Grog, grog!"

Lazarus started to step backwards and then he heard another growl coming from behind him. He turned around and saw several of the Grog creatures. They surrounded him.

The beasts all started to run at him. Lazarus tripped, and fell, scraping his hands. The Grog jumped at him. Lazarus placed his hands upwards in a defensive posture and as he did so he felt a surge of energy. It blasted out of him, hitting the Grog. The creature was thrown far away from him.

Lazarus shook his head in amazement. He stood and surveyed the area. The Grogs stopped attacking him, but walked around him with wary feral eyes. He held his hands up toward the creatures. The Grogs, fearing him, moved away from his outstretched hands. Lazarus wasn't sure if he could create this energy push again. He walked with bravado out of the area, searching for some place to hide and get away from these Grogs. They followed close behind him. A howl was heard at a far distance and the Grogs turned to the noise and bounded off for easier prey.

Lazarus watched the creatures disappear. He looked at his hands. He didn't feel any different, but when he had the surge of power he felt powerful and strong. It was as if this energy was dormant in him since he was a child. Staring at a large piece of broken concrete he focused on it and held out his hand.

Lazarus felt the surge of power again, but it was stronger. The rock burst into shards of powder and dust. He almost fell down in shock. This was something new and exciting, but also a little scary. He wondered what else he could do, but decided to leave this place before the creatures came back. The sun was setting on the horizon and he needed to find some shelter and food.

The backpack he carried had several cans of food: spaghetti, spam and vegetable beef soup. He wished he had a can opener and a pan to cook with. Lazarus was never a Boy Scout and never learned to live in the forest. Yet this was not the wild but a devastated world.

Chapter 10

C indy found herself in a wide field of grass with large holes and fissures in the ground. She remembered being in her office about to call for her manager when the building shook and then swayed. Her secretary ran into the room, screaming in fright. Living most of her life in Southern California she knew what an earthquake felt like and she was about to say something to her secretary, when her necklace grew warm on her skin.

She became encased in a hazy amber colored sphere. Cindy tried to yell at her secretary, but she was whisked away. She broke through the window and the building she was in started to topple and fall. She screamed and screamed. All the high rise buildings fell and she heard the sound of crashing struts and buildings. It echoed with the sound of people shouting and yelling.

Cindy was not sure what happened next. She was flung away, landing in this park. The sphere disappeared and her high heels sank into the grass. She knew where she was. She was in Central Park, but all the landmarks were erased as if a giant had pounded the earth, creating large mountains and picking up trees, flinging them around.

The usual large high-rise buildings that surrounded the outside of the park were gone or fractured. Another tremor shook the ground and she held out her hand to steady herself. She sucked in some air, realizing she had been holding her breath.

She wondered why an earthquake shook New York. *This is crazy*, she thought. Things like this did not happen in the real world, but only in blockbuster thriller movies and she was not in a movie. She heard screaming coming from her right and Cindy saw several people running toward her. A woman and a teen rushed to her with a police officer close behind. He was waving his gun, gesturing at her to move.

Cindy looked around. She was not sure why they were running until she saw something crawl out of the large hole behind them. At first, she knew what the "thing" was. Cindy had seen these insects many times in New York and also at home in California. Yet it was much larger and much more menacing. The insect waved its antennae around as if searching. She also heard another noise. It spoke a word over and over, "Grog, grog."

The large roach lumbered out of the hole and started toward her. The police officer yelled, "Run!" The first creature scrambled to her. Cindy ran because several hundred roaches moved toward her. Cindy tried not to panic but she screamed, looking for an escape route. The roaches were coming from everywhere. The lady holding her dog caught up to her. The officer was close behind. He held his gun and took several shots at the first group of roaches. The bullets slammed into the creatures, but the insects kept moving.

Revulsion filled Cindy. Her feet slipped a few times. She forgot she was wearing her high heels. She flung them off and ran, her stockinged feet barely feeling the grass and dirt.

The man said, "This way."

They ran up a steep hill and turned around a corner. A castle rose above everything, the structure amazingly intact. They ran up the steps to the front entrance, but a creature broke through the interior causing a big hole to appear in the front of the castle. Cindy stopped. They were surrounded. The people around her also stopped. The roaches came at them on all sides.

Terror filled her and Cindy wanted to scream but then she felt her necklace grow warm. Her arms flung outward.

She said, "Duck!"

The police officer looked at her as if she was crazy, but he sensed something was coming because he told everybody to drop to the ground. Cindy was filled with intense light and power. Her body trembled and she suddenly let loose something. Ice shards appeared and shot at the roaches, killing many of the insects.

She heard the sound of squishy explosions. Guts and blood filled the ground. Her body started to fill with white hot energy. She created waves of water from her outstretched hands which slammed into the roaches.

The water pushed trees, dirt, and parts of the castle far away from their position. Cindy's arms felt like lead and she dropped them to her sides. She swayed where she stood. Her spell ceased and her body shook and then she fell to the ground. Her eyesight dimmed and she knew no more.

⌾⚬⚬

CINDY AWOKE, FINDING the officer staring at her. He was handsome with short black hair and an Italian face which was contorted in fear. She noticed his hand was close to his pistol. The sun shone from above in a cloudless sky. She took a long breath and moved to a sitting position. Her body ached and her head felt like it had been hit several times. Gripping her temples, she moaned.

The officer said, "Who are you?"

She brushed back her short blond her, wishing he didn't stare at her with fright.

"My name is Cindy Paulson. I was a manager at Ames and Zucker Financial services."

"I am Dan. The lady over there is Mary and the girl is her daughter, Rochelle." He paused, "How did you do that?"

Cindy shook her head. "I don't know. I just did it."

Rochelle had dark red hair like her mom. She gazed at her with wonder. She said, "Are you a wizard?"

"Sorry," Mary said. "My daughter reads a lot of fantasy books."

Cindy looked to Rochelle. "No. The power just came to me. Officer Dan, where are the other police officers. Are they coming to help?"

He shook his head. "I tried to use my cell phone, but it doesn't work. I lost my walkie talkie while we were running from those things."

Rochelle's young face looked scared. "How did those roaches get so big?"

Officer Dan said, "I don't know. I have seen large roaches before but nothing as big as those things."

"Maybe some radiation leaked out somewhere?" she said.

Dan said, "if that was true then we should be sick or something."

Cindy said, "What do we do now?"

"We should find a police precinct," Officer Dan replied. "Are you fine to move?"

"Yes, give me a few minutes. I'm a little shaky."

Chapter 11

Cindy waited with the others in the group for Dan to figure a way toward his precinct HQ. The police officer scratched his head several times, threw up his hands and said, "I'm not sure. Everything looks different."

He held up his cell phone, showing the compass app on it, but it kept moving round and round. "I thought this would help me."

Cindy said, "Where is your precinct located?"

"It's a block down from Time Square. I believe south from here."

Mary looked off in the distance. "This castle must be the Belvedere Castle. We just have to find the right direction to go."

Rochelle said, "Mom, I think I see the Met from here. But I'm not sure."

They all looked in that direction. The structure was broken and smashed. It could be any of the other buildings lying half exposed to the sun. Yet something was there. They heard a banging noise and a mist started to form around there.

Dan said, "I think I see one of the pillars. I think it is the Met, but it looks different."

Rochelle said, "There might be other survivors."

"We should check it out," Dan said. He looked at them for confirmation. As he spoke Cindy felt something, her necklace, and the stone had started to glow. She needed to be somewhere else but not here.

Mary said, "Your necklace is glowing. It's beautiful."

She looked at it for several seconds as if mesmerized by its brilliance. They all did, and as they did so the stone ceased shining. She had an uneasy feeling about that building and sensed the necklace was trying to tell her something. They trudged along. They stopped several times and had to take a different route because the ground was unsafe to cross. It took them several hours to get there and they were exhausted.

They stood on top of a small hill and looked at the building. It was the Met. She could make out the remnants of the Beaux-Arts facade with some of the front still standing. Cindy sensed something was down there among the wreckage and turned to Mary and Rochelle. "You should stay here. Officer Dan, do you have another gun you can give her?"

He looked at her with a crazy look. "Yes, I have a backup Beretta 9 millimeter."

He took it out of his holster and handed it to Mary, showing her the safety and how to shoot. Mary looked at the weapon in a dubious way, but she didn't argue.

Cindy and the officer starting walking downwards to the Met. The first thing they saw were statues, all types of sculptures from Roman classical to Egyptian and these statues were alive, talking to each other in their own language. Cindy shook her head, amazed. Officer Dan placed his hand on the butt of his pistol.

He scanned around and walked past a group of Greek busts. They talked among each other and didn't pay attention to them. This was wonderful and scary at the same time. She saw a Degas ballet dancer stretching. Dan suddenly stopped walking. He was looking at a man who was sitting on a large gilded armchair, and he was floating and laughing.

The man wore chino pants and a black button-down shirt. He said, "They are all dead. Nobody is alive."

Dan said, "Hello! I am a police officer. Do you need some help?"

The man looked at them for a while. His sandy blond hair was wild, poking up at odd areas on his head.

"Who are you? Are you ghosts or one of these art things? My wife always loved visiting the Met. I don't know shit about art, but boy, did she know."

Cindy said, "Where is your wife?"

The man looked at her. His face softened for a second and then he said, "You can't trick me."

Officer Dan said, "We are not ghosts. We are here to help you. My name is Officer Dan and this is Cindy."

The man said, "What? What? Why are the artworks moving? You cannot be. I have gone crazy. Nobody is alive and you are not here either."

The man stopped floating. His chair skidded on the cracked cement and he stood up and ran at them. Dan didn't hesitate. He whipped out his gun and fired two shots at the crazed man, who stopped in his tracks and was knocked backwards by the velocity of the bullets. His head exploded and all the sculptures stopped moving and talking.

Dan said, "Has the world gone crazy? Nothing makes sense."

Cindy merely stared at the dead man. She was feeling the same way. They walked back. Mary and Rochelle looked relieved when they traveled up the hill.

Mary said, "If we go that way, we should be going south."

Officer Dan didn't say anything and Mary didn't ask them what happened, but Cindy knew they would have heard the shots. Cindy forgot she was walking barefooted. Her black stockings were all shredded from running.

Officer Dan said, "We need to get you some shoes before your feet start to bleed."

Mary said, "What size are you? I always have an extra pair of sandals in my purse."

"I'm size seven."

"I'm a size nine but this should fit until we find another pair of shoes for you."

The sandals were black with an open toe and no back. Cindy tried them on, finding them loose but she could walk in them. A chilly breeze flew around them and Dan directed them to walk near the exit of the park. As they traveled, Cindy had an odd feeling that she was going the wrong way, that she was supposed to find somebody, a stranger named Grace and that this stranger was looking for her.

Chapter 12

A small fire blazed in front of Lazarus. He was inside a small alcove hidden by several broken brick walls and a mound of earth. He was cold and he saw his breath in the air. He felt lucky that it was only April and summer was only a few weeks away. He was chewing on beef jerky and drank out of a bottle of water. The night was quiet. Even the crickets died today. But he heard something coming from behind him so he grabbed a piece of wood and whirled around. A dog came out of the night. It was wearing a collar and it whined as it came into the light. It was not a purebred but a mutt and was shivering in the night.

"Come here, boy."

Lazarus took another piece of beef jerky from his shirt and held it out. He was saving the rest for later, but he wanted some companionship in the worst day of his life. The dog came closer, sniffing the air. It had a long snout and moved with a limp. Lazarus didn't make any sudden moves. The dog came closer and took the jerky from his hands.

"Good dog," he said. He hadn't had a dog for years. His last dog, Champ, died when he was in college, while he was away. He missed that dog.

It chewed the morsel and looked at him.

"Sorry, that is all I have. We will look for some food tomorrow. Come closer to the fire. You've had a long day."

Lazarus rummaged in his backpack and found a small blanket. The dog moved closer to the fire and he wrapped the blanket around him. The dog still shivered a little but snuggled closer to him. Lazarus petted the dogs head and what he thought was water was blood. He looked at its collar and saw the dog's name was Sammy.

Lazarus said, "Ok, Sammy, we will try to help each other."

He looked around and found a large palm leaf on the ground. He placed it close to Sammy and poured some of his water on it. The dog slopped the liquid while Lazarus checked it, looking for where the bleeding was coming from, but couldn't see in the darkness. Sammy was covered in blood and he hoped he could keep this animal alive.

Sammy turned to him and snuggled close to where he was lying on the ground. The dog stopped whimpering and closed his eyes. Lazarus looked up at the stars and the night sky and wondered if God was watching them. His mind was going crazy trying to understand what was happening. He was not sure if he was going to survive tomorrow or the next, but he was sure he had not felt this alive in years. It was sad that it took a tragedy and extreme change to bring him out of the doldrums of his everyday life.

THE MORNING WAS GRAY, the sun hidden by dark clouds. He opened his eyes to the smoldering fire pit. Sammy was not in his sleeping spot. He stood and stretched his arms upward. He dreamt last night that everything was back to normal and he was getting ready for work and then everything changed into an inky blackness. He awoke with his back stiff and his hands cold. He heard Sammy off in the distance, whimpering. Lazarus moved toward the noise.

"Sammy?"

It was the dog, but he sounded different, bigger somehow. Then he saw the blood. It trailed for a few feet to where he heard the noise. His breathing got quicker and he feared he would see something he didn't want to look at. He tried to wipe away from his mind the dead man impaled on the metal rods. He thought about Alice in Wonderland were everybody was crazy and he wondered if he was dreaming all of this and at any moment he would awake to real life.

The sounds of Sammy got louder. He wanted to run and flee away, but there was nowhere to go. His nightmares would follow him no matter where he went. The dog was hidden behind a clump of up-turned grass and trees. He needed to find out what was happening to it, and if he needed to help it out of its misery he would do it. Lazarus realized he was holding onto a large tree limb and he gripped it tightly.

The dog howled to the sky. Lazarus rushed forward and saw it lying in a puddle of blood and shaking all over. Sammy's eyes locked onto his. Lazarus couldn't take it and moved closer to the dog, lifting the tree limb.

He turned his face away, still hearing Sammy struggling. The dogs howled again. Lazarus swung downward with all his might, but before he hit the dog the tree limb stopped in midair. He looked down and saw Sammy holding the tree limb in his mouth, but it was not Sammy. The canine was large and thick muscled. When he looked at the dog's eyes, he started to wag his tail.

"Sammy, is that you?"

The collar was on the ground, broken in two because it was too small to fit this new Sammy. The dog tore the tree limb out of his hands and threw it a few feet away and barked at him in greeting.

"How did you change and get so big?"

The dog licked his face. Lazarus was too stunned to do anything. He patted Sammy's massive head and said, "You look better. We should find breakfast. What do you think?"

The dog barked, but before Lazarus could start back to his camp Sammy ran off.

Chapter 13

Lazarus found Sammy waiting for him a few feet away. He was excited to start the day. They walked among the ruins of the city. The Grogs were roaming around the wreckage of the buildings. He could hear them howling also eating. He didn't want to see what they were eating. With Sammy in tow, the creatures didn't bother them. He was walking past a group of industrial size buildings flattened and smashed by the tsunami. He still held hope that somebody would find and rescue them.

Sammy stopped and sniffed the air. Lazarus looked in the direction Sammy was smelling. It was a grocery store with all the food and goods lying on the ground. Most of the structure seemed intact except where part of the store fell into a ravine. Birds flew around and landed, picking at the food. He also saw a riot of squirrels, rats and other creatures roaming around. Lazarus looked away in disgust.

He was about to rummage among the food when he spotted large Grog creatures sitting in the darkness of the building. He noticed Sammy scanning the darkness, looking at the Grogs. Lazarus petted Sammy's head and warned him to stay away from the area. Lazarus saw a pan and other food items he wanted, but when he looked at the Grogs he turned away.

After walking a few feet he heard a great ruckus taking place behind him. He saw birds taking flight and heard a loud crash and a scream. He didn't look back. Lazarus was happy Sammy was around him. He wasn't as large as a Grog, but he was strong enough to take one in a fair fight.

Traveling a few blocks they encountered another broken store. But this one was not spilling with food and goods. Clothing and household items cluttered the floor and the surrounding area.

Lazarus knelt down, saying, "What do you think, Sammy?"

The dogged sniffed the air. He waved his tail.

"It's fine. Thanks, Sammy."

Sammy almost looked like he waved his head. It was just a gentle nod. Lazarus studied the dog again and Sammy gave him a questioning gaze.

"Ok, let's go find some stuff."

He started walking into the store. Looking around, he couldn't tell where the store began or ended. He realized he was standing in a stretch of a strip mall. So there were several stores in this patch. He moved and looked at the clothes. Grabbing several of the shirts and sweaters, he found his size and placed them into his sack.

He saw a pan sitting by itself.

"Sammy, look, it's a pan. Now we just need a spatula and if we are lucky, some oil."

Lazarus grabbed the pan and looked it over.

"Wow, this is expensive stuff. I could not afford this before."

Smirking he placed it in his sack. After a few more hours, he found a sleeping bag, a heavy jacket, and a large traveling pack. He ditched the old one because it barely fit his stuff. Lazarus had a feeling they would be traveling for a long time after he found the man he was looking for. He also found an axe and a sharpening stone, a can opener and other things he might need.

"So, Sammy let's eat. I found a can of mystery meat."

He looked at a metal can. It read, ham. His mom always called this food mystery meat. He never knew why. He felt a pang of sadness thinking about his parents. He lifted the pin and pulled, hearing a clicking and suction noise as he pried the lid off. The smell made his mouth water. He never liked canned goods, but he was famished. Sammy was also licking his lips.

He needed a spoon or fork but didn't see one. Using his fingers, he pulled some of the meat out and gave it to Sammy. The dog barked and gobbled up the food. He took some himself and ate it. The meat was the tastiest meal he'd had in a long time. He was thirsty and had to dry swallow the food and he made a mental note that he had to find utensils, a canteen, and water. They ate several more cans of ham and some Vienna sausages. They sat on an empty space of asphalt which he cleared before they started to eat. The sun finally poked out of the gray clouds.

"Sammy, it's going to be a warm day today."

Lazarus took off his jacket. He closed his eyes and let his mind direct him. Matthew was slowly moving toward him but he could not tell how far away he was. He stood.

"Are you ready?"

Sammy barked and they started traveling.

LAZARUS SMELT SOMETHING sour coming from the very ground and the dirty crumbling buildings. Sammy pranced next to him and sniffed the air. The fetid scent was coming from the damp areas hidden from the sun. He opened his backpack and took out the small axe, holding the weapon casually in his hand as they walked along a stretch of ground almost stripped clean by the large waves of asphalt and cement.

They had been traveling along a grouping of residential homes, now reduced to broken constructions. Dirt was piled waist-high in some areas and other areas were scrubbed clean of grass and foundations, looking as if nothing stood there.

The odd thing he noticed was the silence. All he heard was his traveling boots and Sammy's paws crunching along the ground. Usually, when humanity still roamed this area before the great wave destroyed this once prosperous city, Lazarus would walk to his apartment and hear the hum of humanity everywhere, from the sounds of men talking in front of their homes to the squelching sounds of traffic driving along the asphalt street. Now, his footsteps sounded loud to his ears and the wind flowed making a restless sound of silence. He hoped somebody was alive and not morphed into a Grog or something worse.

The rancid smell came to him again. Sammy growled, scanning in the area.

"What do you see, Sammy?"

The dog continued to growl. Then he saw it. Somebody stood a few feet away from him. He placed his palm over his forehead and shaded his eyes. Looking at the person, he couldn't discern the figure with the sun behind it. The smell was coming from it. Another figure came out from a backdrop of a dirt mound. Sammy growled.

"Hello," Lazarus said.

They didn't respond to him. The figures were short, about the size of a child of ten, but he sensed waves of hatred coming from them.

Lazarus started to move forward, but Sammy walked in front of him, blocking his way.

"Ok, let's go another way."

He turned and saw more small figures behind him. Lazarus grabbed his axe and moved to higher ground. The figures came closer and he saw them. They all had bald heads, men and women, but they were small, about kid size. Wearing tatters for clothes, they had large luminous red eyes. They gazed at him with no expression until the first creature howled to the sky. All of them started to howl, facing him with a rictus of sharp teeth. Sammy stood close to him and met the first creature.

Chapter 14

The first creature ran up to him with a screech and a snarl. Lazarus backed up a few steps but Sammy launched his large body at it. They met in a booming crash and Lazarus couldn't see who was the victor for the creature slashed with its talon hands and Sammy with his big body moved in front of his sight, blocking his view. He heard a crunch and saw the creature was caught in Sammy's jaws. His dog snapped its neck and threw it away.

Blood splattered the ground in torrents. The creature stopped moving. Lazarus sensed something behind him. Turning, he saw one of the creatures scrambling toward him, moving on all fours like a spider. Without thinking, he swung the small axe at it. He felt the axe sink into the creature's neck, biting and cutting, and deep red blood showered upwards like a geyser.

Something started to happen to him. In his wonderment, he felt something akin to power flow in his body. *Magic*, he was thinking. Holding his free hand aloft he pointed at the nearest creature. A powerful wind blasted at the beast, sending it flying backward. It hit a crumbling brick wall with a thud, destroying the barrier. He turned to see several of the creatures surrounding Sammy.

Running, he pointed toward some of the creatures, flinging them away like leaves. Sammy dispatched the remaining creature with a snap of his jaws. Lazarus stood close to his dog. Sammy was breathing hard, looking for the next attack, but none came. Lazarus held the bloodied axe in his hands and looked at it in a with a mix of horror and bewilderment. "Good boy. Let's get out of here."

He bent down and wiped the axe on the ground. Lazarus felt crude and sad. Even if he was rescued and the world went back to normal, he couldn't see himself sitting in a cubicle again. They walked out of the area. He saw the dead creatures lying mute in various prone positions of death. His magic did this, and he would need to learn how to use and control it.

As they left the area he sensed Matthew was traveling toward him as if they had some communication between them. Yet he was not sure why he felt that way. He also felt something, a need, a drive to find a place he glimpsed in his dreams, a dark place with large cylindrical objects and a place hidden from time and memory that could only be recalled as a legend.

Lazarus noticed the ground changed from cement and asphalt to rocks and earth. Several of the trees still stood with their roots showing. They traveled to a park, large by the look of it, with a small lake that was filled with all types of debris.

He smelt the foul smell again, coming from the tepid waters of the lake. He veered away from the foul smelling water but Sammy kept on looking at the lake. He thought he saw something swimming inside its dirty waters. They moved toward a round cement enclosure where there was a kid's playground. He saw remnants of a metal swing and a monkey bars structure. A few of the poles stuck out at odd angles. He hadn't been to a park since he was in high school.

Lazarus walked by the monkey bars and then the swing. His mind wandered to the last time he was on a swing. It was the day after graduating from Hoover High. He sat on the leather harness. His hands grasped the metal chain links, fingering the cold metal with his fingertips. He barely swung. Next to him was his friend, Cindy. She was also moving slowly.

He was going to college at Long Beach and Cindy was accepted to college back east. She was smart, much smarter than him.

He said, "You are going to do great things."

Cindy looked at him. She flicked her long blond hair. He'd known her since they were in grade school together. They lived a few blocks away from each other.

"You are, too," she said.

They sat in silence for a little while. Lazarus was feeling foolish. He knew he would miss her, but he didn't want to say it because if he did he would do something stupid like tear up and cry. But he knew this was the best thing for her. Cindy was destined for greatness. She was the head cheerleader with the brains of a Mensa student. Cindy was always invited to the best parties. She was dating the captain of the football team. He was not sure why they were friends. They had nothing in common.

"You're just saying that. I'm not like you."

"Look, I'll keep in contact with you. Don't worry. We will still be friends."

"I'm not worried. But if you forget to contact me it's fine."

"So, what are you going to major in at College?"

Lazarus said, "I don't know. What are you going to do?"

She swung a little bit more. "Nah. I think I can swing higher than you."

"Hah, no way."

Lazarus wondered where Cindy was and if she was dead or alive. But, he thought, she must be alive. He saw her in his vision. He shook his head and kept walking. The day turned into dusk with the sun slowly moving down on the horizon. If Lazarus stared upwards at the clouds and the sun and didn't notice the apocalyptic landscape before him, he would be amazed at the sight. The sky was a deep red crimson with highlights of orange and deeper cerulean blue creeping along the edges. The clouds were white and puffy like cotton candy, so beautiful and abundant and close to the ground that he thought he could have plucked them out of the air and tasted them.

"Sammy, we need to find a place to stay for the night, and some dinner."

They'd had a light lunch of crackers a few hours ago and his stomach growled for more. Sammy wagged his tail. He barked and took off.

"Where are you going?"

The dog ran out of sight, coming back with a bag of chips in his mouth.

"Where did you find this?"

Sammy nodded. He followed the dog to another store now open with its contents vomited on the ground. He checked and made sure there were no Grogs waiting to pounce on them.

"So, what should we have for dinner?"

Lazarus found several cans of spaghetti, canned hams, bottles of water and some knives in the wreckage. He also found a saucepan.

"We shall have a good dinner tonight, if we can light a fire."

Sammy barked and pawed the ground. Looking down, Lazarus saw lighters on the ground. He wondered how Sammy knew this.

Chapter 15

Matthew examined his newest find, a large hunting knife with a long edge and rubber handled grip. The blade came with a leather holder. It was sharp and felt balanced in his hand. He swung it a few times to test how it felt and realized he was rather good at edged weapons. A thought came to him. He was, in his earlier days, a martial arts enthusiast and some type of teacher, but his mind closed up to him and he couldn't remember who and what he was or if he was married and had kids. It seemed that his life began in the back alley where the police had taken him and transported him to the large hospital, and that memory slipped from him like water through a sieve.

He sat on a patch of grass next to a half torn wall, tattered and forlorn looking. His back was against the barrier. He had a small fire burning a few yards in front of him. In this enclosed area, he had enough warmth for the night. This was better than before where he slept in a small alley with a dumpster and a cardboard blanket to keep him company.

A name came to him. It was another street person like him, John or Joseph. He didn't know his name. He was just called Clacker, but not because he liked to clap or cause a ruckus. It was because he would clack his teeth at odd times. Clacker was a Vietnam Vet and had some horrible experiences during the war but he never talked about it.

It was several years ago, he thought. Matthew's memory had been murky for a while and things he thought happened yesterday were years ago. It was a night colder than this when they were sitting around a bonfire under a freeway underpass, far away from the businesses and policemen. Clacker was telling him about a time when he had the best pussy in the world.

Clacker would speak a few words and then look away and clack his teeth together, then he would start talking again. When Clacker clacked his teeth he had a faraway look and his mouth would slacken, falling slightly ajar like he was in a trance.

Matthew was not listening because Clacker had a habit of telling a story several times, even Matthew had already heard it. Matthew only kept him around because Clacker always had some food with him, a cracker here and there or a can of food or soup. Clacker had a way of getting food. He went to a homeless shelter. Matthew always stayed away from these shelters because he was known as violent. He wasn't, but they thought he was. Matthew may have hit somebody in line once, when he was getting lunch.

This time, Clacker's story had changed. He usually talked about the time when he was in college when he was in a fraternity and he had a prostitute. Except, he started to talk about the time when he was in the bush waiting for Charlie to kill him.

"Yes, it was a hot night when I sat in the bush with the mosquitos biting my ass, and my best friend next to me. We were sent to scout this part of that god-forsaken jungle."

Clacker stopped talking and clacked his teeth. Matthew turned to him. He had never heard this story before.

"So, I had my gun out before me. We heard noises in the jungle. Somebody screamed and we wanted to run out of the foxhole, but Charlie is tricky. He wants you to leave your hole so he can kill you. So we stayed in our hole. Suddenly, gunfire erupted. I heard my commander yell to fire. I shot my gun and until it burnt my hand. Mortar shells started to fall all around us, but we stayed in our foxhole. Then I turned to look behind me and my friend was dead. His head was split open and his blood was flowing. I screamed and stood and shot into the bush. Charlie was ready for me."

He stopped talking, clacking away. Clacker kept on smacking his teeth, then he looked at the fire, staring at it with such intensity that Matthew thought he was going buggy, a term he had called other street people who leave their minds with the bugs, but keep their bodies in place. Then Clacker was back. He screamed and started to talk gibberish.

"I killed them. I ran into the bush. Charlie was all around me. They were talking in their language that sounded like angry yelling. I killed them all until I was shot in the head."

"You killed them all?" Matthew said.

"Yes, they gave me a medal."

Clackers stopped and clack his teeth.

"You did. You never told me that."

"What? I was saying you should have seen her. She was the best pussy I have ever had. She was tall with the biggest breasts you have ever seen."

"We were talking about the war."

Clackers stared at him in an uncomprehending way. "I can't talk about that."

Clacker started to ramble on with some story he had told him before.

◦≫∾

MATTHEW AWOKE WITH a jerk. He thought he heard a noise and movement coming from the darkness beyond him. It was not yet morning and his fire had smoldered to nothing. He glanced around and saw nothing around him except the broad shelf of debris and broken earth and a tree half out of the ground. Then he saw it coming out of the burnt fires. He had seen this before. A vision, a place he needed to find. He watched the vision like he was watching a TV screen.

He knew there would be war and turmoil and he also saw himself with three others, entering a vast temple underground with light filtering through water. It didn't make sense to him. But they were there through the portal. He knew the man next to him. He was the Leader, the one person who could take them out of turmoil and lead them. Matthew also noticed he was bloodied and barely standing.

He wondered what had happened to him. His newfound powers should protect him. He had been practicing since he knew his element was fire. Magic was finally bestowed on him by the blood of the earth when it was spilled along the land. Yet, destruction reigned when the Bastions were opened. He knew that for sure and he also knew it was his choice and the others to open the Bastions. He shook his head and wondered why he knew all this, but the answer wouldn't come to him. Tomorrow, he knew for sure, he would meet his Leader and comrade.

Chapter 16

Cindy woke early in the morning, hearing the gentle snores of her other companions. Officer Dan yesterday found a building still half-standing in the remnants of structures.

Mary said, "Are you sure this house is safe to sleep in?"

"Yes, it's made of bricks and mortar. It was built at the beginning of the last century. It will hold for at least a night."

They argued a little while longer. Rochelle looked bored. Cindy shook her head. She couldn't understand how a teenager could be bored at a time like this. Night filled the sky with bright stars and dark hues. Some of the street lamps turned on, casting cocoons of light on the street. They finally entered after they heard something clatter in the street beyond.

Upon entering the building, they found blankets and moldy boxes. It was a storage area, unused for quite some time. Cindy slept on the ground with a musty blanket wrapped around her. Officer Dave slept facing the empty doorway.

Light started to creep inside from the open front. Her stomach growled. The only thing she had eaten was some crackers and chips found outside a flattened liquor store.

Rochelle said, "I can't believe this is happening."

Cindy almost jumped from her sleeping spot. She looked over at her. Rochelle held her knees to her chest and was rocking a little. Cindy stood and sat close to her, placing her back against a stained box.

Cindy said, "My mom always told me when times are tough to remember the Lord is there to protect you. And the Lord will help you through your tough times."

Rochelle didn't say anything, so Cindy put her arm around her. They stayed like that for quite some time.

Officer Dan woke when the sun's light shone into his eyes. He jerked and lifted his head.

He said, "Hello, how are you doing?"

He sounded like he was walking down the street, talking to a passerby. She felt he was being cheerful for their benefit.

"We are doing fine," she said.

Mary roused herself and looked at them, rubbing her eyes with her hands.

"I'm hungry. Let's find something to eat."

After they were ready, they stepped out of their shelter. Officer Dave was in the lead. His black police uniform looked careworn and she noticed his shoulders seemed to sag. They had to pick their way through all the fallen debris, glass, steel and other things Officer Dave steered them away from.

She was not in New York when the September eleven terrorist attacks happened. She was still in high school, in her senior year to be exact. They were all sent home from school and she barely had time to talk to her friend, Lazarus. She wondered if this scene of destroyed buildings and dead bodies rekindled some of their memories. She wondered who was still alive to look at this scene. Then, as they walked past a group of crumbling building innards the ground started to shake.

Rochelle said, "What's happening?"

Officer Dave seem to be frozen. The ground shook then rolled as if they were adrift on an ocean.

She said, "It's an aftershock from the quake. Get over here toward a clear area."

They moved a few feet away. It was hard to find a place without dirt and debris jutting out from the ground. But she found an area with smooth asphalt, free of detritus and broken scraps. The shaking stopped as suddenly as it started. Rochelle was holding on to her mom. They all stood, looking downwards.

Dave said, "Thank you, Cindy. I couldn't move. I thought we were, you know."

"I know," she said. "I lived in Los Angeles and know about earthquakes."

He said, "I don't know what to do."

"It's fine. We need to start moving."

"Give us a few minutes," Mary said. Both Rochelle and her mom looked scared and Cindy didn't want them to run away in terror.

"Fine," Cindy said. She thought they should start moving again soon because she sensed something was coming for them.

Dave said, "Do you hear that?"

It was barely audible, but Cindy heard a scrabbling noise, like the sound of thousands of feet moving.

"What's that?" Cindy said. Now it was her turn to be surprised.

Officer Dave turned to them. "Run!"

Mary and Rochelle ran after Officer Dave. Cindy followed them. The sound of running feet became louder and another sound came forth, a low whining noise. Turning behind her, she saw large roaches coming out of every building and fissure. Cindy caught up to her fleeing group. Officer Dave directed them along a street littered with large blocks of cement and asphalt. The dead were scattered among the ruins. Repellant smells emanated from the ground. Cindy didn't care. She ran for her life.

Cindy tried to bring forth her powers, but she couldn't. Terror filled her mind and her actions. The roaches scrambled toward them in a rush of scaled bodies and writhing antennas. A rancid smell of a sewer came to them in a fog, overpowering the air and their senses. She was more than afraid. She was panicked, filled with dread and fear. It felt like an extension of the giant insects. Cindy fell. One of her sandals flew from her and she scraped her palm and forearm. The creatures were almost on top of her. Shots rang out and Cindy got to her feet. The roaches stopped for a few seconds and turned toward Officer Dave. She saw him holding his gun in a shooting stance, firing away.

Cindy knew what was going to happen. She saw the creatures move toward Officer Dave. Looking around, she didn't see Mary or Rochelle. She needed to do something. She screamed as the first roach attacked and hit Dave. A loud crunch of bones was heard. She screamed again. Her arm shot upwards toward the giant insects. Green water peppered the sky and rained on the creatures. The roaches started to scream.

Cindy sensed her power coalescing. Smoke appeared on the creature's bodies. The insects tried to run back into the holes and fissures. Cindy raised her arms high and then downwards. A wave of green acid swept before her, killing and burning all.

Everything ceased. She dropped her hands. The carcasses of the giant roaches littered the ground, smoking in death. She scanned the area looking for Officer Dave. Seeing him lying motionless on the ground she ran to him, noticing that he was not touched by her magic. Standing close to him was Rochelle. Mary knelt by Dave, her hands poised over his head.

"Is he alive?" Cindy asked, kneeling close.

"I don't know," Mary said. "How did you do that?"

Cindy ignored her question and turned him over. He was heavy and Mary had to help her. His skin was turning blue and a blood stain about the size of a fist was on his chest.

He murmured, "Take care of yourself." Then he died.

Cindy saw his eyes change, losing their luster and vibrancy. Rochelle gasped and looked away.

They couldn't say anything for a while. Mary went to her daughter and gave her a hug. Cindy shook her head. She was terrified, not because they were out here in a crazy new world, but because the one person who resembled protection and order was dead. Her eyes misted for a second or two and she wiped away a tear. The fumes of the dead roaches became unbearable.

"We should leave," Cindy said. She kneeled back down and took Officer Dave's holster and gun.

"What are you doing?" Mary said.

"We need something to defend ourselves with," she said.

"I think you can defend yourself with your magic."

"I am not sure I can do that again."

Cindy placed the holster around her hip. She found her sandals and put them back on, noting that she needed to find some more footwear. She stood and they walked away. Mary and Rochelle at first didn't move and then started to follow her.

Chapter 17

S ammy barked several times and then licked his face. Lazarus opened his eyes. The sky was turning blue as the sun crested on the horizon. His body felt like he had been hit by a sledgehammer. He looked at his arm and noticed muscle tone where he didn't have it before. He flexed, and his biceps and forearms popped. Sammy barked again.

He said, "What, boy? What do you see?"

The dog took off like a shot. Lazarus shook his head, hoping Sammy would be careful. They had slept in a small valley with a brick wall behind and large clumps of dirt piled up around them. He knew Sammy would protect him while he slept. This dog was more than a mere animal, but a smart creature that knew what he wanted when he asked, or before he knew what he wanted. Sammy came running back holding in his teeth two large rabbits.

"What do you want me to do with these?"

Sammy placed one of the rabbits on the ground in front of him and trotted away with the other morsel in his mouth.

"Well, you're right. I have to learn to do this."

Lazarus grabbed the knife. He had cooked chicken before, but it had come already prepared and ready for the oven. He found a cleaned surface on a cement stand. Cutting a slit on top of the rabbit he started to pull the fur away from the skin. It came away in a sickening ripping sound. Lazarus almost gave up but persisted in gutting the rabbit, cutting away. When he was finished he had a mess of blood and guts, and a skinned carcass. He was breathing heavy.

Looking around, he saw water bubbling up from a long pipe extending from a building a few feet away. He stood up went over to wash his hands.

He started gathering firewood and found several sticks he could use as a skewer. Realizing he should have done this first made him curse. He felt a little foolish. Sammy watched him with coal black eyes, wondering why he didn't just eat his meal like he did.

When Lazarus finally got all the wood ready, he walked back to his spot and dropped it to the ground. Flies were swarming all over the rabbit carcass. *All that work for nothing*, he thought. He shook his head. He should have got his food the easy way. He grabbed the skinned rabbit and gave it to Sammy, who wolfed it down in several bites.

He found a can of spaghetti and took out the saucepan. But before he opened it, he started a fire. Grabbing a spoon from his backpack, he placed it close to him, opened the can and plopped the mess into the pan. He had to hold the handle close to the fire without burning his hand. After a few minutes simmering it was ready.

He ate his food with his spoon. Everything tasted good, more than good, spectacular. Lazarus had eaten canned spaghetti before. He wondered if the tidal wave had something inside it, something that could create the Grog creatures and give him powers.

He ate everything in his saucepan. He even licked his fingers and cleaned his spoon. He felt invigorated as though he could run a mile. Energy flowed through him and he wondered where this feeling was coming from. He was never an athletic person, and had never had this feeling before. Now, he felt powers course through his body.

He studied Sammy. He was not the same dog that first came to him whimpering and sullen. This was a war canine, ready to do battle against any foe who attacked him. His powers were untapped. He needed to learn more. Cleaning all his pans and utensils with the bubbling water, he placed his things to dry in the sun. Standing a few yards from the ever vigilant Sammy, Lazarus held his right hand up. He looked at a grouping of rocks and broken debris. Focusing on moving the objects didn't do anything. All he sensed was not power or magic, but the tranquil wind blowing around his hair and clothes. Sammy regarded him with a smirk.

Lazarus saw a metal can on the ground and focused on it. The can started to move slightly to the side. He tensed all his muscles and tried to move it more. Getting a slight headache, he wanted to stop, but he kept on staring at the metal soda can. As he did, something else happened. He scanned the can as if looking through a microscope. He saw the blue metal shining in the sun and also sensed the dark liquid inside it. The view was unnerving. He closed his eyes and shook his head.

His body got warm and power filled him. Lazarus wagged his tail. Opening his eyes, he looked at the soda can again, which had not moved. He focused on the object and it started to float upwards. He moved the soda can into a vertical position. Nodding, the can started to turn, over and over again. Lazarus laughed and clapped his hands. The aluminum can fell down and hit the ground with a clunk and thud.

"Wow," Lazarus said. He was amazed. Nothing like this had ever happened to him and he wondered why he was chosen to have these powers. He felt the road ahead would be difficult.

He also sensed he was meant to do something, something important.

Chapter 18

Lazarus and Sammy started traveling again after they finished their breakfast. The day was getting warmer and Lazarus had changed into a gray t-shirt, jeans and tennis shoes. Sammy scanned the wreckage and debris around them. Lazarus thought that if they could find a jeep, or maybe a motorcycle they could travel faster. He knew where he was going. Matthew, the man he was looking for, was walking toward him. He was close. Lazarus was sure about that.

He heard a noise like a thousand beating wings. It was difficult to understand what he saw, at first.

A group of hornets flew together, all in the same color of scarlet and stripes of bright yellow. They made a loud buzzing noise as they flew, sounding like a buzz saw. They moved in unison, upwards, downwards and diagonally. Lazarus crouched behind smashed cement and asphalt debris. He didn't like the looks of these creatures.

The hornets moved closer to him. He saw each of the insects were the size of his hands, with large stingers at the end. The creatures had not seen him yet. His hands touched a large vine. Looking around, he noticed that plants and foliage had started to overtake the landscape almost overnight. A large fern with leaves the size of small children grew through the remnants of a street, spreading its fronds high into the air.

He looked at Sammy. The dog was crouched next to him, staring at the large hornets. Lazarus petted the dog on his head while he scanned the area for some place to hide, away from the insects. He knew a hornet's sting could be hurtful, but these creatures looked like they would kill.

Luckily, the plants and trees shielded them. He wondered why this swarm was just flying around the area. Then he saw a large Grog roaming among the foliage. The Grog sniffed the air. *Great*, he thought. He couldn't escape both creatures. But this was an opportunity to use his powers.

The Grog was coming closer. Sammy started to rise from his spot and Lazarus placed a hand for him to stop moving. He gauged the distance between the swarm and the Grog, which was moving closer to them. Raising his hand, he focused on the Grog. The Hornet swarm was moving further away from them and he only had a minute before the Grog would be on top of them.

He pushed with his magic. The Grog stopped moving. As Lazarus watched the Grog strained, and began to move forward again. He realized it was stronger than his magic. Sammy stood, his hackles rising. Lazarus focused and redoubled his efforts but it was not working. In desperation, he let go of the beast and concentrated on the swarm. He pushed and pulled them toward the Grog. The beast was coming full speed at them. Sammy stood, growling and showing his large teeth. It was the first time Lazarus had seen the dog's teeth and he was glad Sammy was on his side. He was about to give up directing the hornet swarm, when the insects finally noticed the Grog and flew at it. They buzzed louder and massed around the Grog. The Grog stopped in mid-run and fell head first into the cracked cement. Lazarus grabbed Sammy and they ran away into the nearest building. He stepped on cartons of soured milk and yogurt. They ran into several aisles now smashed and lying and on the ground. Sammy moved close to him. From outside, the screaming sound of the Grog trailed off into death throes. The hornet's buzzing became a loud hum.

Lazarus said, "Sammy, let's stay here for a while. Maybe the swarm will leave after they've had their fill."

❧

LAZARUS, SHELTERED inside the building, tore his eyes away from the feeding frenzy. The buzzing noise was so intense that at times he had to hold his hands over his ears to muffle the noise. Sammy sat with his nuzzle close to him, sensing his fear and annoyance.

It was mid-afternoon when Lazarus and Sammy walked out of the building and into the area where they had seen the hornets. The swarm had finally finished eating the carcass. All that was left was bits and pieces of the skull, rib cage and some of the rear leg bones. Everything else was gone except for a messy smear of blood on the ground. Having finished their meal, the insects had disappeared in a fast flying arc away from them.

Walking away from the killing zone Lazarus glanced around the landscape and saw several buildings still standing with most of the inner foundations exposed to the air. He heard a buzzing noise. Glancing at the closest shelter, they ran toward another building. It had a large sign in front which was not broken but showed only some words he couldn't make out, but the containers and shattered cans indicated that it must be a grocery store, one of the larger chains. He was not sure which one because the buzzing sound got louder and he ran into the darkness of the structure.

He smelt something. It was the scent of pizza, spaghetti and cakes. He shook his head. This couldn't be, everything was smashed in the aisles, glass and cash registers. Yet, he noticed the area was clear of debris. It was as if somebody had cleaned the back of the store and the structure. The scent of food wafted in the air. Sammy sniffed and licked his chops. Lazarus nodded to his dog and they explored the back of the building. Scanning the interior, he saw droplets of water still hanging along the walls and dirt along the floor.

"So, there is another survivor."

Lazarus looked around for the man who spoke, but all he saw was busted pipes, boxes of food, metal plates and plastic white bags all strewn on the ground and piled high in several places.

"Over here."

Sammy growled a little but only in fright, not in anger. The man Lazarus saw was floating above the rubble that looked like the meat cutter cases in the back of the grocery store. It was surprisingly intact as if it had not been touched by the water. Yet as Lazarus got closer he knew he was deceived, because the case didn't have any meat in it and the glass was broken in shards. The smell of food came to him again. Lazarus wondered if the man could smell it.

The man was large, bigger than the biggest man he had ever seen in person. Lazarus couldn't help but stare. Besides, the man was floating above him like an avenging angel, holding a large turkey leg in his hands and he had grease flowing down his cheeks. It was almost disgusting.

"Who are you?" Lazarus said.

"I, I am the luckiest man on earth. But let me say, I am happy to find somebody else alive in this wasteland." The man took another bite of his turkey leg. Bits of meat fell on the ground and Sammy ran to eat some of it.

The man said, "My name is Bob."

Lazarus said, "So, Bob, do you have any food for me and my dog?"

Bob waved his hands and buckets of food appeared in front of them.

Chapter 19

Lazarus looked at the food and he was so famished he didn't know where to start eating first. He had a pair of roasted chicken legs in his mouth while Sammy was hunched on the ground tearing up a large roast. The food was better than good. It was incredible. Soda cans and water were also next to it and Lazarus started to drink in large gulps. Bob floated to the ground and joined them in an ecstasy of gluttonous enjoyment. Bob smacked his lips in excitement as he waved his hands and desserts of all kinds appeared in mid-air. Lazarus grabbed a white cupcake and bit into it. The flavor was so intense and sweet he was taken aback for a second. None of this should be happening. He didn't even consider if he was getting poisoned. He trusted this large, red-faced man, Bob. His eating was infectious and Lazarus gobbled so much food that he had to stop for fear of getting sick.

Bob said, "Was that enough, my friend?"

"Yes," he said.

Sammy also howled and kept on chewing on a piece of broiled chicken. Lazarus sat on the ground and stared up at Bob, who floated up into the air.

"How did you survive the hurricane?"

Bob waved his hands. "I don't know. I was working at the Yamaha building. I was a customer service rep there. I didn't see the first wave until it struck my office. I blacked out and end up waking up a block away from here."

"So, you have this power to create food."

It was more of a statement than a question.

Bob nodded his head. "Something came over me. A short of shock, I think, but I'm not entirely sure. The first thing I did was float. I love it. So, do you have any powers?"

Lazarus said, "I have some type of energy to fight the Grogs."

"Those are nasty creatures. I saw a woman change before my eyes. Do you think there was some type of radiation fallout from the nuclear reactors down south?"

"I don't know. But I don't think radiation would give us powers." Lazarus pointed to Sammy. "This dog a day ago was just a small, harmless mutt. Now look at him. He is a war beast. He protected me from the creatures."

Bob floated. He waved his hand and a large pie floated next to him. He took a handful of the cherry pie and stuffed it into his mouth. He chewing was very audible in this structure.

"Bob," Lazarus said, "are you going to leave this place?"

"Nah, I can create food out of the air. I'll stay around here."

"Well, I have to meet somebody. Will you go with me?"

Bob stopped eating and looked at him. "You have to meet somebody?"

"Yes, I have this feeling that I have something important to do."

Bob looked at him in a crazy way. "No, I want to stay here."

"What about the Grogs? They will eventually come here."

Bob shook his head. "I can defend myself. I have conjured food and used it to distract the creatures. I also made a large pie and threw it at them."

Bob laughed. Pieces of the cherry pie were smeared across his once blue button-down shirt. He took out something from his shirt pocket. Lazarus couldn't tell what Bob was holding since it was covered in pieces of chicken, cherries and something he couldn't make out. Bob threw the object at him. Lazarus tried to catch it. The object hit the floor on a discarded bag of potato chips.

"I don't have any use of it, but you are free to take the jeep."

Lazarus grabbed the object, realizing it was a set of keys with a FOB attached to it. "Thanks. Are you sure you don't want to come with us?"

"Yes, I can always find another place." Bob waved his hand and a buttered croissant appeared. He took it and stuffed it down his gullet. Lazarus wanted to tell him that if he kept on eating like this he would grow bigger than this building, but he let that thought disappear. Bob would not listen to him. He had found his place in this new world.

Lazarus said, "Where is the jeep?"

"I parked it in the front somewhere. It has an alarm. I drove it here and I am sure it will still work. Do you know who you're supposed to meet?"

Lazarus shook his head. "I have no clue. I hope this is worth it. I hope somebody will come along and help you."

"Nah, I'll be fine. I have more than I need. I sleep in the back."

Lazarus looked out the front of the broken building and saw that dusk had finally darkened the sky.

He said, "I think Sammy and I will stay here until tomorrow, if that's fine with you."

Bob shook his head, already knowing they would stay. "Sure, I have room in the back for you and your dog. Go ahead and look around. Just be careful and don't stray too far from this area."

"Yes," Lazarus said. He nodded to Sammy who started to sniff around the store.

Bob said, "Do you want a short tour?"

"Sure," Lazarus replied, "but I don't think there is much to see in these ruins."

"Ah," Bob said, "you're wrong. Come over here."

He floated over to the part of the building that was still intact. The food was cleared from this area. Bob moved down an aisle. It was clear of debris and cans and such.

"Did you clean up this place?"

"I tidied a little, but I think somebody was here before me."

Lazarus said, "Have you seen anybody else besides me?"

"No, I thought I saw somebody, but I'm not sure."

"How about dead bodies?"

Bob said, "Only a few bodies outside but not in here."

They came to a corner of the building which had several stacks of wood piled up around it like a fort. It was surprisingly clear and almost looked cozy. Beach chairs were stationed inside. He spied something that looked like a table and the remains of a chair and blanket. But everything looked old, as if it was there years ago.

Lazarus walked inside. He saw around the perimeter food and cans, stacked as if stockpiling to stay here for the long run.

"Did you do any of this?" Lazarus asked.

Bob shook his head. "I don't need to stockpile food. I can make my own. Somebody was here, but they left. I only stumbled in here because it was the first market I found."

Lazarus said, "Was this place dry when you first got here?"

Bob floated next to him and didn't say anything for few seconds. Lazarus looked at him. Bob nodded his head, with a surprised look on his face.

He said, "Well, I never thought of that. Yes, this building and everything around here was dry. How can that be?"

Lazarus went inside the small enclosure and sat on one of the beach chairs. "I have a theory, but I wouldn't know. It's just an idea."

Bob moved closer to him, but his bulk was so large that he almost filled the small enclosure. His body smelt like sweet pies and rotting meat. Lazarus was trying not to gag. Sammy stayed outside the area and began to move down another aisle, sniffing the floor.

Bob said, "Tell me."

"Well, I think the giant wave was magical. And once it hit and destroyed everything it disappeared."

"That's fantastic. But it doesn't make sense, although it would explain some things."

"Yes, Bob, like how you can float and are able to conjure food out of mid-air."

Bob smiled. Lazarus saw chicken gristle on the man's teeth. The air was cooling and he wondered how he kept warm during the nights.

"Do you create a small fire at night?"

"Nah, I always keep warm. It must be from my excess."

He patted his stomach.

Chapter 20

Cindy guided Mary and her daughter over several city blocks. The rubble was so high in places they had to climb up or walk around areas which were too difficult to traverse. Cindy saw the strain she was placing on her small trio when they stopped at mid-afternoon at an area clear of debris. They were all huffing and puffing from the last mountain of rubble they climbed. Nobody was saying much.

Rochelle was looking down at the street and Mary sat against a giant concrete broken base. Her eyes were closed and she was panting. Cindy's feet hurt in the tennis shoes she had found a half a block away in a gathering of broken buildings. They fit but were a little too tight around her toes. She was light headed, since she hadn't had much to eat. They finished off the last of Mary's snacks from her purse.

Rochelle said, "Mom, this reminds me of September eleven. I don't like this."

She sniffled a little and kept looking at the ground.

Mary said, "I didn't think you were old enough to remember." She looked around the broken buildings and rubble. "Yet this is much worse. I don't think a terrorist could have created this earthquake. This is natural."

Rochelle said, "Mom, I don't think so. It's not fair. How come the other cops are not here to help us?"

"I don't know." She stared fixedly at a broken lamp post, now hanging at an odd angle a few feet away.

Cindy said, "That noise. Do you hear that?"

It was a soft sound. So low that Cindy barely heard it.

Rochelle cocked her head to the left. "I think it is the sound of animals."

"Animals?" Cindy said.

Mary looked around. "I think we are close to Central Park Zoo. It should be around here, somewhere. But I can't tell."

They looked for some type of sign, but the broken, dilapidated buildings destroyed the street signs. Then Cindy heard it. A sound like something rustling, and a large growl pierced the air.

Mary grabbed onto her daughter. "I don't like the sound of that."

They all stood, Cindy scanning the street. The creature roared again and she tried to figure out where the sound was coming from.

Mary said, "Let's go this way."

She pointed to a pathway that was clear of the wreckage and junk. They ran forward, picking their way through the rocks and asphalt. A large fissure appeared on their right and they moved around it. Cindy looked into the hole, seeing pipes and sewer water in the crack. And also a pungent smell that pervaded her senses. She felt as if she was falling into the darkness below.

Mary grabbed her arm. "What's wrong?"

Cindy found herself staring at the fissure. She shook her head. "What?" She was groggy as if she was coming out of deep sleep. The roar pierced the litter strewn and ruined street again.

Cindy snapped out of her trance and started to climb a large mound of white concrete and red bricks. She saw an opening at a synagogue. Colored glass was all over the ground and the interior of a temple with pews now moved all around as if a giant pushed them into the center of the structure, where a large hole opened up swallowing most of the interior. They ran inside and saw several dead bodies inside. A man with graying skin was behind the pulpit. A large stone had completely buried the man save his head and his right hand.

Mary said, "Rochelle, don't look."

Another body was buried under the destruction of the walls. Outside, the sound of a creature scrabbling up the mountain of stones was heard. The creature sounded very close. A sniffing and a scratching noise were audible to Cindy's ears. A growl and a snarl and then the scrabbling sound again. The beast was large. Mary pointed to a large pile of stone and a hiding place behind it. The sun poked from the fissure through the roof top.

They ran and stooped below the large awning, going inside the hiding hole. Rochelle and Mary went in first. There was no room for Cindy to get inside. She turned and stayed in the shadows, staring at the area they had come from. Her mind was racing. Fear gripped her and she wanted to run and flee, but she stayed rooted to her spot.

The creature growled, a low guttural sound that sounded like grunting, almost a yelping sound. The creature's head came through the opening of the temple, a long snout and tiny beady eyes scanning the interior. It was a brown bear, but it was changed. It had brown scales like an alligator. The claws were as long and thick as daggers. It could easily rip her apart in one swipe.

Cindy was frozen with fear. She saw the bear's muzzle was coated with red blood. She held her breath as the creature kept looking inside, sniffing. Her breath left her lungs in a rush and she nearly screamed. The beast's ears perked up.

Cindy tried to conjure some type of magic like she had with the roaches. But nothing came forth. Her mind was too focused on the death stare of the creature. The bear turned to look behind it. It growled and started lumber away with a waggling motion of its scaled haunches. The scrabbling noise of the creature's claws striking the stone was heard again while it climbed up and out into the street.

She waited in the darkness, it seemed like forever, and finally took in a long breath. Her body trembling, Cindy turned and saw Mary and Rochelle climbing out of the small hiding place. They didn't speak for a few seconds. They merely looked at the opening where the creature stood.

Mary spoke first. "What was that thing?"

"Mom, I think it was a bear," Rochelle said.

"Yes," Cindy said. "I think you are right. But it didn't look like a bear."

Mary said, "Has the world gone crazy?"

Nobody said anything at her outburst. In fact, her daughter came closer to her mom and placed her arm around her shoulder.

Cindy, who didn't have any kids and who thought parenthood was nonsense, saw how the daughter gave comfort to her mom where Cindy thought Mary should give strength to Rochelle.

Cindy shook her head. "New York doesn't get earthquakes like Los Angeles. Something has happened." She sighed and then said without thinking, "Magic."

Mary looked at her. "What did you say?"

"Did I say something?" she said.

"Yes," Rochelle said. "You said magic."

"I don't understand why I said that. But it makes sense. Magic, like the tales of Merlin and in Lord of the Rings could do this."

Mary had a wild look in her eyes. "No, I don't think so. This must be some kind of government experiment that has gone wrong. Or maybe a virus?"

Cindy said, "Maybe you're right. We need to find some place to stay. Where should we go?"

Rochelle said, "we should go to the police Precinct Officer Dan was talking about."

Cindy agreed. "Yes, I think we are heading that way."

Mary studied the dilapidated temple. "I think we are on 65th street. This is the Jewish temple there. I had a friend who came here." She paused and stifled a cry welling up from her throat.

Rochelle said, "It's ok, Mom. Maybe, your friend is still alive."

Chapter 21

Running and yelling were all Grace could remember. She was working at the New York, New York Casino. She was a front desk clerk. She had started her workday, an early shift starting in the morning until mid-afternoon. Dale, the Front Desk Manager, was walking behind her. Last night, he had given her a stern lecture about flirting with the tourists who flock to Las Vegas.

He had said, "Grace, be careful. I know you are young, in your mid-twenties. But for God's sake don't pretend to be friends with these people. They don't care about you. They want to gamble and win big. You are here only to help them spend that money." He gestured to the many cameras pointed upwards. "We are also watching. I want you to understand we are also watching."

"Yes, sir. I was being nice," Grace said.

She had been a front desk clerk for over five years and had worked at many of the other casinos. Dale nodded to her as he passed. There were several people standing in line ready to check into the hotel. She saw the regulars, locals who lived around Las Vegas, roaming inside the front of the casino. She could tell they were locals. They looked sad and forlorn with a hungry look in their eyes.

Grace was passing out a new set of pass card keys to the tourist in front of her. The other front desk clerk to her right was checking in another guest.

The first sign that something was wrong was the sound. It was not a rumbling but more of a swooshing sound. People ran inside from the front sliding doors and somebody screamed. Grace stood poised with a card in her hand.

The man in front of her turned around. His credit card was in his meaty thick hand, ready to give to her. He made a huffing noise like the sound of a dog panting. Dale walked to the front entrance as people ran past him, glancing back. Grace, for some reason, remembered seeing a small girl with her dad holding her hand. He yelled something Grace could not understand until it was too late.

He yelled, "The sand, the sand."

Dale got to the front of the double glass doors. Grace was about to grab the man's credit card when all hell broke loose. Dale turned from the front entrance and said, "Run!"

The loud sound of wind whined in Grace's ears. It was so loud that she covered her ears. Then the doors exploded inward. Sand flew inside the interior of the casino with a wind so powerful, it picked up the slot machines on the casino floor and pushed them like leaves in an autumn breeze. Grace fell backwards and hit a wall behind her. The front desk covered her for a brief second until the world turned tan and sand filled her nostrils and mouth. She tried to scream but sand filled her throat.

Darkness encroached her sight. Grace was dying. She tried to move and stand but her body felt like lead.

Sand and dirt started to fill the small space she was in. She pushed upwards but the sand made her fall back. And all this happened in the space of maybe ten seconds.

She recalled the time long ago, when she was a little girl playing in a playground at her elementary school. She was digging a hole with a blue plastic shovel and placing it into her red bucket. It was recess time and she was sitting with her best friend, Melody. They were in the corner away from the other kids in her class, talking about the new boy who had come that day. His name was Matthew, and Melody thought he was cute with his sandy blond hair.

Grace said, "That's gross. You shouldn't like boys. They touch worms and pick up insects."

Melody said, "But this Matthew has a cute smile."

Grace looked over and saw Matthew standing by himself, looking shyly at the swings a few feet away from them. Grace thought Matthew was cute in a quiet sort of way, as though he would like books and such instead of running around playing ball with the other boys.

She must have kept staring at the new kid because Matthew noticed her looking at him and he quickly turned away.

"Grace," Melody said, "stop that."

"What?"

She found herself placing the sand, not in her bucket, but at the side. She was essentially picking up sand and placing it to the side of the bucket, making a small pile.

"Why do you do like digging? It's a small kids game."

"I like it," Grace said. But she didn't tell Melody why she liked digging. She liked the smell of the earth and dirt.

GRACE AWOKE TRAPPED in a pile of dirt, with sand and debris flowing on top of her. The heady smell of earth came to her and she breathed it in with relish. Part of her mind knew she was dying, but she felt elated. She felt something else, too. Her right index finger started to get warm and then she remembered the gift she'd found in front of her apartment. She thought it was a gift. She had found a package at her doorstep and inside the box filled with white popcorn packing was a small velvet box. Inside that was a silver ring with bits of black stone embedded around it.

She was surprised the ring fit so well and she decided to keep it. Now, her finger hurt with warm pain. The feeling started to spread through her body. The roaring sound of the sand storm filtered all around her, making her think and feel she was trapped inside a living earth tomb and that she was going to be the next Cleopatra. She actually smiled and sensed something had changed. She was inside an invisible barrier and saw herself being lifted away from her entrapment. Before she got get a good glimpse of the inside of the casino, she was thrust upwards in a violent jolt that erupted through the ceiling, breaking through the steel beams, girders and then the rooftop. It was so fast everything around her blurred as if she was on a roller coaster back in Magic Mountain, flying through the air. The air flowed around her and she saw the ring on her right finger glowing an intense brown and coal black.

All around her, the sandstorm raged, banging against the invisible barrier surrounding her. She had never felt so deathly scared and exhilarated at once. The heat of her body was pulsating with the glowing of the ring and it made her gasp. She couldn't fathom what was happening to her. She thrust her hands out before her and saw that the sand storm around her reacted to her movement. Sand started to gather around her palms as if it was magnetized. She clenched her right hand. A plume of debris and sand developed out of her small shelter. She lifted both of her hands above her and a line of dirt flowed upwards into the heavens. She was laughing.

Chapter 22

Grace, in her invisible cocoon, didn't know how long she was suspended up in the air looking down at the raging sand storm destroy the city of Las Vegas. The horror of all the dead overwhelmed and terrified her. She was not sure why she was chosen to be a survivor. Nothing made sensed to her. She recalled from the news on her radio saying the weather was going to be hot with no signs of storms or even clouds. The world had changed in a blink of an eye and she was here to witness the beginning of the end. She felt something in the pocket of her work uniform. It was her cell phone. She laughed and took it out, but didn't get any reception. Grace tried the Internet and couldn't get a signal. Everything was dead.

She noticed the sand storm was lessening and she saw the tops of the building and streets. Most of the casinos and structures were almost obliterated, covered in sand, and she thought she was not in Las Vegas at all but an odd land where humanity had disappeared from the face of the earth. Her bubble started to move down to the ground.

She hovered over the top of the Statue of Liberty, covered in tan sand. She saw the top of the flaming torch and parts of the other buildings of the New York New York Casino. Grace always looked up to the tops of the casino marveling how beautiful it was, but now everything was an empty husk of its former self. Her feet touched the sand. The storm had dispersed, leaving a clear sky. Before her, she saw an alien landscape. Tops of buildings punctured the ground, broken and shattered. She then saw the bodies everywhere in various death poses. Some were bloodied pulps, with only a hand or a leg sticking out of the sand.

She thought she was standing in a vast cemetery and she was the only living person left, but then she heard somebody crying. It was a man, a few feet from here. He was bruised and bloodied, but alive.

Grace started walking to him. Her bubble had disappeared as soon as her feet touched the ground and she was free to move. The man saw her and held up his hand to stop her. His eyes were wide with pain. Grace didn't know what to do. She kept moving toward him. Just seeing somebody alive in this carnage made her want to help. The man knelt to the ground and his body started to contort. He flung himself into the air and fell onto his back. He was making an odd noise. Then he said something over and over again.

"Grog, grog."

His body grew larger and feathers sprouted from his body. His face also changed, a large beak replaced his nose and his eyes became smaller. In a matter of seconds, the man changed into a large winged avian creature, looking like a cross between a large vulture and a hawk. The creature said, "Grog, grog," but it did not sound like a human, but a bird.

The avian creature spread its wings and brushed the sand off itself. It screeched, and shot itself at her. Grace was stunned and held her hands out to protect herself. A wall of sand shot up, creating a protective barrier. The creature hit the wall with a loud crunch, but she could hear it trying to get through. Suddenly she saw the large bird fly into the sky, circling her several times and trying to attack her again. She lifted her hands up and sand shot upwards and hit the creature.

Grace saw the bird veer off to the left. It looked at her and squawked loudly. She heard the sound of Grog, mixed with a large squawk. Another voice joined the first creature and Grace turned around. Several of the dead bodies rose from where they were sitting

and eyed her. She saw malice in their eyes. One old lady transformed
into a large orange cat with yellow glowing eyes. It growled and
padded closer to her. The flying bird answered the cat's growl and
both creatures launched themselves at her.

Grace held out both of her hands and pointed at the creatures,
but instead of sand, large boulders and pieces of concrete came out
from the ground and hit them. The bird turned to the side at the last
second.

Grace back-peddled, searching for another place to hide. She had
killed the large cat but missed the bird. The flying creature squawked
again and flew away from her.

Grace watched as the bird moved away towards the horizon.
She took a deep breath. Looking around she turned, but didn't see
any other Grog creatures roaming about. Her mind was on fire. She
was not sure how her new powers manifested. She never had any
predilection for this sort of power. *Hell*, she thought, *people don't just
change and become mutant creatures.* She had always like rocks, stones
and gems. She even had a small collection at home of white and black
gemstones. Grace would stare at these stones for hours. She glanced
at the ring on her finger. The black stone could be opal or onyx. She
was not sure.

She walked down the slope, her feet sliding along the shifting
sand. Her body felt strong but at the same time bruised, as if she had
exercised the night before. She scanned the horizon. The clouds covered the sky, hovering over the sun. It was not warm or even hot, but
cool like the desert in the night. She thought this was odd. It should
be hot at this time in the summer, blazing hot like this morning. She
walked away from any of the dead bodies she encountered. The hill
moved steadily lower. Her feet sank deeply into the sand, her black
tennis shoes becoming filled with sand and dirt.

A cold breeze peppered her with swirling sand and silt and she
noticed her ring had started to glow an intense white, not burning

her skin, but making her feel good, better than fine. She thought she could run a mile without breaking a sweat. Walking down the dune, she didn't notice her feet were not touching the ground anymore but were, in fact, floating. She was intently studying at her ring and didn't realize she had soared up a few feet from where she was walking.

With a short scream, she saw herself dangling in mid-air. She felt an odd sensation of being weightless, and then she realized she was controlling this. Grace focused and moved down to the ground, but before she touched it she started to move forward, still not touching but propelled forward, and she smiled. *This is amazing*, she thought and kept the floating sensation. It gave her stomach a flutter.

Drifting a few feet, she scanned ahead looking for some type of destination. She was not sure what she wanted to do. She should be looking for survivors or a shelter, but she felt blank from shock and didn't know where to start. She wondered if more of the Grog creatures would attack.

Then she wondered if she had been affected by radiation, or worse, a plague, and she didn't know it. But what type of radiation would cause her to have such powers and people to morph into those creatures? Then she recalled the odd dreams of the last few weeks. Dreams that she thought were nothing, just fantasies made by the mind from events that happened during the day or years before, but what she had been dreaming was consistent.

She saw a vast underground chamber with large round structures inside it. And then something changed and she flowed past the structures into another world, an ancient metropolis. She was with three other people. She recognized one person, little Matthew from her childhood.

Yet she didn't understand how her dream related to this freak sand storm. Grace propelled herself downwards. She saw the sands had opened up, revealing the street below. It was the main strip, the street where all the casinos were located. Locals and tourist from

California called it the new strip because all the newer casinos were built there. The old strip where the older casinos were housed were several miles from here.

She floated lower to the ground and saw a fake mountain now covered with sand. She knew she was in front of the casino called Treasure Island.

The front entrance was completely covered by sand and silt. The large hotel, built in the shape of an open "V" was located next to the casino. The building was now smashed from the top to the bottom with only bits of the internal structure showing to the sky.

She heard something. Somebody called her to enter the hotel.

Chapter 23

Grace had a prickly feeling at the back of her neck and she sensed something guiding her. She floated toward an area at the back of the casino. The sun's rays fell on her as the clouds move beyond the mountains but the rolling fog of dust still covered the sky.

As she flew around the back area of the casino she saw more twisted steel and pieces of the interior, from the slot machines and gambling tables to wood and metal frames scorched by the sandstorm that raged just a few hours ago. Then she saw the bodies and body parts. It was a slaughter. Most of the dead had almost no skin, with bone showing through. Blood flowed all over in large puddles.

Somebody screamed. Down below a little boy ran from several large wolves the size of cars. She flew toward the kid, yelling for the wolves to stop. The foremost wolf was about to jump at the boy and Grace focused on a shattered piece of concrete. It shook and then the concrete flew up, hitting the first wolf square in the face and barely missing the boy. A loud crunching noise could be heard.

She flew and stopped in front of the boy and the wolves. The boy looked at her for several seconds, not understanding if she was a friend or another creature.

He said, "What? Who?"

Grace lifted her hands and said, "Duck."

The boy jumped to the ground. Asphalt and cement shot from behind her and hit all the wolves, splattering their bodies in a shower of dirt and debris. The boy looked at her for a few seconds, his mouth open.

She said, "You're safe now. What's your name?"

"My name is Lawrence. My parents are dead."

He said this in such a non-emotional way that Grace felt sad. "My name is Grace. I was working at the casino when the storm hit."

She thought she was babbling and stopped talking. The boy came up to her and gave her a hug. He was crying softly. He said, "I thought everybody was dead."

"How did you survive?"

"My parents made me stay inside the bathroom."

Tears started to flow down his cheeks and Grace wiped them away. They didn't say anything for a while.

She said, "Those wolves, where did they come from?"

"From the people," the boy said. He looked around, checking to see if more monsters were coming to get him.

Grace said, "Yes, I saw people changing, myself. Let's get out of here before more come."

She looked around and realized they were trapped in this small, devastated area.

He said, "Can you take me up?"

She nodded. "I'm still learning. But I'll try."

She smiled in spite of the situation they were in. "Get closer to me."

A snarl was heard in the distance and Lawrence came closer to her. She grabbed him and focused inside herself, but the feeling of weightlessness didn't coalesce. Lawrence looked toward the right and saw two large apelike creatures poke their heads out of the debris.

"Oh no!" he said.

The creatures bounded and shot toward them in graceful and fast movements. Grace grabbed Lawrence and willed herself to float. They soared upwards in a dizzying movement. The two large creatures tried to grab them with their claws and Lawrence held on to her with such strength she couldn't breathe.

She said. "We're fine, now. You can relax."

Lawrence still held her. He was looking down at the ape creatures. They snorted at them and pounded the ground.

"Grog! Grog!" the creatures said up at them.

"Don't look at them."

She directed their ascent away from the Treasure Island casino. Lawrence slowly let his grip lessen around her waist. She noticed she could have them float together without exerting herself. It was easy, she thought. Lawrence looked around without even marveling at the powers she possessed, as if this was normal circumstances to be running from dangerous creatures and having your world change in a second.

He said, "Look over there. I think there is a convenience store."

She scanned the area Lawrence was pointing at and saw a liquor store looking almost the same as before the sand storm. She was instantly suspicious and stopped to study the area.

"I don't know," Grace said.

Lawrence said, "I don't see any creatures around there and I'm getting hungry."

Grace was about to explain that she didn't have any money, then realized it didn't matter now. She noticed several of the casinos and buildings around the small store made a perfect barrier from the storm. Yet, she still thought this didn't explain how the store sat unbroken.

"Sure, but be careful and stay by me."

Lawrence nodded to her and they started to move down. Sand and broken plaster and steel covered the parking lot and around the store, making it looked like an oasis in this odd broken landscape. She landed them close to the entrance. One car, half displaced by the sand, was parked in the front. The car's doors stood open. When they got closer she noticed the large glass windows of the store were broken. She shook her head and realized this place was just as broken as the other buildings surrounding it. The sign on top was half gone, with the other half stating, "Liquor". Their feet crunched as they got to the double-doored entrance.

"Let me go first," she said. She grabbed the door handle and pulled it forward. It was a bad move. Pieces of glass rained on them and she and Lawrence stepped backwards, but the shards of glass stopped in mid-air. Grace was holding up her right hand to shield her face. She waved her hand and the glass flew away from them, striking the side of the building.

Lawrence asked, "How did you do that?"

She shook her head. He didn't question that they could fly and she could shoot large concrete slabs at the mutated creatures, but he questioned this.

"I don't know. Follow me."

Inside it was dark. The store was only one large room. The shelves and food were mostly on the ground, and on the right was a waist high glass structure that was the counter area. The cash register was gone, as well as the shelves that held most of the hard liquor containers.

The food packages were all open and covered with sand. Nothing looked edible. They moved to the back area.

Lawrence said, "What's that?"

Grace saw it and said, "Stop. Go back out."

It was the body of the dead shopkeeper, except it was pulverized to such an extent it was unrecognizable. Sand was piled on top of him or her. Blood was smeared behind him. The sand storm had blasted through the front door where he stood. There was a back area but the door was still closed.

Grace turned behind her and saw Lawrence standing at the front.

Chapter 24

Grace nodded to Lawrence to wait. She started to the back door and tried its handle but it was still locked. The door had held through the storm although the metal surface was scratched and pitted by the sand. If she wanted to get inside there, she had to find the key.

She went back to the dead body and gazed at it for a while. The key would either be on this person or somewhere else. Lawrence outside was getting restless.

She said, "If you hear anything call me at once. Ok?"

"Yes," the boy said.

Grace placed her hand over the body and willed the sand and debris to move. Nothing happened at first, and then the sand and debris shot up and broke through the roof of the store.

"Sorry," she said. She needed to learn how to use her powers. She took a deep breath and checked the dead body. The head was smashed in. The dead man was wearing a blue and white checkered shirt and blue jeans. Blood flowed from the many wounds he had sustained. She knew it was a man by the hair and body mass.

Grace went to reach into the man's front pockets but stopped herself, about to gag. She shook her head and moved backwards and almost fell when she slipped a few times on candy bars. She had an idea, but first, she needed to move outside and take a deep breath.

She met Lawrence in the front and he nodded to her. "Did you find anything?"

She said, "Not yet. There is a locked door, but I can't find the key. But I have an idea. I am not sure if it will work."

She walked away from him, looking for the biggest stone or cement block. She realized her powers focused on the same things, sand, rocks and debris.

"Aha," she said and turned toward Lawrence. "Can you move away from the front?"

Grace watched him move a few steps and nodded to him. Placing her hand in front of a large asphalt piece on the ground Grace focused on it. It was as large as a car, but it began to move. She felt a sudden heavy weight push against her. She was not sure she could do this but she redoubled her efforts and the asphalt piece started to shudder upwards, closer to her.

She focused on moving it closer to the front of the liquor store when a shout came from within.

"Hey, stop!"

She saw a woman about her age rush out of the store. She wore a white shirt and jeans. Her face had a cut on her cheek.

Grace instantly stopped. The cement piece fell to the ground with a large thump. The woman was Asian and spoke with a slight accent. She came directly at Grace.

The lady said, "Don't do it. You could have killed me."

"I'm sorry. I didn't think anybody was here."

"You thought nobody was alive."

"Well, yes," she said. "My name is Grace, and this is Lawrence."

" Joan." She scanned the area. "My dad will be pissed." Then she turned away and looked back at the store. Joan's body seem to sag and she moved closer to the car parked in front. Tears started to flow.

Joan said, "He should have let me die. He drove here in a hurry and threw me into the back storage room. That fool!"

Her body convulsed and she started to cry in agony. Grace realized what had transpired here. She looked at the Toyota Tercel with its door open. Joan's dad had seen the impending storm, ran inside and locked his daughter in the back storage area. Grace came closer to Joan and hugged her.

Lawrence turned away and stared into the collapsed city.

⚜

JOAN STOOD IN THE FRONT. She didn't want to go back inside. Grace rummaged in the large storage room. The walls were lined with metal and the air was cool. It looked more like a meat locker than a back stockroom. She saw rows of food, candy, alcohol and bottles of water and soda. She grabbed two bottles and some chips and candy.

Lawrence and Joan were talking. She heard Lawrence say he was from California, Orange County.

Joan said, "Do you live by the beach?"

"It was a few miles down."

"Your family must be rich," Joan said. Her words came out stifled, as if she was trying to form them before she spoke them.

"You will pay for those later," Joan said.

Grace was surprised she asked her to pay but said only, "Sure, we need to find shelter, or maybe a police officer."

Joan said, "Right. But I'm staying right here."

"Did you hear what we told you about the creatures? It won't be safe here by yourself."

"I'll take my chances. I can stay in the store room. You'll come back when you find help?"

Grace scanned the skies noting that the sun was setting.

"Let's not be hasty. We'll stay here tonight and then we shall see tomorrow."

They gathered wood from the many broken buildings and debris along the route. It would be an endless supply. Joan stopped complaining about her dad's store but merely looked at the devastation before them. They left the dead body inside the store and nothing was said about it. Grace knew they should bury the body but there no place to dig. Everything was broken and the ground was cement. She was thinking about maybe building a cairn by placing stones and cement on top of the body, but she didn't want to tell Joan her idea. She glanced at Joan seeing that this new situation seemed to settle on her. *Hell*, Grace thought, *she's trying to get a handle on what is happening.*

Joan told her to use the lighters they found on the ground to light the fire. They cleared an area and built a small bonfire. The fire roared before them. It was getting cold.

Joan stood and went to her dad's car and popped the trunk. She took out several blankets from the back and gave them to them.

"My dad always had these things in the back. He was always scared we would be stuck in the desert."

Joan shook her head and looked at the liquor store. "He paid attention to this stupid store more than me and my mom."

Grace placed the checkered blanket around Lawrence and they scooted closer to the fire. Joan stood, staring at the store. Her hands were clenched. She looked as if she was going to kick or punch the wall or something. She looked at them and then at the fire, then sighed and sat on the cement. She absently brushed off a few curling piles of sand from her clothes.

Joan held a package of cookies and started to eat its contents.

Lawrence said, "Are you going with us?"

She nodded to him. "There is nothing for me here."

Grace said, "Good. I am glad that you are coming with us."

Grace was eating a chocolate bar and drinking a bottled water. She said, "I think we should take turns watching tonight."

"I'm not sure about those creatures you talked about but we should. I'll take the first watch. I'm not sleepy."

Grace fed more wood on the fire. "Sure, I'll take the next watch."

Lawrence said, "I can help, too."

"No, not yet. You need some sleep. I don't know who is still alive and if those Grog creatures will attack us at night."

Joan said, "I have a tire iron in the trunk."

"Any other weapons? A gun?"

"No, my dad didn't believe in guns, but inside the store, there should be a bat and another tire iron."

"Aha," Lawrence said, "we can be an army with tire irons."

Joan smiled. The boy's optimism was infectious.

He said, "Will we be changed into those creatures?"

"I don't think so," Grace said, looking around the fire and at them.

"How did you do that with the rock?" Joan said. Her blanket was around her shoulders.

"I don't know. I just have the power to move things."

Joan said, "You told me how you fought against the bird and wolves."

Lawrence's face got animated. "You should have seen it. She killed those beasts and then we floated here. It was incredible."

Joan said, "I don't believe it."

Grace didn't want to explain it again to Joan. They had been talking about this for the last several hours now. They didn't have any powers like hers.

She said, "Well, it's true. I didn't make up those stories. I need some rest."

She stood and brushed off the sand from her polyester pants. She always hated this uniform. As soon as they found a clothing store, she would change, she thought. It was not considered looting because they needed these things to survive, and when this crazy new world finally went back to some type of normalcy she would pay.

Part 2

The Circle of Four

"Deep into that darkness peering, long I stood there, wondering, fearing, doubting, dreaming dreams no mortal ever dared to dream before."

— Edgar Allan Poe, The Raven

"A beast can never be as cruel as a human being, so artistically, so picturesquely cruel."

— Fyodor Dostoyevsky, The Brothers Karamazov

Interlude 2: The Report

Notes:
While reading and researching the historical stories of the time before the Breaking of the Seals, it did not escape my attention that this was a time when magic was not as natural as the air and rain. Magic had been repressed and contained in the Bastions for eons.

I was born into this world drinking magic from the teat of my mom. Many of my older colleagues were survivors of the zero day of the Breaking of the Seals. This report was only a prelude to a much bigger project on the accounts of that time, but reading the many interviews I decided I couldn't finish this project in my own lifetime.

I also forgot to add definitions to a few things and people who are in this informal report. I will add more when needed.

Definitions:

Bastions: Giant containers holding the magical essence of the earth. Held in many key locations. (See: the map of the world). However, not all the Bastions were found.

Grog: A mutation through magical means. (After the magic was released, many of the human population became a Grog). Each mutation would change the hapless human into fantastical creatures such as a wolf, bird or insect. Note: A scientific inquiry is in progress to determine why so many people changed to these creatures. No progress has of yet has been made in finding a reason for these strange occurrences.

Alpha Wizard: Powerful being who has command of elemental magic. There were only four during the two year reign of terror and they are reported to have been more powerful than the Wizards during the current age.

Magic: The essence of the earth which can imbue a person with command of the elements (air, wind, fire, earth and steel)

BREAKING OF THE SEALS: Survivors

Survivor: Charles (Charlie) McGee

Interviewer: John Haskins.

Digital Audio: Recorded twenty years after the Breaking of the Bastions

John: Hello, Charlie, I know you have retired from the Army corps of the United Nations. Can you tell me your occupation during the Zero day?

Charlie: Is this thing on? (The sound of rustling and audio feedback)

John: Yes, just speak into the microphone.

Charlie: Oh, sorry. I was a private in the Marines. Oh, that was so many years ago, son.

John: So, Charlie. What can you recall? Where were you stationed in the Marine Corp?

Charlie: (Long pause). Yes, I was stationed in Camp Pendleton close to Oceanside. It's not there anymore.

John: So, tell me what happened during that day?

Charlie: What day? Oh yeah, the zero day. If I can recall, Camp Pendleton was hit with a large wave. I was eating chow at the mess hall when I woke on the ground, still holding my tray. You know, son, you remind me of somebody. Was your mom's name Doris? I used to date a woman named Doris in my younger days.

John: No, my mom is not named Doris. Please continue with your account.

Charlie: Oh yeah, right. I forgot where I was. So, my base was destroyed. But I was a marine and we always fight. So, I wandered a bit. I've seen some crazy things in my lifetime, son. But when I saw a man, a man from my squad, change before me into one of those creatures I nearly soiled my pants. (A chuckle).

John: A Grog?

Charlie: Whatever that thing was called. It saw me but didn't attack. I was dead to rights if it did. I ran to my barracks. But it was not there. The building was gone.

John: So, what did you do?

Charlie: I did what any good marine would do. I found a gun. But most of them were wet and destroyed. Those blasted beasts were all over the place. I found a marine who been ripped apart by a Grog.

John: Did you help him?

Charlie: You're damn right I did (a slight crackled laugh). I grabbed an M16 and started shooting. I hit the bastards.

John: How did you know the gun would shoot?

Charlie: I just did. It was my talent from then on. I can tell by looking at things how to fix them and if they will work.

John: When did you learn this talent?

Charlie: It was after that day when the tidal wave hit the base. I was never good at mechanical things, but then I could fix anything. It was great.

John: (rustling of papers) I see that you got a distinguished blue star in the fight at Camp Pendleton.

Charlie: Yes, it was odd. I only killed the creatures that were killing the marines. Anybody would have done that.

John: We will talk later. Thank you.

⊙≪≫⊙

CHARLES (CHARLIE) MCGEE is a distinguished soldier during the new republic. He has lost some of his memory and I will try to induce some recall by an attempting an experimental reading of minds spell.

Side note: Something odd happened today. Two men came into my office. They introduced themselves as New Republic Agents. I have never heard of this division before and I was not going to tell them anything. They asked me if I was working on a book about the history of the Breaking. I had to tell them no. I have hidden my notes and manuscripts in my home from then onwards. I don't trust anybody. I had to tell my students and graduate students not to tell them about my book.

I am going to finish most of this manuscript. The odd thing about the two men who visited me was that they did not look human. I wondered if they were elves. We have not seen them since they were mentioned in the accounts and histories.

I believe these elves are the aliens we are always hearing about in abductions and in old magazines. I wondered how these government agents learned about my small project. The time is late and I am getting tired. I will keep writing these history manuscripts and will complete everything I can before I give this to the next historian, because we have to be the beacons of truth in this age of change and darkness.

Chapter 25

Royce ran up the next hill, moving at a steady pace. His four legs moved gracefully through the landscape of sand and dirt. He was heading toward the city closest to the base. Sitting back on his haunches he glanced at the grouping of small shrubs and cactuses dotting the area. It was night and the moon was shining above. He howled into the sky.

Another animal came to him, a large bird. The creature landed before him holding a small fox in its beak, placing it on the ground. Royce knew this was an offering. He growled and grabbed the morsel, ripping it apart and finishing everything. He howled again.

His body started to tingle and change. He shrank and morphed back into himself. It hurt a little but not too much. Royce stood dressed as himself in his army fatigues. The bird waited for him. It squawked, "Grog! Grog!"

Royce glared at the bird. He said, "You can change back."

He knew the bird was a human before, but the bird just looked at him.

Except, something was odd. He was not himself. He was different. He looked at his hands and saw his fingers were still shaped as claws. He touched his face and felt fangs. He was a man with wolfish features. He also felt his hair. It was long and flowing, like a mane.

"This cannot be."

He could speak sentences. Royce turned to the large bird.

"Do you have something to tell me?"

The bird squawked a few times and said, "Grog, grog."

"So, you did see one of the intruders? She was an Alpha wizard. She is in Las Vegas. It does not matter now because I am stronger than an Alpha. I can kill them one by one."

The bird squawked again. He nodded for the bird to fly back. He would take care of that woman, but he had something to do first. Royce would find more creatures at the city of Barstow. This Alpha girl, even though she was powerful, would be destroyed by his army. She would have to wait.

He roamed around the desert for a while, recalling that it was the Mojave Desert. The first place to visit was his small apartment. He sniffed the air. There was something in the air, magic, but deep magic. It filtered the very air and marinated everything with a tangy feeling.

He said, "Thinners, are you here."

Something flashed before him. It was like looking at a computer screen, but it was floating before him, transparent and glowing. On the screen were the Thinners. They were small, and he could only see the top half of them, but they looked different. They wore dark black cloaks and stared at him with long faces and bright green and blue eyes.

"Royce, you will be our savior. You will kill the Alphas and give us back the charms so we can come back."

"I thought you are here? I saw you in the base."

"You don't understand. We were not there. The Alphas have the key to helping us. You have to bring them to us."

Royce nodded. "Yes, I will do that. I have been bested by them, but I shall exact my revenge."

The creature said, "Yes, whatever you desire, but find the ancient device and destroy it. And Royce, stop calling us Thinners. We are not elves."

He growled at the Thinners.

"Hah," the creature said, "you don't know the history of your land. You will do as we ask. We have given you power, real power. But you cannot do the task. Remember, underneath the caverns, you let them open the Bastion portal."

"I will find them. I know where one of the Alphas is located, but she is strong and I need more allies."

"We will leave this in your hands."

"I will kill and destroy them and the device."

The screen disappeared and Royce was left excited about his new charge, his new job. He always knew he was destined for greatness. He felt he would receive accolades and awards like his father. His parents would finally respect him. He nodded. Moving closer to an open space of dirt and sand, he focused and started the change.

His body convulsed and he hunched to the ground. His fingers and legs morphed into canine paws and his face stretched, revealing large sharp teeth. When he was transformed into an Alpha wolf he howled into the heavens, a loud and forlorn sound. He waited for a reply, but no creatures answered.

He ran at top speed, trying to push his new powers. He moved in a blur, passing hills and covering miles in several hours. He arrived close to his apartment in the early morning hours. The city of Barstow had changed. Usually, it was a small sleepy town, a place that tourists from California passed on their way to Las Vegas without giving it a second glance. Except, the usual fast food joints and the freeway were usually open at this time. But this time, it was not. And everything was destroyed or broken, like tonka toys thrown away by an unruly child. Sand was everywhere, in large piles over each and every building and structure Royce encountered.

He howled at the slowly rising sun. Royce felt that the Alphas had created this catastrophe. They should never have opened the gates. He padded around a blasted Burger King opened like a hard boiled egg, cut and seared at the top. He was hungry and he wanted something to eat. He sniffed and found the refrigerated back room. Inside was half frozen meat, potatoes and other food stuff, but everything was covered with sand and other dirt. He didn't care. He ate everything that looked edible.

Royce jumped out on top of the roof. He saw outside a group of creatures, animals that were once human, waiting for him. When they saw him they all bowed their heads with respect. He saw the group were mostly wolves, but with a scattering of insectile creatures and a few large birds. He howled at them. The beasts all growled in unison, "Grog, grog."

Royce's army was growing. The next thing he needed to do was destroy the first Alpha. She was in Nevada and he knew what needed to be done. He growled his command and sent the other birds to join his disciple.

Chapter 26

The city of Los Angeles lay like a huge creature, cut open from neck to tail with its entrails glistening and bloody in the sun. Matthew woke from a fitful dream. He was standing with several people inside a spacious cavern, staring at large containers he needed to open. Somebody shouted for him to flee, but he attacked a man holding a large gun that thundered bullets all around him. The bullets tore into him.

He jerked from his prone position and opened his eyes at the destroyed landscape. He heard the sounds of water raining down upon the ground. He had traveled this land for several days.

His dinner last night was roasted rabbit cooked over an open fire. He had learned this somehow in a far away memory that he couldn't recall knowing or even understanding.

Matthew stood and stretched, looking around for any creatures and people roaming about the devastated land. He had slept under a freeway that was still intact, the underpass over him keeping him cool in its shade. The day was getting warm and Matthew took off his thick jacket and scarf. He sensed something was amiss. It was as if an impending darkness came over him with an evil creature watching him, ready to pounce and dismember him. He didn't see anything but the feeling hung around him like a blanket.

The last few days he had been practicing his new powers. One thing that he learned was his infinite ability to conjure and manipulate fire. He held out his hands and pointed at a patch of bare earth a few yards from him. He focused and sensed power radiating from his chest. Fire exploded from his hand and struck the wood pile and flames shot upwards.

"Wow," he said.

He waved his right hand in a circle and the flames started to circle. Matthew almost clapped his hands in delight, but he didn't. *Now*, he thought. He had been practicing his powers for several hours and he hoped he could perform this. He focused on the fire and watched it dance before him. He saw it curl around the wood, eating the air and destroying the debris.

He became the fire and sensed his mind and body going into his powers. The flames rose higher and higher, then he concentrated and let it become whisper-thin like a concentric tunnel. He envisioned the fire going through a pipe. He held the fire still and placed both of his hands downward in a covering position. He smothered it with his mind. Smoke arose from the stack of wood and debris.

He was holding his breath and took a deep gasp of air. His body trembled slightly as if he had lifted something very heavy and his muscles tingled with the use. His powers were developing. He sat in a large cement block, still feeling that something was going to attack him. He thought he would never be ready no matter how many hours he practiced his magic. This growing evil would always be more powerful and destructive than he would be.

Matthew relaxed his body and mind. A howl pierced and punctured the air sending goose bumps along his back and arms.

The noise was not coming from around this area or even in Los Angeles. The noise was coming from within his mind and inside his very bones.

Matthew heard the sound of the enemy and knew the adversary was far away from him. He would have to confront this person one day. He heard the howl again and had an odd feeling that he knew who this person was and had met this person before. It was from somewhere in the far reaches of his memory. But his history was lost to him, like a sea of ideas and patterns which shifted around him and changed like a jigsaw puzzle with pieces that don't fit. He glanced at his ring and looked at the stone embedded on it, noticing it glowing a fiery orange-red.

A name came bubbling up to the surface of his unconscious, Royce. He didn't understand how he could know this, but he was certain. Royce had changed. He had become this Alpha wolf beast.

Matthew shook his head. He needed to find the Leader to show him his true destiny. He was destined to find this ancient city and unlock the Bastions.

Matthew went to his supplies. He had a backpack stuffed with food and a long knife he found in rubble inside a large store.

Then, in a corner of the shade, he spotted a large creature staring at him. It was as big as the Grog wolves he saw roaming among the wreckage of the city, but something was different with this beast. It looked like a dog, not the feral grog beasts he had seen before. It sniffed at the air and waited. The creature didn't attack him or even growl. Matthew lifted his right hand and a small flame sprouted over his palm. He had seen enough carnage and beasts killing and didn't want to be the next victim.

"Wait!" A voice as clear as the sky shot into the bottom of his shelter. A man walked closer to him and said, "Are you, Matthew? I have been looking for you."

He knew instantly who this person was. Matthew went on one knee. "Yes, my name is Matthew. You must be the Leader I have been searching for."

Chapter 27

L azarus didn't know what to make of this man, Matthew. He watched him in a reverent way which made Lazarus feel a little uneasy. He was not sure why Matthew had called him the Leader several times.

"My name is Lazarus," he said again. "This dog here is called Sammy. It's nice to meet you."

Matthew stood and nodded. "Thank you. Now, we can start our quest."

"Quest? I don't know what you're talking about."

"We were given the task to find the way, the doorway."

Lazarus shook his head. The man was clearly delusional. He didn't understand why he had been compelled to find this man.

"Do you know what is happening?"

Sammy came closer to Matthew and sniffed him, looking at him in an uncertain way. Matthew petted Sammy's head.

Matthew said, "The world has gone through the change. I have seen the storehouses of power, now broken and laid waste. The seals have been destroyed."

"How do you know this?"

"I have seen this in my dreams. I had been seeing visions for years. I always thought I was mad, but now I know I am not. We were meant to find this the ancient city."

Lazarus noticed that Matthew, even though he had new clothes, had a rough exterior and burnt skin. His hair was all in disarray. Lazarus thought he looked like a survivor, but then on second thoughts, he realized that Matthew had the look of a man living on the streets even before the storm destroyed California.

He said, "Have you seen other people?"

"Well yes, but they are dead. I have not seen anybody alive."

Lazarus nodded, "Yes, me too. That band on your arm. Have you been in hospital?"

Matthew regarded him with surprise and glanced down at his wrist. "Yes, I was in a hospital when the first wave hit."

"Did something odd happen? Like, did an invisible barrier save you?"

Matthew nodded. "It was divine providence. We were chosen."

"So, this ancient city, what do you know about it?"

Matthew shook his head. "I thought you would know. Did you have the visions?"

"Visions? No. But I have been having odd dreams for the last several weeks."

Matthew rubbed Sammy's back. The dog panted and moved closer to him.

"We have to find the others."

"There are others?" Lazarus knew Matthew was right.

"You know what I am speaking about, Leader. We have to find the others before we set out on our quest."

"This doorway you spoke of. Where is it?"

Matthew glanced down in concentration. "It is hidden from me. We have to find the others before we find the doorway."

"Ok, we will find the others," Lazarus said. "I'm hungry. Do you want any food?"

"Yes, I have some in my backpack."

Lazarus held up his hand. "Sammy can find us some food. If you can skin the animal then we can have some meat."

"I'll start a fire," Matthew said.

"Yes, I have seen what you have done," Lazarus replied.

Matthew said, "Do you have powers?"

"Well, yes I do, but I don't really understand it." Lazarus nodded to Sammy and he bounded away to find some food.

Matthew nodded. "What is your elemental?"

"Elemental?" he asked.

"Yes." Matthew gave him an odd look like Lazarus should understand what he was talking about. Matthew's eyes were glassy and his hands were very expressive when he spoke.

"You know what I'm talking about, man. Every Mage has their own element they can conjure and command. Mine is fire."

Matthew held up his right hand and a flame sprouted above his palm. It was the size of his fist. He smiled and Lazarus noticed that Matthew was missing some of his front teeth.

"I'm not sure."

Lazarus thought about the things he had done over the last few days, magical things. The only time he exerted power was when the Grogs or a swarm of insects were going to attack him. Sammy had been his protection since he defeated those creatures.

He thought about it and said, "I think my elemental is wind or air. I guess."

"Show me."

"I can't just do it. It doesn't work like that with me."

"Try," Matthew implored, holding his arms out to him.

Lazarus moved a few paces away from him and glanced at a group of stones and debris on the ground. He placed his hand out like Matthew did and focused. He tried to move the stones. Nothing happened. He tried to concentrate again. A small wind came up but that was it.

Matthew stared at him with utter fascination. "You are too stiff. You need to relax. You can do it."

"I'm not sure. The only time I used magic when somebody attacked me."

Matthew smiled a crooked grin. Lazarus saw Matthew's missing teeth and had to look away from him. Without warning, Matthew jumped at him. Flames rose up from the man's hands. Lazarus pinwheeled backwards, almost falling back. Sammy was too far away to react to this sudden movement.

Lazarus held up his hand in a defensive manner and a strong and powerful feeling overcame him. It was like being cold and hot at the same time. Lazarus suddenly soared up to the sky away from the impending flames. He held up his hands away from Matthew. He tried to stop the magic, but it released from his body. Lightning shot out of him hitting a nearby decrepit building. It destroyed and demolished the remaining structure which created a cascading effect. The structure started to fold on itself.

Lazarus tried to stop the power but it poured forth from him like a waterfall. Then the magic ceased and he fell the ground. He had no energy. The sound of the collapsing building reverberated in his ears and a plume of thick dust obscured everything before him.

"Impressive," Matthew said.

Lazarus couldn't see him through the haze. But he saw Sammy padding up to him covered in dirt and almost laughed.

Chapter 28

L azarus Venti couldn't recall much about his childhood because, as he thought, there was nothing to recall. He moved through his grade school and junior high as a spectator, watching his life pass him by like a person viewing a television show, laughing at some things and smiling at the right times, but not really participating. The only time he felt comfortable was when his uncle Jack came to visit his home.

His uncle was a large man. He told extravagant and highly entertaining stories. He was a doctor on a cruise ship that went to different and exciting locations.

Uncle Jack had cruise tours on both sides of the west and east coasts. Lazarus only saw Uncle Jack when he was in California and only for a few hours. His mom was always concerned about Uncle Jack's safety. They constantly squabbled about him going on another cruise. She thought he should find a job at the nearest hospital and settle down. Uncle Jack always laughed at her, stating that he was happy gallivanting around the world seeing exotic locations and sometimes, when his parents and Uncle Jack thought he was out of earshot in his room, Lazarus would listen and hear Uncle Jack talk about his many girlfriends he had in these distant ports. His dad always laughed at these stories.

Besides these fun visits from his uncle, Lazarus saw his own life punctuated with boring situations and happenings. He never had many friends and he pretty much stayed to himself. He liked math and history in school and had good grades in everything. Lazarus felt he was unremarkable. His parents had him take up baseball, touch football, soccer and a gamut of other sports. He was not good at anything athletic. They even encouraged him to play an instrument, the flute, but he was not good with that as well. He was an average kid with an average mind.

His mom talked to him once about Uncle Jack. They had finished dinner and his dad walked over to the living room to watch TV. The sound of a comedy sitcom sounded in the house, laughter and people talking excitedly.

His mom took a few plates away to the kitchen and then came back to him. Lazarus was about to go to his room and read a Justice League comic he bought the day before with his allowance money when his mom said, "Lazarus, I know you idolize your Uncle Jack. But I don't want you to end up like him."

"What, Mom? Uncle Jack seems happy."

"You were just like your Uncle Jack when he was your age. He didn't have many friends. I always tried to help him in school."

Lazarus was feeling uncomfortable about this conversation. "Mom, why are we talking about Uncle Jack?

She sat closer to him. "Your Uncle Jack is in the hospital. He has cancer."

"What? But he's a doctor. Shouldn't he know?"

"Yes, he did. But, son, cancer is sneaky. Sometimes a healthy person has cancer and doesn't know."

His mom placed a hand on his arm. He didn't know she was holding his arm. She didn't say anything to him. Maybe she was waiting for him to do something, or cry.

In a daze, Lazarus looked up. He saw his dad standing in the hallway. His dad, usually a loud and gregarious man, stood mute. They all looked at each other for a few seconds. The sound of the television sounded loud and the laughter sounded forced and unbelievable.

His father cleared his throat. "Uncle Jack is at the hospital downtown. We can still make it to visiting hours, if you want to see him."

"Yes!" He was startled at his voice.

His mom nodded. They ended up at the hospital half past seven, well past the time posted for visiting hours, but the attendant at the desk waved them through toward the elevators. Lazarus didn't understand this then, but years later when his mind was able to accept the futility of life he realized that the nurse let them through after visiting times because his uncle was dying, and the nurses always let relatives visit their loved ones if the time was dire.

Lazarus and his parents entered a white room with two beds in them. The light was closed. He saw his uncle lying on the bed at the far corner. The other bed was empty. His uncle's eyes were closed, but he opened them when they came inside. Uncle Jack had lost a lot of weight since he had last seen him. His skin sagged on his face and arms.

"Hello, my favorite nephew is here."

Uncle Jack smiled and Lazarus gave him a hug.

He said, "Will you be fine?"

"Sure I am. This is nothing. I'm here for some minor stuff."

Lazarus heard his mom crying softly behind him and knew this was bad.

"Are you sure? Cancer is bad."

"I can beat it. Don't you worry. It was like the time when I helped the people on board my cruise ship. These doctors here are top notch. I need to talk to your mom for a second."

Lazarus went outside and waited in the hallway a few feet away from the nurse's station. His dad sat close to him. Lazarus watched the nurses moving back and forth down the hallways. He felt numb, wondering why they had to be here at this time of night. They could have come here tomorrow.

"Dad," he said, "will Uncle Jack be fine?"

His dad took a while to say anything. "Your mom will be mad that I told you. But you are old enough to understand. It doesn't look good. He is having emergency surgery tomorrow to try to take out the cancer. He has a fifty-fifty chance. You are not going to school tomorrow."

Chapter 29

Matthew realized that the Leader, Lazarus, was a very powerful wizard. He shouldn't have pushed him to use his magic, but Lazarus didn't see what he could. He saw the raw talent and power Lazarus possessed. It was written all over his body. The magic flowed around him like the very air he breathed.

He even had powerful allies. His pooch, Sammy, was a war dog and would protect him to his dying breath. Yet these Grog creatures were dangerous and they needed to find more allies to help them on their quest.

It was night and Lazarus was warming his hands near the fire. Sammy had caught a few rabbits a few hours ago and they'd had a meal of meat roasted over a fire. Matthew sat on the dirt. They had moved their camp a few blocks down, deciding to stay in a small structure which looked like a large open space parking lot, but was now covered with huge blocks of cement, asphalt and pieces of the building, creating a barrier around their area.

"Lazarus," he said, "what do you command for me to do?"

The Leader looked at him in a strange way. "I need to think. I don't understand all this."

Matthew nodded. The Leader was not ready. He did not know what he could see and do. Lazarus was still thinking he was in the old world.

Matthew said, "I will gather supplies for our trip."

"We cannot be the only people alive. Somebody must have survived."

"Yes, I believe you are right, but we don't have time to look for them."

Lazarus turned to him. "Why do we have to start this quest that you keep talking about?"

"He is coming. The Dark Creature."

"You mean like a Grog?"

Matthew saw something pass through his mind. He shook violently and looked away. Suddenly, everything around them seemed darker and colder.

"No, he is more than a Grog. He is stronger. He will come with an army of creatures."

"How do you know this?"

"They have come to me in my dreams."

The Leader scanned the flames before him. Sammy was curled up next to him and he moved his head upwards, scanning the camp. Since the incident today when Lazarus destroyed the remnants of a building, the Grog creatures had disappeared. The last few days the Grogs were all over the decimated landscape eating and killing any people they encountered.

"Who do you see in your dreams?"

"The elves. They are talking to me. They are helping us, but they are far away in a distant place."

Lazarus was quiet. His silence was punctuated with the crackling of the fire.

He said, "We can both go to sleep. Sammy will watch over us."

Lazarus petted the top of his dog's head. Matthew was not sure if the Leader believed him.

"Sure."

He grabbed his blanket and bedded down for the night. The ground was still warm from today and he felt comfortable.

LAZARUS WATCHED AS the big man turned over and went to sleep. He wondered why he had sought this man because he was clearly not well mentally. Sure, Matthew knew how to control his magic and had some answers to his questions, but these answers were suspect and crazy. It gave him more questions. They should be looking for more survivors and a place to stay.

He knew he wasn't some type of adventurer or hero to find these people Matthew was talking about. This quest to find a doorway to an ancient city was crazy and ludicrous. They might end up being killed, or killing each other.

Elves, why did this man dream about elves and quests? It was sheer madness, but everything that had happened the last few days was crazy. Only in thriller books and movies could a world turn upside down in a split second. He tried to recall what he did the day before the tidal wave destroyed his building but couldn't remember the last normal day of his life.

He wondered what Uncle Jack would do in this situation if he was alive. He fed more wood to the fire in front of him. With Sammy next to him and Matthew, they should be able to survive and maybe thrive in this crazy place. The last few days he had wondered about other survivors and also about the police or even the army. Somebody must have survived.

The bracelet on his wrist glinted in the firelight. He stared at the golden-silvery rings and at the stone attached to it. The opal had been silent since the first day of the catastrophe.

He shook his head. His uncle would take command and be the leader on this quest Matthew kept talking about. If he should lead shouldn't he know more than the Matthew, shouldn't he have the visions and ideas? He reached down to Sammy and petted his head. The dog wagged his tail and gazed at him. The animal could look furious and huggable at the same time.

Lazarus stood and grabbed his sleeping bag. They had abandoned the jeep a few miles away from here because the roads were impassable, but he wondered if they could use the car. He would ask Matthew in the morning about going back to get the jeep.

But for now, he would get some rest. He unzipped the sleeping bag and fell among the folds. Sammy padded to him and slept close by. The animal's warmth was almost like a blanket covering him. He had been lucky to find a companion such as this. The dog wagged his tail as if knowing his thoughts. Lazarus closed his eyes and was promptly asleep.

At the edges of wakefulness, he saw the opal on his bracelet start to glow.

Chapter 30

Lazarus woke with Sammy licking his face. He dreamt last night of watching TV while lying in his soft bed. He was watching a sitcom about several friends in New York doing almost nothing but get in odd situations. He saw himself as one of the friends in the sitcom and his girlfriend had come over to his apartment, but his ex-girlfriend surprised him by showing up at his doorstep. It was a stupid dream, not a vision liked Matthew had.

"It's ok," Lazarus said, "I'm awake."

The dog howled. He jumped up from his sleeping place ready to fight. The first thing he noticed was the sound. He heard birds and other things, animals screeching in the distance. A large tree shaded them from the sun, but a tree was not here yesterday. Lazarus stood and looked around. Green ivy covered the large cement blocks and debris. A forest had sprung up overnight while he was sleeping. He climbed up a mound and studied the area. Trees and plants covered the landscape of Los Angeles. Nature had overtaken the manmade structures.

Matthew said, "I woke and found this. It was the magic that came forth."

"From where?"

The big man climbed up toward where Lazarus stood. He towered over him. Lazarus only reached up to Matthew's shoulders. They surveyed the land.

"I don't know. I get dreams, but I don't really know where they come from."

"So, this magic, where has it been all these years? Why now?"

Lazarus' face was warm. He wished everything was the same again. He never wanted to have these powers. He wanted to be back at his apartment again, working at his job, doing mundane things.

"I don't know. We have to find the others and then maybe we can find out."

The sound of cockatoos was heard and also another animal he could not name. It was like being in the Amazon forest.

They started a fire in the clearing, working silently. Its warmth felt good in the coolness of the morning. Their breakfast consisted of berries and nuts they found a short way from their camp. Grass shot up from the ground, covering the uneven pavement and dirt. He couldn't believe this vibrant forest had sprung up overnight. When he scanned ahead the forest only began around where they slept, not pushing beyond a half a block from where they camped.

Water was in short supply, but luckily Lazarus had filled several canteens from a pipe that jutted out from a building before he encountered Matthew. They would have to find another water source before they set out.

"Matthew, I think we should find the jeep I abandoned a mile away from here. Then we can go find the others. But where are we going?"

Matthew stared at him. Lazarus wondered if he heard him, but Matthew was not looking at him but upwards into the canopy of leaves and tree limbs.

Lazarus turned and saw a large panther moving among the trees. The animal was muscular and sleek. It didn't spot them, but was hunting other game. Sammy was growling next to him. The panther didn't look any different to other large cats he saw in the zoo and he wondered if this animal had come from the local zoo.

He held his breath as the panther left the area. Matthew was still looking up at the trees and he shook his head.

"Wow," Matthew said, "did you see that?"

The animal was smaller than the Grogs but still impressive to look at while he roamed among the vegetation.

"Yes, I'm glad the panther didn't look at us to be its next meal."

Matthew said, "It didn't look odd."

Lazarus understood. This animal looked normal. So, he thought, not every creature was changed by the magic.

"We should leave. Sammy, did you get your breakfast?"

The dog had been eating a small rabbit caught in the morning, but the carcass lay Sammy's feet because he was staring at the direction in which the panther had gone.

"What's wrong?"

They heard a loud growling sound and then another noise of something larger growling back. The death cry of the panther was clearly audible. Sammy's hackles stood up. He looked like he wanted to run at the sound, yet he stayed next to Lazarus, growling.

Matthew looked at him with magical flames already poised on his upraised palms. The large growl didn't sound like a Grog or any creature he knew. Then he thought about the swarm that killed the Grog a few miles from here.

They packed up their supplies and belongings and Matthew whispered, "Which way to the jeep?"

Lazarus pointed and they started moving. He hoped the creature was not traveling to their destination. It took several hours to tramp through the forest and the sun was high above when they came out. The day was getting hot and humid and his clothes stuck to his back. He peeled off his long shirt and changed into a T-shirt and shorts. He wanted to change out of his thick walking boots, but decided to keep them on. The heat didn't affect Matthew. He still wore his large jacket and carried his backpack.

"Can we stop and take a short break?" Lazarus asked.

He looked down at Sammy who was panting. Matthew nodded and they stopped underneath the shade of a dilapidated structure. Lazarus's feet were sore and his body ached from climbing over the many scraps and detritus that covered the streets. He was still trying to get used to the empty roads and buildings which were full of people a week ago. He hoped this devastation only covered Los Angeles and they would eventually meet somebody when they reached their destination.

Matthew sat in the shade next to a broken cinder block and checked the area. The sky was clear, with small birds visible. Lazarus heard the sound of monkeys and looked up to see a group of chimpanzees moving between the broken buildings.

He said, "Matthew, where are the dead bodies? There must have been people killed in this wreckage."

"I did see some bodies in the first few days but they all seem to either be eaten by the Grogs or to have disappeared."

Lazarus nodded. In this new world, he didn't know what expect. There had to have been a couple of million of people living in LA. They all couldn't all have changed to Grogs.

"You know, on the first day, I saw some people. There was a large man who could conjure food and also a man who was skewered by metal."

The big man nodded.

Lazarus said, "Shouldn't we find them?"

Matthew was quiet for a while, squinting into the sun. "We have a quest. We have to complete it."

"Is this quest more important than helping other people?"

"Yes."

"These elves you talked about. Did they start this catastrophe?"

"No. We started this a long time ago."

Lazarus looked away from the big man. He was getting angry and he shouldn't. He clenched his hands and stared out at the decimated world. It was odd, he thought, how he heard the news about the terrorists in the Middle East destroying the American way of life, but something altogether different destroyed everything in one day.

He couldn't believe the whole United States was annihilated. It wasn't nuclear weapons that did this, but something hidden in the past.

Chapter 31

Lazarus's Uncle Jack died a few weeks later after he saw him before his surgery. His parents mostly stayed at the hospital with him in tow, taking turns visiting with Uncle Jack. He watched as his uncle shrank from the many chemo treatments and surgeries he endured. Lazarus's Junior High let him graduate even though he stayed penned up at the cancer ward. Lazarus did his homework during the day and at night sat next to his uncle.

Uncle Jack seemed to change from a man who told many stories to a quiet man who stared at the images on the TV. They watched everything from game shows to sitcoms. After the first week, his dad took him home to get a few clothes and to stay home for a while. His friend, Cindy, came over to visit with him. He was in his living room with their neighbor, Carol, an old spinster. Her husband had died several years ago. He heard a knock at the front door.

Carol stood and walked over to the door and opened it. He heard a girl speak to Carol.

"Is Lazarus here?"

"Yes, who are you?"

"I'm his friend from school. Cindy."

Carol didn't seem to know what to do. She turned to him.

"It's fine. She's a friend."

"I don't like this. You can't have a small girl visit you. It's indecent."

"Don't worry. We'll talk in the dining room. You can see us from the living room."

Carol didn't move but then she nodded. "Ok. Sorry, I'm old-fashion. And you need to talk to a friend, under the circumstances."

He walked up to the doorway. Cindy lived in the house at the end of the block and they went to the same grade school and junior high. They had been friends because their parents were. They even shared a crib together as babies.

He led Cindy into the dining room and said, "Do you want something to drink? I actually don't know what we have in the fridge."

"Maybe something later. I wanted to know how are you doing?"

"I'm fine. And my parents want to thank you for getting my study guides and homework."

She smiled. "You would have done the same for me."

"Sure," he said with too much confidence. In a corner of his mind, he knew wouldn't have helped her if the roles were reversed and he felt foolish and sad. He had been so numb since he first heard his uncle was sick. He didn't know what he felt. Cindy looked at him with her big blue eyes, twirling her blond hair with her hand. For a brief moment, he sensed a stirring of adolescence come into his mind and body. He felt something for her, something he couldn't understand since his emotions had been in a maelstrom of sadness and fear for his uncle and for his parents, fear of the ultimate taker of lives - death.

Cindy touched his hand briefly. "Are you ok?"

"I think so."

Tears formed in his eyes and he had to look away from her. He wanted to embrace her and stay within her arms for a long time, but he heard Carol stirring behind him.

She walked up and said, "Do you kids want some chocolate chip cookies? I can make a batch."

"Sure."

Carol lumbered into the kitchen. "There is also milk."

Lazarus said, "Thank you."

"Let's watch TV," Cindy said. "I think there is something funny on tonight."

"Do your parents know you're here?"

"Yes, I told them. And today is Friday. I don't have any homework tonight."

They sat side by side in the living room. Carol was in the recliner. They watched a movie about aliens that tried to take over the world. Lazarus had seen this movie before and even seen this in the hospital, but he didn't care. He munched on freshly baked cookies accompanied by a glass of cold milk. For some reason, he wanted to hold Cindy's hand, but he squashed that idea. She was way too pretty and the boys in her school always pestered him to introduce them to her.

The next day Uncle Jack passed away in his sleep. Lazarus vowed to himself he would never try to achieve more than he had already, that staying on the easy path was the way to go. His uncle showed him what would happen when somebody traveled the world and had rich experiences. Even after that, there was only pain and death.

LAZARUS DIDN'T UNDERSTAND why he was thinking about his uncle and about his friend Cindy. Sammy walked next to him as they climbed the decimated sections of Los Angeles. Lazarus was perspiring and all his thoughts about his old life seemed inconsequential and naive. If he survived the next day or the next month, it would be a miracle. He didn't have survival skills like Matthew or animalistic senses like Sammy. He was ill prepared to traverse this new land. The forest started again with trees sprouting from the ground, breaking through the pavement and buildings. A smattering of colorful birds, all different shades of blues and green chattered away on the tree limbs.

He was amazed at first seeing so many avian creatures in the one place. He was thinking about the swarm of hornets and he froze. Matthew kept on walking forward toward the canopy of birds.

"Matthew, stop! Remember the swarm that I told you about."

The big man didn't slow. He held up his hands and the birds flew up into the air in a whoosh of feathers and squawks. Lazarus felt the stirrings of his magic, but it was different. He didn't feel any malice or rancor coming from the animals. He heard something. The birds landed close to Matthew, standing on any surface they could find.

Lazarus said, "Do you feel that?"

"Yes, the birds are talking to us. They are telling me the Grogs all left and headed east, away from the city."

Lazarus shook his head. He didn't hear any of this, but Matthew's magic was different to his. He was about to ask Matthew another question but the birds all took flight and disappeared into the broken rubble and walls surrounding them.

"Why did they leave?"

Matthew was staring up at the birds. "I don't know. I thought I could talk to these birds, but they said a few things and left." He turned his face up and lifted his hands again but the birds flew away from him.

Lazarus had an idea, but he didn't want to alarm Matthew. He sensed that something, or someone, was directing them. Yet, he didn't feel like they were being led like marionettes attached to strings. Lazarus almost looked upwards to the sky wondering if these entities were watching them now. He wondered if it was the elves and then shook his head. He was being paranoid.

They started traveling again. The birds disappeared and no other animals came to them.

A thought came to him, that he should have gone back home to check on his parents before embarking on this journey. He was being selfish. But he knew that the reason he didn't go home was because he knew they were dead, or worse.

They found the jeep still parked at the beginning of the freeway before the broken debris destroyed the path. Lazarus checked his pockets and for a split second thought he had lost the keys, but then his hand touched them. He pointed the FOB at the car and pressed the open button, but nothing happened.

"Shit!"

They looked around. This was the only car in the vicinity that was not destroyed or lying on its side.

He said, "The battery must be dead."

It had half a tank of gas, so fuel was not the problem.

Matthew said, "What should we do?"

"Well, we can look for another battery or find another car."

Matthew nodded.

Chapter 32

C indy woke from a long nap. They had been traveling along a broken strip of streets, coming closer to what they thought was Times Square, but the closer they got the more the path was impassable. They had to double back a few times and climb a few hills piled with the remains of large buildings and apartments. Mary and Rochelle didn't talk through this long day. At mid-afternoon, they decided to stop and rest. They had not eaten anything since the morning. They raided a small store, smashed and shattered with its contents of food scattered among the debris and decimated material of buildings. She had a backpack filled with other items from the store next to her while she slept.

Cindy looked up from her small hiding place in the overhang of a bus stop, which for some reason was clear of rubble. She heard something. It was dusk and the sun was going down on the horizon. She sighed, looking at the skyline and remembering a few days ago how buildings and structures had dotted the city. She heard the noise again. Cindy had slept through the afternoon. She looked for Mary and Rochelle. They were not within her sight and she felt a little trepidation, thinking the Grog insects had got them or something else. She stood and brushed off the dirt from her pants.

Cindy heard the noise again, a clanking noise, and she moved toward it. Her body trembled while she picked her way up the street. She spied a long pipe on the ground and she picked it up for protection. The clanking noise was to her right. Cindy stopped and listened for anything that would help her figure out what was happening. She wanted to yell for Mary and Rochelle but she stopped herself. Her mind screamed for her to flee, but she had to find them, no matter if they were alive or dead.

She saw a large mound of cement, asphalt and debris. The sound was coming from that area. Goosebumps developed on her arms as if a cold breeze flew by her, but it was warm in New York, and that was odd because it had been cold for the last few weeks.

Cindy started to climb. She held the large pipe in her hands, clasped in a two-handed grip like a baseball player. She turned to look at where she slept today but it was hidden by the stacks of debris. The clanking stopped and it was eerie hearing the wind flowing through the devastation. The first thing she saw didn't register in her brain until she saw everything.

Before her blood and gore spread out among the various rocks, bricks and glass. Even though it was dusk, the blood was glinting through the glass. Entrails splattered all over and Cindy couldn't tell if this was one person or two. Then she heard the clanking noise. A metal pipe attached to a large cord hung over the carnage and it was covered in the gore. And the pipe swayed in the wind hitting a metal siding. She thought she saw a ripped piece of a scalp with long dark red hair attached to it sitting below the pipe.

Cindy turned and vomited to the side. She wiped her mouth and climbed down the embankment. Her stomach recoiled again like a venomous snake and she doubled over clutching it. The images of the entrails and blood floated in her mind. She ran down an opened lane and then stopped herself. She needed to know if Mary or Rochelle was alive. If one of them survived, she would have to find them. Cindy steeled her nerves and took a deep breath. She needed to think. She decided to travel half a block away and break camp. Tomorrow, she would come back and look again. The sun finally disappeared into the night.

Cindy walked a few feet, looking around, but finding nothing that looked promising. All she saw was more broken buildings and bricks. Finally, she saw a small structure that was half broken and opened in the front. She was thinking of making a small fire. The nights of New York were chilly and she had enough wood and paper to create a fire. She touched the bic lighter in her pocket. Rochelle had grabbed a few lighters when they found the store in the morning. She checked the small backpack and took out a bottled water, now almost done, and some licorice and potato chips. She had saved these for dinner tonight.

Cindy went into the small structure. It was relatively clean even though most of the walls were ripped and broken. She cleared an area and found several slabs of wood and paper for kindling. She placed the wood in the middle of the clearing and added the newsprint around the bottom of the mound. Grabbing the lighter, she flicked the spark wheel and nothing happened. She flicked it several times and a flame erupted.

She placed the flame to the paper and lit the bonfire, holding her hands closer to the warmth of the small blaze. The surrounding structure would protect her from anybody seeing the light. She didn't want to sleep because she was afraid the creature that had done all that carnage was probably still out there, moving and looking for more food.

The fire caught quickly and warmed the area around her. She sat on the bare cement. Her body started to get warm, not from the fire blazing before her but from inside her chest and arms. She sensed a calling from something or someone. She felt a pulling toward somebody, in the same way, that two magnets are attracted to each other. Cindy knew it was a person and this person was far away from her. Somewhere on the west coast, she thought, and she believed this calling meant that she was going to do something, embark on a journey to somewhere.

She shook her head. This was crazy. Pulling her hands away from the fire she wondered if all this was an elaborate experiment. She envisioned a scientist appearing and telling her the experiment was done and she could go back to her old life.

Her hands started to move in an intricate pattern and a globe appeared before her, made of water. She marveled at it. It was the size of her fist and it floated close to her. It was transparent so that she could see the broken buildings and walls through it, and then an image appeared. It flashed like a television screen and she was amazed to see a man looking at her, but not really seeing her.

It was her friend, Lazarus. She almost touched the globe.

Chapter 33

Matthew watched as the Leader sat across from him. Lazarus led him toward several cars along the stretch of highway. Most of the cars had rotting dead bodies inside them, a macabre sight in the dim light of dusk. They stopped a few feet away on the clear area from the freeway. The tidal wave had pushed most of the vegetation and cars far off in an area, piled high like building blocks. Most of the people had died inside their automobiles that were smashed and buried in the debris.

He cooked them a dinner of roasted rabbit. The war dog, Sammy, was becoming invaluable to their quest. Matthew wanted to smile and jump for joy because all these years people thought he was crazy, but now he was destined to be on a journey and complete his quest. It had finally happened, but not the way he expected.

He had dreamt about this quest for years, since he had been living on the streets and before, in a different life. He held a memory in his mind. He thought he saw himself standing in front of a group of people in a vast auditorium. They were listening to him. He was a teacher of something, but he couldn't recall what he taught. It was fuzzy, like seeing through a murky and dirty glass.

He also recalled a beautiful brunette woman, who, he thought, was his wife. Matthew shook his head. This could not be. He didn't want to remember, it hurt him. His life was chaotic, moving from place to place and living on the streets, fighting for every meal and running from the police. Nobody understood. He had to embark on this quest.

The elves visited and told him. He was supposed to meet this Leader and find the ancient city. But this catastrophe which had destroyed Los Angeles was not something he thought would happen. And this Leader of his, Lazarus, was not the person Matthew thought should lead them. He seemed fussy and inexperienced with living out in the wild and the streets. He was not like Matthew, who had been on this quest for years. Matthew took a large stick and poked the fire. For some reason, the elves had picked this man to be their Leader and Matthew had no choice but to comply. He didn't have a choice so many years ago and he didn't have a choice now.

Visions and memories came to him. He remembered he was a teacher, a teacher of something at a college. Then he saw the brunette woman again. She was hugging him and smiling. They had many good times together and then he remembered a small child whose name was Lizzy. She died. The fuzziness of his brain encroached into his sight and mind. He did not want to remember. Pain and sadness were all he felt. He also saw a large carousel. The kind you would see at a carnival filled with fantastic sea creatures, horses and animals. It was turning and turning and he saw himself sitting on a white horse with Lizzy in front of him as they rode up and down and round and round. They waved at the brunette lady as they rode the horse and all was good.

Matthew's brain hurt and he grabbed his temples.

Lazarus said, "What's wrong? Are you hurt?"

The Leader was on his feet staring at him with sadness and shock in his eyes.

"It was the carousel. I don't want to see it. She is gone."

"Who is gone?"

Sammy also stood and glanced around warily.

"Nobody, it doesn't matter."

Matthew didn't want to explain to Lazarus about his old life because they were gone, gone like the many pills and medicine they gave him when he was a patient at the hospital, the sanitarium where others liked him stared at nothing and secretly wanted to leave but didn't dare to because the orderlies watched them like a hawk.

⚜

LAZARUS WAS CONCERNED about the big man. Matthew grabbed his head and howled like a banshee to the sky. And when he tried to ask him what was wrong, Matthew would not tell him. Lazarus thought Matthew was deeply disturbed and should be on some kind of medication. He wondered if Matthew would go crazy, use his powers, and decide to kill him and Sammy. The big man was quiet now, staring at the flames of the fire and pushing the logs with a long stick.

Lazarus lay on his sleeping bag. It was a cool night but not cold. They had checked all the cars on this part of the warped freeway and the cars either had dead bodies or were destroyed beyond drivability. They might have to walk the rest of the way.

He sensed somebody watching him. He thought he saw a brief flash, a light came close to him and then it was gone. Gazing at the area, he saw nothing but cars piled on top of each other, but the feeling of being watched was still there. It was like being in a store with people all around you staring and gawking at you. This presence was familiar, as if he knew the person and he knew where he needed to head, and it was far away.

Matthew said, "You know where we should go."

Lazarus was surprised he knew. He wondered if he could read his mind, but then understood it was something else.

"You felt it, too. You sensed the other person watching us."

"Yes, there were eyes on me. I don't like eyes on me. It makes me feel wrong."

"Do you need extra medication? We can try to look for something."

"No! I don't need those things. Not after..."

Matthew gazed at him with eyes that had so much hurt in them that Lazarus had to look away and study the fire. There was something in Matthew. Something he didn't want to remember and Lazarus didn't want to coax him to tell him. Some things should be kept secret.

Chapter 34

A wind buffeted Grace as she floated up and looked around their surroundings. Joan had decided to leave with them the next day. They stayed an extra day at the small store, gathering supplies and figuring out what they should do. Even though Grace had lived here for several years she didn't know where the nearest police station was but Joan said it was down a few miles from here. But Grace couldn't tell where they were. She scanned for the landmarks of the casinos, but all she saw while she floated in the sky was mounds of sand dunes. Eventually, she saw something she recognized, the 15 freeway. The sand dunes covered most of it.

She said, "Joan, I see the 15 freeway."

Grace floated too high and they couldn't hear her. She looked down and saw them staring at her. She was about to start to descend back to them, but turned away to look behind her and she saw something that almost made her shout. A wall of sand was coming to them. They needed to find shelter. But then she remembered that her powers could protect them. She descended.

Lawrence sensed something. "What did you see?"

"I saw the 15 freeway, but I saw something else. Another storm is coming toward us."

Joan said, "What do we do?"

Grace heard a whining noise and the ground rumbled. She started to radiate intense heat from her chest and arms. She heard the beating of her heart. The wind blasted through their small area in front of the store.

Lawrence said, "Grace, what should we do?"

The boy grabbed her arm. Grace looked at her hand and saw the ring on her finger start to glow.

She said, "Gather close to me."

Joan and Lawrence moved close to her. The wind started to whine louder and Grace felt power gather within her. It was as if the power of the storm raged inside. She lifted her hands and a white glowing barrier surrounded them. The sound of the storm was deafening. The ground shuddered and a wave of dirt, ground and sand hit the barrier.

Joan tried to speak to her, but Grace couldn't understand what she was saying through the noise of the storm. She focused and they floated into the maw of the tempest. Lawrence hugged so her tight that she almost couldn't breathe. Her magical powers seethed and thundered inside her. She felt the fury of the storm. Grace had never felt so powerful. She moved her hand downwards. The sand storm changed into a large hurricane. Large chunks of building walls, stone and other things she couldn't recognize flew around them. They were inside the eye of the storm. The deafening sound faded to a whine. And Grace knew that if she let the glowing force field disperse they would be torn apart.

Slowly, by degrees, the storm started to lessen and change direction, leaving them. They were floating several hundred feet from the ground. Grace saw that Las Vegas was completely covered by sand and dirt. She couldn't see the 15 freeway or the store. The sands of nature finally took over the manmade structures. She descended to the ground.

"Where are our supplies?" Grace asked.

Joan said, "I have them in my backpack."

"I also have some food in my pack," Lawrence said.

"I tried to speak to you, but you were in a trance," Joan said.

Her face was flushed with sadness when she gazed at the area where her father's store was covered with sand. Grace saw sand dunes everywhere she looked. Nothing could have survived the second tempest.

Joan said, "What do we do now?"

"We leave. There is nothing holding us here. Even the creatures must be dead."

The sun was high in the sky and Grace felt the heat burning into her skin. She lifted her hand and sand floated above them, creating a canopy shading them from the heat.

Lawrence said, "That's neat."

Grace was about to speak then an odd feeling came over her. She needed to find him, the person who would show them the pathway, the doorway to the ancient city. A place they all needed to find. It was The Calling.

Lawrence said, "Do you hear me?"

"What? Sorry, I didn't hear you. What did you say?"

"You said that you have to find him. Who are you speaking about?"

"I don't know. But I know where we should go. We are going to California."

Joan said, "That is hundreds of miles from here."

"Yes, I know."

"How do you expect us to get there from here?"

Grace was not sure but she was sure about one thing. "You don't have to go. I need to do this alone. We will find you a safe place."

She said this with conviction and realized there really was no safe place anymore. The safest place was with her.

Lawrence gave a sad and sheepish look. "Where are you going, and why can't we go with you?"

Grace shook her head. "Lawrence." She knelt by him. "I don't mean I will leave you alone right now. But when we find some people to help, you can go with them."

The desert looked desolate with some of the tallest buildings poking through the surface. A wind picked up and she sensed her powers had changed and morphed into something more powerful and stronger. She knew where to go and she felt like a compass pointed due west toward the Leader, but she also sensed something else, a deep vastness of strength had been released into the world and was changing everything.

"Come with me for now. It's up to you."

Joan and Lawrence had no choice at the moment. Las Vegas was swallowed by the sands of magic and nature. They nodded in agreement.

"So be it."

She knew the first place they would go would be the State Line. There were several casinos there and hopefully the buildings were still standing. Grace saw the remnants of the 15 freeway snaking out of the sand several hundred feet away. With her magical compass showing where to go she decided this was the path toward the State Line.

Grace said, "We don't have to walk."

Her powers had grown and she knew she could easily levitate all of them. Grace focused her powers and they all floated off the ground.

Joan yelped.

Lawrence said, "Whoopee, let's go."

They started to move across the sand. The wind buffeted their clothes.

Chapter 35

Grace and her group soared higher. Lawrence yelled in joy. Joan looked pale and didn't say much during their travel. Grace wanted to go faster, but looking at Joan's face made her fly slow and closer to the ground. After they left the remnants of Las Vegas, they had to fly several miles until the bottom of the actual ground showed. The sand storm which covered all of Las Vegas create mounds of hills which made the ground disappear. The freeway became a two-way lane. Several abandoned cars stood mute on the stretch of the street. Most of the automobiles had the doors either ajar or smashed open.

She said, "Lawrence, don't look at the bodies or inside the cars."

Most of the dead were ravaged by a creature or ripped apart. Grace knew the wolves must have done this damage and she moved away from these scenes when she could. Grace called for a stop in the afternoon. Her mind and body were getting tired, and they had finally reached the outskirts of the State Line where California and Nevada divided. She saw the tops of the casino, Buffalo Bill, Gold Strike, Nevada Landing, and Whisky Pete's still a half a mile from their position. They took several candy bars and drinks from the packs and started to eat. They were covered head to toe in sand and dirt even though Grace had shielded them the best she could while they traveled. She wanted to take one of the cars stranded on the road, but none of them were usable.

She created a sand shade over them and they ate on a barren area of the ground. Stunted bushes and shrubs were scattered along the landscape. Lawrence drank most of his bottled water.

"Slow down," Grace said. "We need to conserve our supplies."

He nodded in agreement. Grace didn't know what she would do with these two. She couldn't bring them along with her, for her mission was dangerous, or she imagined so. She turned to the casinos still far off in the distance and she realized something.

Joan said what she was thinking. "The casino's lights and signs are on."

Joan shielded her eyes and peered at the casinos. Grace followed her gazed. Even in the blazing sun, she could see the lights and signs were on but she was not sure. She wanted to start their journey again and rush toward the buildings, but her excitement was tempered with having seen the carnage and terror the Grog creatures caused in Las Vegas.

Lawrence said, "We should go. Maybe we can find my parents there."

Grace came closer to Lawrence and knelt by him. "I thought your parents died in the hotel."

His eyes grew huge and he nodded. She saw his mind was trying to comprehend this awful truth.

"I know. But I sometimes think this is a nightmare and I will wake up back at home."

"Yes, I think the same thing."

She gave him a hug. He stifled a cry. Joan looked away from them.

⁘

GRACE HAD AN ODD FEELING looking at the Casinos. They hid behind a sand dune between Whisky Pete's and Nevada Landing several feet from the road. She was not sure if the lights were on or if the heat of the desert was playing tricks on them. Yet she felt a fore-boding around her mind and her body. She wanted to fly to this casi-no and see if somebody, anybody, was alive, but it looked too easy.

Joan said, "I think we should go. We need to know if somebody is there."

"I don't know," Lawrence said. "It looks wrong."

Grace understood. The casino looked wrong.

"They have already seen us."

Joan was right. They could have seen them if they looked out the windows. But who would be looking, that was the question.

Grace knew they didn't have any weapons. They had her magic to defend them, but what if they surprised her and knocked her out? The others would be defenseless.

"We could wait until nighttime and then check it out," she said.

"Yes, let's do that," Lawrence replied.

Joan looked nonplussed and shook her head. "I want to go now."

"No, we should wait. There's something wrong. Can you feel it?"

Lawrence said, "Yes, I can feel it too."

Joan started to stand. "I don't care. You are not the boss of me. My dad always bossed me around and now he's dead and I will do what I want."

She started to walk forward. Grace shook her head. She couldn't make Joan do anything. But she knew she was right. She watched Joan walk down toward the Casinos. It would take an hour to walk there. She should go with her but she had an obligation to protect Lawrence. He was a minor and couldn't look after himself. And she thought it was imperative she found a safe haven for him.

Grace moved Lawrence a few feet down toward a high sand dune to watch Joan walk the last few hundred feet to the nearest casino, Buffalo Bill. She saw a large fake mountain with the roller coaster that maneuvered in and out of the casino. Dusk was coming with the cool breeze of the desert. Lawrence lay on the ground watching Joan.

The lights of the Casinos were on and bright. Joan reached the parking lot which had several cars stationed in neat rows, as if people had arrived for a weekend of fun.

A flash came from the sky and clouds appeared out of nowhere. And then a noise like thunder arose and Lawrence moved down. He looked away from Joan, his eyes darting around.

He said, "Should you help her?"

Grace's eyes were transfixed on the lights and the buildings. She sensed deep magic awakening from the very earth. She was about to fly toward Joan when her slim figure disappeared. First, she was walking down an embankment in the dim light, next she was gone.

"Where did she go?"

Lawrence was next to her. She felt his hot breath on her arm.

"Look!"

The ground rippled and moved like water. Grace sensed the leviathan before it broke through the surface of the ground. It rose higher than the tallest buildings of the casinos and roller coaster. The leviathan was a long scaled worm with a round open maw. Even from their vantage point, Grace could see the many rows of razor sharp daggers in its mouth like dozens of shark teeth, all in concentric rows.

The giant worm reared up high and stopped in midair. Grace almost screamed while Lawrence next to her was mute. The leviathan fell to the ground and disappeared into the sands.

Lawrence clutched her arm, digging into her skin.

"What is that thing?" he asked.

"I don't know, but I don't want to walk down there and find out."

Grace was searching for Joan but she was nowhere to be found. She had disappeared underneath the sands. Grace placed her hands on the ground. She was not sure if she could do this, but she gave it a try. She focused her senses outward toward the Casinos, trying to find out what was hidden underneath.

Her mind started to flow through the sands, feeling the layout of the earth. It was a harrowing experience as though she was being swallowed into the ground. Yet her body was still on the surface. Lawrence was her anchor. The boy still held her arm and he didn't say anything to her while she was in a trance. She sensed the leviathan under the buildings and structures. It awoke and came into being after the magical storms brought forth destruction. The creature's mind was not open to her, but she saw its lair. It was a large cavern filled with dead bodies. Grace scanned and saw Joan. She was eviscerated and dismembered. Other smaller worms were feeding on her. Grace couldn't take it and rushed back to her body.

She awoke from the trance in a breathless small scream.

Chapter 36

Cindy took a deep breath and tried to gather her will to do the task before her. She waited until mid-morning to go back to the gore and blood. She told herself it was not her responsibility to find Mary or Rochelle, but they did help her when she was in trouble and she needed to know if they were dead. Cindy had hoped that when she woke in the morning she would find one of them, but neither appeared. She was surprised the magical water globe she conjured last night was still floating close to her position. She sensed the globe had watched her through the night, protecting her and making sure nobody caught her unaware.

She stood and recalled last night how she had seen her old friend, Lazarus, inside the globe. Was this a vision, she wondered, or a memory? Yet, she knew she had to find him. He was alive and he was the Leader. She stood and brushed off the dirt from the rugged khaki pants she wore and had found in the remains of a clothing store. She almost laughed. If anybody saw her attired like this, they wouldn't recognize her from her power suits and the dresses she wore at work. She shook her head. She was postponing what she needed to do. Walking back to the area where she saw the blood, her mind tried to give her the hope that Mary and Rochelle were not dead. They fled somewhere far away and they were fine. She muttered something under her breath. Great, she thought, she was going crazy, becoming like the many street bums who populated the parks and streets of New York.

Cindy climbed a hill of rocks and bricks. Her boots gave her better traction than the sandals she wore a few days ago. Then she felt the pulling again. She needed to find Lazarus and not look for Mary and Rochelle. The thought was so strong she almost turned around. She said out loud, "No!"

Magic came out of her. A gush of water flew from her and struck against a small wall that still stood. The small wave destroyed the brick wall into small pieces of concrete and debris. It dawned on her that her powers were water based in nature and she could conjure magic at any time, but she didn't know how to control it.

She wondered if she could do other things. Her mind wandered and she shook her head. She needed to get this task over with. Cindy walked to the place she had napped the day before and looked around. She was not sure if this area was the place. Everything looked the same, just a mess of broken pieces of brick walls and concrete. Large cracks peppered the streets and at certain places yawning fissures. Then she recalled the sound of metal hitting against metal had led her to the gruesome scene. She waited and tried to hear the sound again, but to no avail. The pipe had either fallen or the wind couldn't make the pipe strike against the metal siding. She was almost relieved that she couldn't find the gruesome scene again.

Cindy was about to leave and start to check other areas, when she heard the sound again, the incessant noise of pipe banging against metal. It was the death knoll that brought to her to the corpses which lay in a heap of junk and refuse, to tell her to look and watch and tell her she couldn't help them and she didn't protect them. She started to travel to that noise, being careful not to fall or hurt herself.

Cindy stopped and saw the heap of rubble that hid the gore. Her body started to shake and she couldn't move for a while. Then she took a deep breath and started to climb. She heard the banging of the pipe and then something else, a buzzing noise. Cindy climbed to the top and stared at the blood and gore, but it was covered by hundreds of flies. Her stomach curled and moved like the buzzing insects. She looked away but then she saw something. It was Mary's purse, blood-stained and cut into pieces, and then she saw a leg and then Mary, lying on her stomach, cut into ribbons.

Cindy said, "No, no."

She wanted to look away but she could not. Cindy had to look. She gazed away from the gore. And saw another hump covered with flies. Maybe it was Rochelle.

Cindy's mind reeled with pain. She wondered why the creatures didn't attack her. It didn't make sense. She looked away and saw the water globe was not next to her. She placed her hands in fists. Magic crackled.

The globe appeared and it was transparent, filled with water and with lightning crackling along its surface. Cindy's anger boiled over. This should not be happening. She should be at her job in her high rise building talking about accounts and money. The smell of death wafted in the air and she moved back down the small hill. She wanted to say some eulogy to the dead, but she didn't know what to say. She should bury them.

The crackling noise from the floating globe and the buzzing noise of the flies made her angrier. She held up her hands before her, focused at the small hill and gathered her magic. A blast of water hit the mound and an explosion rocked the space. Debris and stone fell backwards covering Mary and the gore. The flies flew upwards in a swarm. The insects were a cloud of incessant buzzing. They moved in formation and Cindy thought the creatures were going to attack her.

But the flies hovered for a second and disappeared. She sighed and looked at the resting place of Mary and maybe her daughter, Rochelle, and nodded. The water globe changed into a clear droplet as it moved close to her and in the second before it was about to touch her it disappeared.

She left the vicinity and moved toward Time Square, the only place she hoped she would find somebody alive.

Chapter 37

Cindy started traveling again, roaming through the passable areas of the streets. She thought the time was growing short and that she had to find Lazarus because of some undefinable disaster looming over them, but she thought the disaster had already happened and she needed to learn to survive in this strange land.

She thought some type of military response should have occurred and the skies should be covered with helicopters and airplanes searching for survivors. But the skies were clear. She wondered why the greatest nation on earth didn't have a plan in place for this type of catastrophe. Cindy walked through a passage filled with decimated buildings and debris.

She hoped the creatures that killed Mary and Rochelle were not watching her right now, ready to attack. She tried to listen to any sounds and scan any dark hole or fissure, but there were too many places to watch. She focused and the water globe appeared. She wondered if she could give this thing commands.

She said, "Change into a bird."

The globe started to transform. It grew feathers, talons and a beak. The falcon flapped its wings and took flight. It squawked and flew around her. Cindy watched it fly and move along the wind's currents in the sky.

"Wow," she said. "I didn't know I could do this." Cindy clapped her hands. "Alright, I want you to protect me."

The falcon squawked and flew close to her and then soared high above and plunged down by her. She felt protected.

Cindy started to move along the street. She traveled through the many broken and demolished areas almost indistinguishable from the other places she had traveled. Cindy was not even sure she was moving in the correct direction. Then she saw a large sign on the ground. Parts of the marquee were shattered all over the ground and surrounding area, but she clearly saw two large letters "RA". Cindy realized she was in the wreckage of the Radio City Music Hall. The falcon high above squawked at her. She looked up into the air.

"What is it? What do you see?"

She shook her head. The echo of a memory of the famous Radio City Music hall hit her. A year ago around Christmas time she had was invited by a man, Charles, she thought, to watch the famous Radio City Rockettes dance. She knew Charles was trying to impress her because she was from LA and she was new in town. Cindy was impressed. She loved the large round amphitheater with its Art Deco embellishments and the many sculptures and murals all over the interior. It was dizzying. When they took their seats and watched the statuesque Rockettes dance in formation, she tried not to gawk like a teenager at her first prom. Cindy didn't want to show how eager she was because she didn't know this man, Charles, and she didn't want to end up sleeping with him.

The falcon squawked at her and she had to gaze at the bird. Something was wrong. The bird flew high in the buildings, swooping in and out of spaces.

She said, "I see you. What is wrong?"

Cindy couldn't understand her bird. She shook her head. This was crazy. She was speaking to an animal. A loud noise thundered and she instinctively ducked her head. It was the sound of a gun. Cindy felt a pain in her chest and clutched at her skin. The falcon fell to the ground. It was shot. The bird hit the street in a sickening, splattered sound.

Before she could look around to find who shot her bird she heard a noise from behind her. A rock barreled at her and struck her on the side of her temple. She fell close to her falcon.

Her body hit the pavement in a bone-charring bounce. She felt the pain inside her and heard voices. Cindy tried to move but she couldn't get herself to stand or even turn her body.

"You shouldn't have done that. The Council will be mad that you hurt the woman."

"Nah, she will be ok. This one is special. She has powers."

"The Council will not like that you spoilt the girls."

"She will be fine."

A strong hand grabbed her and maneuvered her toward a waiting jeep. The car was scarred and dented all over. They moved her to the back of the opened trunk, placing her inside in a gentle manner. It was like being carried by two human giants. The door closed.

Cindy heard the men talking outside. They were arguing for some reason. After a few minutes, the two men opened the door. The jeep started and the vehicle started moving. Her head hurt and felt tender. The jeep jostled and moved down the road.

After a few minutes, she tried to moved her hands and legs, but saw something surrounding and binding her. It looked like a rope but it glowed and was semi-transparent. The rope made her light-headed and drowsy. She needed to be calm and stay awake but the constant moving and jostling made her sleepy. She closed her eyes.

CINDY WOKE ON A COT and looked through jail bars. She shook her head. She should have woken when the car stopped but she didn't, and she would pay the price. She looked at the other cells and saw a familiar person. It was Rochelle, unharmed and looking at her.

"Rochelle. I thought you were dead."

Rochelle didn't respond. She seemed to be in a daze. She murmured, "My mom is dead. They took me here."

"Where are we?"

"We are at the police station."

Cindy was surprised the building was still standing and the jail was still in working order. She was curious about how Mary was killed, but she didn't want to ask Rochelle at this moment. She seemed confused.

"Are you ok? You seem to be acting odd."

"I don't know. They have powers like you."

"Who are they?"

"They are called the Council. They control the creatures around here. They are different. They are not human."

"Why didn't they kill me when I was napping?"

"They didn't want to kill you. You are powerful."

Cindy was surprised and shocked. She wished she knew more about her powers.

The screech of doors opening was heard down the hallway. Footsteps echoed down the chamber and two large men approached her cell. They were tall, over six foot each and almost identical twins except one had dark brown hair and the other was bald.

The bald one said, "The Council wants to see you, Cindy."

Chapter 38

Cindy was led out of the police precinct and out toward the front door. Before she was taken out of her cell, the two large men placed the magical ropes around her. It was dim inside the interior of the police station and Cindy had to squint as she exited the building.

In front of her captors, she saw a group of people all looking dazed and confused like Rochelle. She stared at them.

The bald man turned to her and said, "Move it!"

They pushed her toward a squat building which was partly intact. The front of the structure was open for her to see inside. They mounted the steps into a hallway clear of debris and fallen furniture. People shuffled up and down the stairs, looking like zombies.

Then she sensed them. They were saying in her mind. "Obey. You're safe here."

Cindy started up the steps behind the two large men and the people crowding the stairs moved away from them. She felt lulled by the voices of the Council but she felt something else. It was the necklace she wore. The stone burnt her skin and when she held it in her hand the voices in her head ceased speaking.

They walked to the second floor where she saw more people milling around the hallways and corridors. The people all turned to her and stared. The necklace she wore was hidden underneath her shirt, but she felt the people could see it on her. The heat of the stone was almost unbearable but she didn't want to alert her captors or the people surrounding her. The two large men stopped at an open doorway down the left hallway. Light spilled from inside, sunlight glittering off the two large windows inside the cavernous room.

Cindy couldn't see their faces at first because they were sitting in several chairs with their backs facing the large windows. She only saw their silhouettes. She noticed the four people were not shaped like people, but something bigger.

The voice speaking to her had a guttural sound. "You are the Alpha wizard. You must have the stone. I feel it."

She said, "Who are you?"

"We are the new world order."

Nobody said anything and Cindy thought they wanted her to feel amazed. Inside her mind, she heard the voices talking to her.

"You will submit to us. We are the new world order. You will obey us."

She looked at him and the others and said, "No."

He moved so fast that he blurred when he attacked her. Cindy held up her arms in a warding gesture. The ropes around her broke in a snap. The attacker hit an invisible barrier before he could touch her. All she saw was a large furred body and sharp teeth. It was some type of canine. She moved back a step.

The creature sat back in his chair again.

He said, "You are powerful like the Master told us. You will give me the stone."

"No," she said again, but with more conviction in her voice. She smelt a musty scent like wet dog fur and wrinkled her nose.

"So be it. We have your friend in our jail cell and if you don't give us the stone she will suffer the same fate as her mother."

A creature appeared before her. It was not one of the Council. Several other creatures came from behind the first. It was the large insects that chased her and her companions in Central Park.

"Also," the man said, "I will let these insects devour all the people who still survived the quake."

She fingered the smooth stone. It was cool to the touch and didn't burn her skin like it had a few minutes ago. She also heard something, a sweet song that sounded familiar to her. She couldn't place it.

"Give me the stone."

"If I give you the stone, will you let these people and my friend go?"

The man considered this and the five other Council members started to chatter amongst each other.

"No, we think not. This is not a democracy. You have to comply or we will kill one person each minute until you give us the stone."

The man-beast nodded and a man came forward, holding hands with a small child. Her eyes darted around to the Council and then at Cindy.

"What?" she said. The small girl was coming out of a trance.

The man-beast said, "Hello, Charlotte, do you know why you are here?"

"We are protected by you."

"Yes," the man-beast said. "Do you see this lady next to you?"

Charlotte nodded her head. "She is beautiful."

"Ask her?"

The child turned to her and cocked her head to the side as if listening to somebody.

"They want you to give the stone to them. You understand. The Council is here to protect us from the creatures."

The bald, thick man who brought her there took out a long dagger. It glittered in the sunlight pouring inside the room. He handed her the weapon.

Charlotte took the dagger into her small hands. She looked into Cindy's eyes. "Give them the stone."

Charlotte pointed the sharp point of the dagger toward her stomach. Cindy knew what the Council was doing and that it was her choice to let this sweet little girl to kill herself or not.

"Stop!" Cindy said. "I will give you the necklace."

She unclasped the back of the necklace and pulled the stone with it. She palmed the charm and gave it to the bald thick man. Charlotte instantly dropped the dagger and stared at it as if it was a snake.

The little girl's eyes glazed over and she looked straight ahead. She was back in a trance.

"Good! You shall be our guests until our Masters tells us what to do with you. Take her back to her cell."

Cindy sighed in relief and followed the guards out.

Chapter 39

Cindy sat on her cot trying to figure a way to escape. Rochelle had been moved from her cell a day before. The guards, the two large men, who brought her here, came at night. They would check on her and then leave. A woman brought her food twice a day and a group of men cleaned her cell once a day. They never talked or looked at her. Each had the same dreamy and frozen look on their faces. She tried to talk to the young woman who brought her food. She was a brunette and she looked to be the same age as her. But when Cindy tried to speak to her she didn't say anything. It was like talking to a robot. Except, Cindy thought, the last time she brought her breakfast and Cindy said, "Hello." She gave her a small nod.

The next day another person was brought into the jail. It was an older man who had a beleaguered look to his face. He didn't understand why he was brought here. The two burly guards pushed him into the cell.

"I should not be in here. I am an American citizen."

Cindy noticed the man had a magical rope tied around him like she did when she first came here.

"Get in there," the jailer said. "The Council wants to talk to you."

Cindy, for the first time, noticed the bars of her cell glowed a little. The man's cell also glowed. These prison cells were made for magical people like her.

They placed the older man in the cell directly across from her own prison. He grabbed the bars and shook his head. He wore a torn up blue suit with a stained white shirt. He looked as if he was a teacher or professor at a college.

The man saw her and said, "Hello."

"Hi," Cindy said.

"How long have you been in here?"

Cindy was not sure but she said, "I think for several days."

"Great," the man said. "I don't understand why they bound me in this rope. I can get out of it without trouble."

She said, "The rope is for your magic. What can you do?"

"How did you know?" The man gazed at her and then squinted. He absently placed a finger close to his head like he was pushing up the frame of glasses. "It's funny," he said. "I had to wear glasses since I was a teenager and then after the earthquake I have perfect vision. Sorry, I have not introduced myself. My name is Robert Lang."

"My name is Cindy Paulson. And to answer your former question I knew you have magic because I have magic myself. And this is the reason why you are not in a trance like the others."

Robert said, "I can read minds and also talk to animals. It was odd at first. I survived those Grog creatures by listening to rats and mice."

Cindy nodded. "I seem to affect water and use it as a weapon."

"Wow, I would like to see that."

They were silent for a while.

Cindy said, "What did you do before the earthquake?"

"I, well, it's hard to explain."

"Tell me. We have time."

"I worked for the government. I analyzed and created reports for threat assessments on the American people."

"Are you with the CIA or Homeland security?"

"Well, it does not matter. I officially worked for NSA but I directly reported to certain high-ranking officials. But all this doesn't matter now."

"Did you know this was going to happen?"

"No. But there are layers of secrets that I am not supposed to know."

"But you do."

"Cindy, how do I know that you aren't here to spy on me?"

"You're paranoid," Cindy said. "You have to trust me. I would not be part of a government cover-up."

Cindy gazed at him and looked away out toward the jail cell's window. The only thing she saw from here was an alleyway and a partially destroyed wall.

Robert said, "Well, I don't have any choice. They will probably torture me and get the info."

She shook her head. "You don't understand. None of that matters. Look around you. People are changing into beasts and we have magic, real magic."

Cindy fell silent. She looked down at her hands. If she could use her magic, she could free the people enraptured by the Council. She knew she had the power to do so and looking at Robert she could see he was thinking the same thing.

She said, "We need to help these people. They are trapped by beasts."

"The Council," Robert said.

"Yes," Cindy said. "You knew about them before."

Robert sighed and then nodded his head. He looked around the cell.

"Before all this happened I was reading a top secret report about something underground. Some type of government facility that housed some type of energy. And this Council was trying to find it."

She gazed at him and saw not a regular person, but a man who was the keeper of secrets, who only spoke to clandestine circles not divulging anything, but Robert had a wary look to him as if the years had not been kind to him.

He said, "I didn't pay attention to this at first. We had other terrorist reports more pertinent to my superiors. But I noticed the CIA and NSA were devoting a lot of men and time to find this Council. I thought it was odd."

Cindy wanted to ask him questions, but she feared if she did he would stop talking.

"I could have stopped this, all of this."

"No, you couldn't," she said. "The earthquake was a natural happening."

Robert said, "You had a necklace, a stone that glowed."

"What? How do you know about that?"

"I accidentally found and opened them. But I am getting ahead of myself. I knew you were one of the Alpha mages. I don't need to read your mind to see your magic."

"Wait, you knew all this was going to happen?"

Robert shook her head. "Alas, I did not know. I was visited by somebody, but you would not believe me if I told you."

Cindy said, "If you told me it was aliens, I would believe you. All the crazy things that have happened are like being in a Grimm's Fairytale."

He said, "It was not aliens, but they were mistaken for aliens for eons. I was visited by the elves."

"Elves, you mean people with pointed ears like in Lord of the Rings movies?"

Robert shook his head. "Well, they don't have pointed ears. But they are taller than us and they look different."

"So, why did they visit you?"

"I have asked myself that question many times in the last few days. I think I was the only person who could find the stones."

Cindy sat back on her cot, wondering what was going to happen next.

Chapter 40

Cindy said, "What do these stones have to do with this earthquake and magic?"

"I really didn't understand at first. The elves wanted me to get the stones and deliver them, but the Council was also watching me. And they have powerful people."

"So, this Council is the people here?"

"Some of them are here. I uncovered a cabal, a secret society. They lurked in the shadows and were worse than the people I worked for, and deadlier."

"What happened?"

"I got the stones. It was not easy, but when I was about to deliver them to the Elves I was captured. I had to hide the stones, but something happened when I opened the case the second time. The stones flew away and disappeared. I fled my home. And then this happened."

"How did you know I have a stone?"

"Well, I was not sure but those two brutes who brought me here were talking about you. When I saw you I was sure you had one of the stones."

Cindy shook her head. "You were looking for me?"

"Well, somebody like you. You were not the only person who received the stones."

"What?"

"Yes, there was four stones in all. And you have to find the other stones before the next full moon."

Cindy shook her head. "The Council has my stone. But I don't know if I believe you."

She studied his clothes and wondered if this absent-minded professor look was a way to get her to do something. But his crazy story almost made sense. Cindy did sense another person, her friend Lazarus, and she needed to find him soon.

Robert said, "Don't worry. I think I can help you. But you need to get the stone and leave now."

"You said I needed to find these people who have the stone before the full moon. What is going to happen?"

He looked directly into her eyes. "I don't know. But I do know it will be really bad."

"Wait. Let me think."

This was going too fast. She needed to take a breather. The door opened and the two tall brutes came back into the jail. They went directly to Robert and opened his cell.

"The Council is ready for you."

The bald jailer snickered at him. When Robert passed through outside into the corridor, Cindy heard his voice in his head. The bars of her cell started to glow, but Robert said in her mind, "When you see the sign, you need to use your magic."

Robert's voice suddenly ceased as if something or somebody stopped him from talking. Cindy fidgeted. She was not sure what she was going to do but she felt something was going to happen soon. She stood and paced around her small cell. Then an image bloomed in her mind. It was almost like watching a grainy TV screen.

Cindy saw Robert standing in front of the Council she saw him talking but she couldn't hear any voices. She understood this image was coming from Robert and his own magic. Then Robert took something out of his pocket. It was a small box, but she knew what was going to happen. She covered her ears.

THE EXPLOSION ROCKED the building and instantly her powers came back to her plus the necklace with the stone. The necklace floated in front of her and the stone glowed and blinked out of her sight. She felt the necklace wrap around her neck. She pointed. A large wave exploded from her fingertips and destroyed the brick wall. The smell of smoke and fire wafted in the air. Cindy jumped through the opening. People were screaming and running around. She ran into the streets and surveyed the scene. People were dead in front of the building where she saw the Council and the structure was a smoldering ruin. Scanning the fleeing people, she looked for Rochelle among the living or the dead but the scene was chaotic. Fires started to break out among the other buildings. The remnants of New York City would burn to the ground unless she did something.

Cindy was about to run to the closest burning building when a group of people rushed to her in blind fear. She held up her arms in a defensive movement, but something happened. Her body grew warm and she floated upwards in a rush of air. Cindy yelped, not in terror, but in surprise.

She found herself hovering a few feet above the ground. The crowd of people didn't even notice. They kept running until they were out of her sight.

She calmed herself and knew her plan of action was to stop the fires. She didn't know if she had enough power or magic to do it but the time to think was over. Lifting both of her hands up to the sky, she concentrated. Her body started to vibrate slowly and a warmth flooded her skin. It was not burning nor scalding but was like being immersed in a warm bath.

Rain appeared on the street, pouring over the buildings on fire. The smell of ashes and soot flooded her senses and she focused her will and power on creating more rain. Her body started to shake as if she was being pulled in several different directions. She was not sure if she could keep up this conjuring.

Cindy dropped her arms and her feet touched the ground. She was exhausted beyond anything she had felt before. Shaking, she looked around and noticed the people were not running like before. They were looking at the smoking buildings. The rain poured from the sky, but was slowly petering out. Without her mind concentrating on the conjuring, her magic was ceasing.

Cindy swayed where she stood and was about to fall when a man grabbed and pulled her to an open area. The man looked at her with awe and also with a little fear. The fires ceased and a calm came over everybody around her. They turned to her.

Cindy was not sure what to say. A girl came toward her and knelt. She realized it was Rochelle.

She said, "I thought you were dead."

Cindy merely nodded.

Chapter 41

Grace and Lawrence camped out for another day in the hot desert sun. She decided to move their camp across the way toward the casino, Buffalo Bill, away from the Giant Worm's lair. She erected a sand shield over them to keep them cool during the day but the scorching heat gave them scolding winds which created a blast of burning air.

After she saw the Giant Worm's lair Grace knew Joan was already dead. It was foolhardy to try to save her. Joan died as she walked toward the casinos.

Grace debated circumnavigating this area and try to make it to the next city, Victorville, which was hundreds of miles from here. She looked through her dwindling supplies and knew they were not going to survive on their meager provisions.

They needed to get into the Casinos and see if they could find more food and water. Plus, if they could take one of the cars in the parking lot it would be a lot easier traveling. Lawrence didn't complain. He was made of sturdy stock and she was glad to have him around. They had talked at length about their plans to enter the casino, Buffalo Bill's. She saw the billboard lights were still on. She realized that a week ago she would have laughed at the prospect of raiding a store, any store, but now the stakes had changed and she had to act like a grown up and make grown up decisions.

Grace had seen the Giant Worm several times since they camped out here. It seemed to thrive on the sun, moving along the sand as if it was water. She could see the trails the creature left as it traveled but they disappeared after several hours, making the ground look perfectly smooth. And this was the reason why Lawrence, as well as herself, thought the casinos and the surrounding areas looked so unreal, so wrong. They could not have seen it at first but recognized it through their instincts.

Now she was at a crossroads. She needed to make a decision to leave or try to enter the casinos. Lawrence was not sure. He wanted to run away. Maybe go back to Las Vegas to find more people. She decided to fly over the sands and enter the casino, Buffalo Bill's, at night when, she believed, the Giant Worm was not active.

The sun descended below the horizon and a cool breeze flew around them, giving a much needed respite from the heat. They had a small meal of beef jerky and drank the remaining water they had. Grace waited until the stars appeared in the sky and the calmness of the scene descended upon them. Inside, she was quivering with emotion and sadness brought about by the death of Joan, but also for herself and the trials she would have to endure over the next few months or years. She nodded to Lawrence and the small boy, the little man, brought out of the terror of his parent's death to her, grabbed her hand. His palm was moist with perspiration.

Grace nodded and then they flew upwards, higher and higher until the winds pushed at them in gentle, but persistent hands. She knew the higher they were the better, and as they sought the upper atmosphere she started to sense the other one, the Leader, the man she was supposed to find and become part of the four.

She shook her head. The Leader was close, but she needed to concentrate because any wrong move would cause them to die and she couldn't have that. She looked at Lawrence and smiled at him. They started to fly across the sands, moving against the winds, watching the bright lights of the casino's sign and marquee becoming brighter and bigger. Below them, the sand started to shake. She glided faster to Buffalo Bill's main building, hearing the sound of the roller coaster as it moved on its track and the casino's large sign of an Indian headdress and the picture of the buffalo looming closer and closer.

They were about to reach the parking lot with the cars parked in neat rows, when the Giant Worm suddenly reared up from the ground and stood quivering between them and the casino. Up close, Grace saw that its body was segmented in scales, with a mouth as large as a semi-truck. She saw the teeth glittering in the moonlight. Each tooth was as long or longer than her arm. She heard a squealing noise that penetrated her head. Lawrence, next to her, cried out in terror. Grace stopped moving and flew backwards away from the large creature. The Giant Worm jumped back down into the sands and disappeared. It happened so suddenly Grace almost thought it was a mirage.

"Lawrence, I want you back in a safe place. I can place you back in the desert and do this alone."

"No, we talked about this. It's all or nothing. Let's do this again."

Grace soared closer to the buildings. The wind was flowing past them and tears were springing from her eyes. The Giant Worm reared up in front of them again. Grace held up her hand and pushed. The creature roared in pain and fled back down its hole. She smiled, they had a chance. They starting flying toward the front doors of the casino.

The creature appeared around them without exploding from the ground. It floated and encircled them in its body. Then it roared. Grace shot up into the sky and soared toward the hills. The creature followed, speeding toward them.

She focused and several shards of rock and sand shot at the Giant Worm. The projectiles struck its rough hide and bounced off harmlessly. Grace and Lawrence flew closer to the ground and the creature followed. Grace conjured a sandstorm and hit the creature several times, knocking it to the side. The beast roared a violent scream.

The noise punched them as if it was a solid object and they fell to the ground.

Before they struck the sand, she pushed her hands down and they skidded upwards. Grace saw the Giant Worm fly above them, covering them with its massive body.

She said, "Lawrence, I'm sorry. I tried to protect you."

He smiled and nodded.

Chapter 42

G race accepted her fate, but couldn't let Lawrence die. She did something she was not sure she could do, but she tried nonetheless. She wrapped Lawrence in a bubble of dirt and sand. The creature's large bulk was about to smother them. She focused her will, and Lawrence disappeared and reappeared far away. She hoped the little boy materialized at the front steps of the casino, but the creature's considerable body blocked her from seeing Lawrence. Her magic was dwindling and she floated down to the ground.

Grace accepted this. She didn't expect herself to even get this far in life. She had grown up in Las Vegas. Her mom was a gambling and drug addict who sometimes did sex acts for money. Grace was shipped to her aunt's house half a mile over from her mom's dilapidated apartment when she was thrown in jail for stealing.

Grace was going down the same life as her mom. She started stealing and taking drugs. Her aunt Betty told her if she didn't clean herself up she was going to be in jail like her mom. Somehow, Grace changed, graduated high school and got a certificate in hospitality from the community college of Southern Las Vegas.

The darkness encroached into Grace's thoughts. She thought she was about to feel the beast's teeth tear into her, but something else happened. A bright flash of fire exploded before her. The creature roared and dove back into the ground while sand sprayed all over like water. She stood with her arms upraised in a defensive gesture.

A voice in her mind said, "Hurry, fly upwards. We are here to help you."

She soared up into the wind and the night. Searching around her for the voice she saw a jeep coming straight at them from the road honking its horn. A man stood on top of the roof holding a large ball of fire in his hands. He was looking around for the Giant Worm.

Grace sensed the Leader was here. He drove the car and they didn't understand the predicament they were all in. The Giant Worm suddenly appeared before the road, overshadowing the car's headlights. The man standing on top of the car was howling like a mad man. He was actually yelling at the creature.

The Giant Worm came directly at the car and dove at it and as it did so a large fireball erupted and hit the creature's face. Grace felt the shockwaves coming from the encounter. The beast plunged into the sand hill toward the right of the street, missing the car by several feet. Plumes of sand and dust flew in the air.

Grace was frozen for a second until she heard Lawrence's voice. He was yelling from the entrance of Buffalo Bill's glass doors. He was jumping up and down, trying to get her attention. Grace couldn't leave the Leader and his comrade to fight the Giant Worm by themselves. She nodded to him and flew closer to the jeep. The car entered the parking lot and the driver stopped honking and parked close to Lawrence.

Grace waited for the Giant Worm to attack but it didn't appear. She sensed it was wounded but not killed. She floated to the front entrance of Buffalo Bill's casino, noticing that next to this casino was another hotel, The Primm Valley Resort.

GRACE HUGGED LAWRENCE and led them inside through the double doors. She saw that the lights of the interior were on and groups of people were watching her, moving closer as they entered. Nobody spoke for several seconds. She felt she had entered a fairy tale, walking into an enchanted forest.

The Leader came up to them. He was normal height with salt and pepper hair. He was unremarkable, so normal she would have never had given him a second look in a crowd, but his eyes gave him away. They were fiery with intelligence and something she would understand later, compassion. A huge dog came next to him.

He said, "My name is Lazarus Venti and this is Sammy."

He shook her hand and Lawrence's hand. Grace saw a bracelet on his wrist and recognized the stone that sparkled and glowed. She absently combed her hair with her fingers, knowing she must look a mess. Lawrence held out his hand and stroked Sammy's back.

"My name is Grace, and this Lawrence."

The other big man moved closer to them. "I am Matthew."

They all shook hands with him. Grace felt the power between them. It was like electricity being discharged, yet she felt somebody was missing. The silence between them was not awkward but comfortable. They needed to be together for some purpose that she hoped Lazarus would explain to her.

A man dressed in a suit and tie came forward. "Hi, I am the manager at the casino. My name is Bob. We have been trapped since this whole nightmare started."

Chapter 43

Lazarus, sitting next to Grace, wondered again about their destination. He had been directed to find this short woman with brunette hair. It was a beacon from his inner mind that she was in trouble. Matthew and Lazarus found a jeep and gassed it up at a gas station which was still in working order and rushed hell bent down the freeway toward Nevada. They drove through the many cars littering the path. He sensed some creature was about to devour her. Getting closer to the bright casino lights, Matthew opened the window and somehow jumped on top of the car, yelling and screaming like a mad man. Sammy barked from the back of the jeep.

When they saw the huge scaled worm about to smother Grace, he yelled, but Matthew was quicker. He shot several large fireballs at the beast. It hit along its massive body and then he saw the worm's sightless eyes stare at him and Lazarus felt his blood freeze with terror. Yet Lazarus honked his car's horn feeling the rush of magic mixed with his terror and exhilaration.

Lazarus wanted to attack this beast. He almost stopped the car because he wanted to look into the creature's eyes. He wanted to battle and kill this beast. Yet his rational mind prevailed. When the large worm rushed and dove into the sand and disappeared into the hills, he steered the car toward Grace, who flew to the front entrance of Buffalo Bill's casino. Matthew jumped back into the passenger seat.

For the next few hours, they sat in a food court in a place called the Dog's House. They ate hamburgers and hotdogs. Sammy sat close to his feet to eat. Bob talked about how they tried several times to escape the Casino, but the Giant Worm killed all who tried to flee. Only a handful of people were still left from the eighty who were ensnared in the hotel. Some of the tourists decided to leave anyway by themselves, rushing into their cars and flying down the road, but they all died in the maw of the creature.

Bob said, "You were the only ones who actually made it inside here. But I have a question for all of you. How did you do those things?"

The Whisky Pete's manager looked at them as if they were not people but superheroes who did powerful deeds, but Lazarus didn't feel that way.

Lazarus said, "I don't know. I think we all acquired our powers after the disaster. Does anybody here have powers?"

Bob shook his head. "No, we're all the same. Except, there is somebody here who is not right."

"What do you mean?" Matthew said. The big man was eating his second hot dog. His hand was smeared with mustard and relish. He knotted his brow.

Bob said, "After the sandstorm, he changed. He was once a blackjack dealer who would never hurt a fly. But he changed. This man became violent and hair grew all over him. And I swear he was not the same person."

Lazarus said, "As if the man became a wolf."

"Yes," Bob said.

"Where is this man?"

"His name is Eugene and we have in trapped in a storage room."

Lazarus said, "He is already gone. He escaped as soon as you left him alone."

Bob said, "How can you know this?"

"He is a Grog and he went to his master," Matthew said.

"What is a Grog?" Bob looked at them with an incredulous face.

"A creature that was once a human, born from magic. These Grogs become mindless animals which only destroy and kill. You are lucky he didn't come back and kill you."

Bob said, "I can't believe you."

He stood and motioned for several of the other people waiting in the lobby to come follow him. They moved to a back area of the casino at the back of the dealer tables and slot machines.

Lazarus noticed there were only a few children here. And realized that most people didn't stay here for a vacation, but traveled to the bright lights and money of Las Vegas and children never came along on these excursions, because Las Vegas was an adult playground and children didn't have many places to go except the casino Circus, Circus.

A couple in their mid-twenties followed close behind them. He was tall and thin and she was a beautiful blond girl who did not look like she was twenty-one. They both had the look of shock, fear and desperation as if death lingered in the air.

They went down several flights of stairs. Most of the people stayed on top of the main floor. Bob had the burly man follow them.

He said, "I had several of the men contain Eugene when he changed. He still looked human until we placed him in the storage room."

"When did you feed him last?" Lazarus said.

Bob said, "I don't remember."

Before they entered the last corridor on the way to the vast storage room Lazarus noticed Grace and Lawrence following them and he told them to leave and go back to the main casino room.

Lawrence jutted his chin upwards. "I go where Grace goes."

She looked at the little boy and shook her head. "You're right. I shouldn't have him down here. Come on, Lawrence, let's go back."

"I want to see the man-beast."

"No, let's go. Sammy, I want you to protect Lawrence."

Sammy padded closer to the little boy. Lazarus watched them go. He knew he would have to separate Lawrence from Grace, because where they were going was more dangerous than this place and a little boy needed to be in a safe area. Bob continued, going toward a brightly lit corridor.

"Eugene is down here." He pointed toward a metal door now closed and bolted. Bob produced a key and was about to open the door when Matthew stopped him.

"Let me do this."

Bob didn't argue. They all saw the power Matthew possessed and he was large, built like a linebacker. Lazarus was surprised how this man, who was a vagrant for years, was still huge. Matthew took charge, grabbed the keys from Bob and opened the door.

The hinges screeched as Matthew pushed opened the door. He rushed inside and Lazarus followed close behind. Several bright lights were on showing a rack of destroyed metals shelves and debris. The walls were covered with claw marks along the surface. Lazarus looked around but couldn't see the hole until he was almost on top of it. The hole was in the corner of the room and a cool breeze came from the opening.

Bob said, "Wow! Eugene did this?"

"He's not human anymore. He is a beast."

Bob gaped around the wrecked interior. "What could we have done?"

"Nothing, he would have killed somebody. From what I have seen these Grogs usually go in packs and he went home to the calling of his Alpha male."

Bob said, "They have a leader? I don't want to meet this creature."

Lazarus said, "I hope you won't."

"What are we to do?"

"We first need to find a destination and then leave."

"What do we do about the Giant Worm?"

Lazarus said, "Leave the creature to us."

Chapter 44

Bob held a meeting in the main casino area of Buffalo Bill's. Lazarus studied the handful of twenty or so people. They crowded in a clump and stayed away from them.

Bob said, "These people will help us escape this place, but we need to decide where we should we go from here."

A few people said they wanted to go to the west coast, San Diego or toward Utah. People argued Utah would be a better destination because it was a landlocked state and hopefully would not have sustained some type of catastrophe.

Lazarus said, "We should go to the other casinos and Whisky Pete's and see if anybody is still alive."

"No," Bob said. "We need to think of the welfare of these people here."

Matthew said, "I will go and find out."

Lazarus said, "Wait, let's think this out. We need you to stay here and protect these people."

Grace spoke up. "How can you people be so heartless? We need to find out about the other survivors."

Nobody spoke for a few seconds and then Grace said, "I'll go. I can fly over there."

Lazarus said, "I'll go with you. I think I can learn how to fly. I feel it is possible. But Lawrence, you need to stay with Matthew. He needs help here."

The boy stared down at his feet. "Ok, but you need to keep Grace safe from harm."

His eyes looked so earnest and scared that Lazarus wanted to give him a hug. He wondered how this boy could still be strong. He saw his parents killed and other horrors in Las Vegas. Nothing could erase those memories.

"I will. You can watch us from the hotel windows."

Lawrence nodded. His eyes looked so sad.

Grace said, "Everything will be fine. Lazarus is our Leader and he will know what to do."

Lazarus was not sure about that. When it came to the fight with the Giant Worm, Matthew was the one who used his powers. Lazarus was not entirely comfortable with using his magic.

He said, "When should we leave?"

"I don't know," Grace said, "I thought the creature only came out during the daytime, but I was wrong."

Bob inclined his head. "The Giant Worm seems to only come out when somebody tries to leave. It doesn't matter if it's daylight, morning or night. The creature comes out."

Lazarus nodded. "What makes the creature come out of the sands?"

"Well, I never thought about it in that way," Bob said.

"What do you remember?"

"It could be the vibrations when the car moved along the road," Bob said.

Grace said, "I don't think so. I flew, and the creature knew I was there."

"How about the smell?" Matthew said.

Lazarus looked at the big man. He was smart, and street smart.

Bob said, "Maybe, but it wouldn't matter. As soon as he travels beyond the parking lot, the beast will come."

Lazarus said, "So we should try to make it over now."

He was thinking they should think this over before they left.

"I can take you over with me. We can fly together."

"I can't fly. I think. But yes, I will need your help."

They moved to the front entrance. Lazarus thought it was odd being in a casino and planning for battle. He thought how many tourists had stopped here before they either entered Las Vegas, or made it the last stop before going home to California. He recalled he had stopped here before and even played a few hands at the gambling tables to try to recoup his money.

Lazarus said, "Isn't there a small shuttle that connects both casinos?"

Bob said, "We had one. But nobody wanted to get inside that thing and ride it across."

"Does it still work?"

"Yes, I supposed. But I don't think you should try to use it."

Lazarus said, "I was thinking about using it for a diversion."

"What are you going to do?"

"I think if we start the tram and wait until the worm shows, maybe we can fly across without being seen," Lazarus said and then looked over at Grace. "Can you fly very fast?"

"I think so. I've never tried."

Lawrence said, "You can do it. I've seen you fly. You can go very fast."

Grace nodded at the small boy and he smiled. She beamed as she looked at Lawrence. Lazarus noticed how beautiful Grace was and he wished he didn't need to take her to the other casino.

Bob said, "I will have somebody start the tram. You will see it move down the track."

Grace said, "Can you also have the roller coaster run?"

"That sounds like a good idea," Lazarus said. "It can maybe cause another distraction."

Bob said, "Sure, I can get somebody to do that. But I hope for your sake this will work. What will happen when you want to come back?"

Lazarus said, "We'll figure something else."

Bob said, "You should find a way to get us out of this trap. We can go to Utah. Forget about the other Casino."

"You think this is a dumb idea," Lazarus said.

"Yes, I was thinking about the Grogs you talked about. They are also out there."

"We can protect ourselves from the Grogs. It's the Giant Worm we have problems with." Lazarus paused and then said, "Let's start."

Chapter 45

Lazarus and Grace stood at the front glassed entrance to Buffalo Bill's casino. They could feel the heat radiating from outside. It was mid-morning and they'd had a small meal of eggs, bacon and toast, even though, Bob said, they were running out of food. It seemed they had food for another month. They decided that whether or not they made it to the Whisky Pete's casino they should make plans to leave. The sound of the roller coaster was audible from where they stood.

As the tram started to move along the tracks they stepped outside in the stifling heat. Looking around, Lazarus didn't see the creature come out. He glanced into the lobby and saw Lawrence, Matthew and Bob gazing at them. If the Giant Worm didn't show, they would still try to make it over but they would be careful.

He felt this would work. They watched as the tram started to move slowly toward Whisky Pete's casino, getting near the middle of the track. The sand on the right started to shake and buckle as if something was swimming underneath the surface. The creature surfaced and moved toward the tram.

Grace said, "Are you ready?"

"Yes," he said.

They floated upwards. The Giant Worm appeared and reared up into the air. The beast moved slowly, placing its huge mouth near the tram but it didn't attack it. It dove back into the sand.

Lazarus said, "Go, now."

They flew toward Whisky Pete's, the sign getting bigger as they came closer. They soared up high and plunged into the front entrance of the casino.

The creature burst underneath them and tried to attack. Before Lazarus could say anything Grace swiftly flew to the right. Lazarus saw the razor sharp teeth and the maw of the worm's gullet. He yelled. Grace grabbed his waist and they flew faster, moving around the back of Whisky Pete's casino.

Lazarus felt impotent. He wanted to help. He was the Leader, after all. He reached into his mind and body and tried to conjure something. Touching his bracelet with his right hand, he heard the sweet music he heard before and a warm tingling came over him.

They streaked toward the back buildings, moving fast. The air rippled their clothes and his eyes teared as they darted close to the buildings. When the creature reared up before them it rose higher than the tallest structure he had ever seen. Grace abruptly stopped their descent and backed away. His stomach lurched.

The worm opened its massive jaws and screeched a high whining noise. It was different to its roar and he felt a heaviness come over him. They started to descend.

"Grace, wake up!"

She tried to speak but what she said sounded muffled. His sight was going dim and he realized that they had underestimated this creature. He told himself not to close his eyes, repeating it several times, but he couldn't help it. His eyelids felt heavy. He screamed inside his head, again and again, to wake up. But his eyelids closed.

But then Lazarus heard something, the sweet music. It spoke to him and he thought they were not floating above a ravenous worm creature, but dancing in the heavens. The feeling was so pervasive that he smiled and held Grace closer as if they were dancing.

A burning feeling came to his head and arms and he awoke with a start, focusing on his magic. They were ascending higher into the sky. The creature roared and as the beast's mouth opened Lazarus shot a wicked lightning bolt into the creature's gullet. The spell came out of him in a rush of power. He expelled a vast amount of magic which exhausted him. Grace woke and shook her head. She kept them from falling as she looked down at the Giant Worm.

The creature's mouth opened so wide that Lazarus thought he heard the dead inside. Then he heard a cracking noise. The lightning boomed as it exploded and the creature's body burst outwards. Grace shot away from the scene while pieces of the worm flew all around them. She stayed protected behind the walls of Whisky Pete's hotel. The pieces of the creature rained down, smoking entrails and skin hitting the ground in sickening thuds. Then the smell hit them. It was nauseating. Grace let go of him and he wished they had kept holding each other. She held her arms up and pushed some of the innards away from them.

Lazarus should be doing something, but he was tired and confused. He didn't know how he created his magic or how he could conjure it again. His body vibrated with power and he wanted to use it again, no matter the consequences.

But he didn't feel entirely in control and he didn't like that. It was like when you swung on a swing tied to a tree next to a river. Most kids, not him, would love to swing back and forth and then jump into the water, but not him. He didn't like the feeling of weightlessness right after he kicked off from the swing and plunged into the depths of the lake. It made his stomach queasy. But now he wanted to use his magic again. It felt free and right.

After a few minutes, they heard a loud thud and then a squeal. They didn't have to look. The large worm creature was dead and the carcass smelt like day-old cooked fish. The scent assailed their senses and they rushed to get inside the building.

They moved to the nearest door which was locked. Grace was about to leave and check on the next door, but Lazarus shook his head.

"Stand back." He hoped he knew what he was doing.

He backed up a few steps, turned both of his hands up with his palms facing the door and focused. A wind came out of his outstretched fingers and blasted the door which caved in and flew down the corridor, hitting the wall opposite them. The sound was deafening.

They rushed inside and down a hallway lit with fluorescent lights, fleeing the scent of the dead worm. They were in some type of office areas of the casino.

"Ok," Lazarus said, "we can stop."

He was exhausted and he bent down on his knees to catch his breath. Grace sat in the hallway. Lazarus's face was smeared with dark soot and she absently brushed it off.

"Yuck!" she said.

They looked around. This was a service area of the hotel. It was quiet, deathly quiet. And Lazarus felt something dark and evil in this building. He stopped and Grace looked at him.

"What's wrong?" she asked.

"Something is not right here."

Chapter 46

Lazarus led the way through the maze of corridors and hallways, the feeling lingering in his mind and body. He wanted to flee and burn down the casino. Yet nothing assaulted them, there no dead bodies or the scent of rotting corpses. All he heard was the soft hum of air conditioning keeping the building cool. They walked the length of the bottom floor of the hotel and saw the sign announcing the location of the casino and the front desk.

Moving down the carpeted hallway, they both heard the sounds of the slot machines and something else he couldn't describe. He didn't like the sound.

Grace said, "What is that?"

"I don't know."

He led the way. They walked into a bright room with slot machines and tables and they stopped as soon as they saw the scene before them. He wanted to run and never see this again, but the eeriness was imprinted on his mind.

The people they saw were clearly dead. They sat on the chairs and dealer tables. And they were covered with thin nebulous strands almost liked spider webs, but the strands glowed and the corpses were opened like ripe fruit went bad.

Grace said, "What can do this?"

Her voice sounded too loud to his ears. They heard the sound again. It was like scrabbling legs, and then they saw it. A creature hung on the ceiling. It was a once a man but had long insectoid legs coming out of its body and a large abdomen like a spider. For a split second, Lazarus felt such horror that he almost laughed. He thought, *This is what a spider man should look like.* They heard the silk web blowing in the wind.

Grace grabbed his arm and they started to move toward the exit. Then the creature spoke, "Ah, don't leave me. I'm lonely."

Lazarus didn't want to stop but the man-creature moved fast and blocked the exit. Grace held up her arm.

She said, "Don't come any closer. We have magic."

The man-creature stared at them with multifaceted eyes. Lazarus wanted to scream but he stifled his fear.

He said, "Yes, she is right. Don't come any closer. You killed these people here."

"I can't help what I am."

They heard the insectile scrabbling noise again and he realized it was not the man-creature before them making the noises. Looking around them he saw hundreds of spiders about the size of his palms running toward them. With a sickening feeling, he knew how the people died, and understood why the corpses looked like overripe opened fruit.

"Stop. We have magic."

"Hahaha, you don't have power. I have the real power."

The spiders started to scramble toward them. Lazarus conjured a circle of fire around them. He didn't will the magic into existence. He just thought it and the magic happened. The flames crackled, destroying and burning the spiders. He smelt the scent of burnt tar. The man-creature screamed and came at them.

Grace held up her hand and the ground erupted above the man-creature. He scrambled backwards away from them and Grace missed.

Lazarus moved to the exit, the circle of flames keeping the spiders at bay. He wanted to destroy this casino and everything in it.

The man-creature hissed. "You cannot be a vessel to my children. You are tainted."

They exited through the glass doors and out into the heat of the sun, where the smell from the worm carcass assailed his nostrils.

Lazarus grabbed Grace's hand and they flew upwards. When they were safely away from Whisky Pete's casino, he let out a sigh of relief. They scent of the dead worm was still in the air and he almost gagged.

Lazarus flew them across the street to Buffalo Bill's, past the parking lot with the many cars, and stopped at the front doors of the entrance. People stood in the sun watching them. He descended toward Matthew and Lawrence. As soon as their feet touched the ground Lawrence sprinted across and hugged Grace. She looked surprised but hugged him back.

Bob stood with the handful of people. He still wore his suit and tie in the stifling heat. He said, "Wow, I saw what you did to that worm. You saved us." Bob walked closer to Lazarus and clapped his hand on his back.

Lazarus didn't know what to say. He merely nodded, then said, "Let's go inside. It's too hot to stand out here."

Bob said, "Sure, the smell is bad."

Lawrence was babbling something to Grace about how they saw them fighting the worm and it was the greatest thing he had ever seen, better than the movies and better than any sports event his father loved to watch.

The coolness of Buffalo Bill's made Lazarus relax. He said, "Can I get some water? We have to discuss some things."

Bob said, "Sure." He nodded to somebody and the girl left. Lazarus sat at the nearest chair he could find. It was a slot machine with the lights still on. He barely looked at it because weariness enveloped him and all he wanted to do was sleep. On the screen was

the number four and he thought it meant something, but he was not
sure.

They crowded around them. Lazarus recounted what Grace and
he had seen at Whisky Pete's casino. Bob nodded, surprise in his eyes
when Lazarus spoke about the spider creature.

"You all have to leave soon. He will try to come over here," he
said.

Matthew said, "We should go back there and kill that thing."

"No, we aren't murderers. We have to be better than that. We
have power, more than most people, and we have a responsibility to
do the right thing."

Matthew shook his head and walked away a bit.

Bob said, "If what you say is true we should leave in a few hours."

Lazarus nodded. "Yes." He looked over to Whisky Pete's casino.
"We should post guards until we get out."

Bob nodded and followed his gaze. "Yes, that's a good idea. We
decided that we are going to Utah. You are more than welcome to go
with us."

"Well, I have to talk to Grace and Matthew. We have to decide
what are going to do. Bob, do you have a private place to talk?"

"Yes, my office."

He looked at Grace and then at Lawrence and Sammy. He had
an idea, but he needed to talk to Grace about that.

Chapter 47

Lazarus, Matthew and Grace crowded into Bob's small office. The room was furnished with a desk and several metal drawers. Everything was neat and clean. It was as if Bob could come back to work and have business as usual, but they all knew that was not going to happen. Lawrence wanted to come to this meeting, but Lazarus told him they needed to talk alone about grown up things. The boy was unperturbed and still wanted to come. He was waiting outside in the hallway, patting Sammy. The dog loved being around Lawrence and they never left each other's side.

Lazarus sat behind the oak desk and they sat across from him. The room was small and Matthew's body seem to overtake the whole room. He squirmed in his small chair.

Lazarus began, "I think we should have Lawrence and Sammy go with Bob to Utah."

He stared at Grace. Her eyes widened and her mouth quivered for a brief second, but she nodded. "Yes, I believe that is the best for him."

"Sammy will be his protection and when all this is over we could all go to Utah."

Lazarus didn't believe they would survive whatever trials that were waiting for them, but the future was not set in stone.

Grace said, "Yes." Her eyes betrayed her. She didn't look sure about leaving Lawrence, but knew she couldn't let him go with them.

"Matthew, where are we supposed to go?"

The big man looked at them. He said, "We are missing the last person. The power of four."

"What did you say?"

Matthew had said his last statement as if he was in a trance. "Oh, what did I say? We are missing the last person." Matthew looked to the side. "She is coming to us."

Lazarus's left wrist felt warm and he looked at his hand. The stone attached to the bracelet on his wrist glowed a bright hot white. Grace held up her arm and also Matthew. They both had rings with glowing stones. They sat transfixed, looking at the stones.

He instantly knew where they had to go and he knew by looking at each other what faced him. He saw a pyramid. It looked like a Mayan temple but it was underground. He didn't know about Mexico and the pyramids there, but thought all the structures were above ground.

Matthew growled, "We need to wait for the last person. She will come to us."

"Where should we go?"

"You already know."

"So, we will go to Mexico."

"The pyramid is not in Mexico."

"What? Where is it?"

Matthew shook his head. "I'm not sure." Matthew blinked several times.

Grace said, "I think it is somewhere in Texas or somewhere. I believe that is where we should go."

The stones winked out and were normal again. Lazarus felt the rightness of all this. It was their destiny.

He said, "Cindy."

Shaking his head, Lazarus didn't know why he said his old friend's name. It was eerie but he instantly knew who the last person of their party was.

"Who did you say?" Grace said.

"Cindy," he said again. "She's the last person we need to find. But the last I heard Cindy was back east somewhere. New York, I think."

The big man, Matthew, said, "Yes, that is correct. She is the last person."

Grace said, "Should we find her?"

"No, Matthew is right. She will find us. Let's ask Bob if there is a car we can take."

THEY ALL LEFT THE OFFICE and Lawrence jumped up from the ground. Sammy waved his tail and panted. Lazarus patted the large dog's head and Grace knelt on one knee facing Lawrence.

"We have something to talk about," she said.

Lawrence said, "I have something to tell you."

Grace nodded.

The boy said, "Sammy and I were talking." He looked down at his feet. "We knew you wanted us to go with Bob and the others to Utah."

Grace sucked in her breathe. Lazarus was about to say something but he stayed silent.

Lawrence continued, "We will go with Bob. Right, Sammy?"

The dog looked at Lazarus for confirmation. It was an odd look for a dog.

"Yes, Sammy. It's fine. I want you to watch and protect Lawrence. He will need your help."

The dog's eyes almost pooled with tears and Lazarus had to look away. It was odd he should feel this way toward this large mongrel. He patted the dog's head, wishing he could take Sammy, but he had a sneaky suspicion that he couldn't go where they were going. They walked back toward the front of the casino.

Bob and his group were readying supplies. Each of them carried several sacks and backpacks. Bob held a bag filled with water and food stuff. He stared at them as they came up to him.

"So, you decided," Bob said.

"Yes, we are headed toward Texas. Do you have a car we can use?"

"Well, yes. It's a jeep and it's all gassed up. It was mine," he said. Bob held up his hands. "Don't worry. We have another car we can use."

Lazarus nodded and a thought came to him. He knew exactly where they were heading and would tell his group when they were leaving.

Bob helped them gather supplies and place them into the jeep. Lazarus and Matthew transferred the other things they collected from the car they had arrived in.

When everything was packed they gathered once again at the front of the casino. Bob and a group of two men sprinted to them, puffing from the exertion.

Bob said, "Something is coming."

He pointed toward Whisky Pete's Casino. Lazarus saw the man-spider creature scrambling up the street and behind this creature were hundreds of spiders.

"Get to your cars!" Bob shouted.

Everybody ran to their vehicles. Lazarus and Matthew were already at their jeep and looked for Grace. She was hugging Lawrence. Sammy padded behind the small boy. Lazarus realized they couldn't leave without helping the others escape.

He said, "Grace, hurry, we need you to drive the car!"

Matthew said, "They're coming."

"Matthew, help me fight this creature. I will help you fly."

"I don't like heights."

"Don't worry."

Grace came running up to them. The other cars started up and they moved onto the desert, heading south. The spiders advanced faster than he thought.

"Grace, I want you to drive south from here. We will catch up to you later."

Grace understood and jumped into the driver's seat, started the car, and sped off.

Lazarus focused and flew upwards with Matthew close behind.

The large man yelped a little but steadied himself, looking up at him.

Chapter 48

Cindy smiled and hugged Rochelle. She wanted to leave as soon as she smothered the fires and helped restore order after the Council members were killed. They wanted to elect her as the new head of the citizens of New York, but she explained she had to go. Rochelle wanted to go with her but Cindy told her that she had to embark on a dangerous journey and that Rochelle needed to stay with this small group of survivors.

Cindy explained, "I might not come back. Rochelle, you need to help rebuild New York. I need a place to come back to."

Cindy became known as the Great Mage of New York, the person who saved them from enslavement and stopped the raging fires from engulfing the remains of the city.

Rochelle walked with Cindy. The young teenage girl was quiet. She had gone through many tragedies, from losing her mom in a horrific way and then being enslaved by the monsters of the Council. In front of Cindy was a large bird conjured and created from her water globe. She could make her globe change into anything. The bird shimmered in the daylight. It was made out of water, but was solid. Other people stood several feet away from them out of respect, but also, she suspected, out of fear. Cindy was the only person besides the Council with the command of magic. And this was power.

The large bird placed her right wing down.

Cindy said, "I will try to come back when I am done."

"If you come back," Rochelle said.

"Yes," Cindy said.

She mounted the bird by stepping on its outstretched wing and sat on the creature's back. Cindy waited until Rochelle moved back to the waiting people. She waved a goodbye to them and patted the bird's neck.

The bird unfurled its wings and started to flap. A gust of wind arose, spraying the onlookers with dirt. Cindy and the bird lifted and flew. The sensation of weightlessness gave Cindy an air of happiness and joy. She thought this was how the Wright Brothers must have felt when they had their first ever flight.

Cindy knew her destination. She felt the Leader and his group had finally met and felt their magical echoes. It was seared into her brain. She steered her bird moving due south, watching the scene of destruction move past her. Her heart became heavy staring upon the many broken streets and buildings. The once thriving metropolitan city of New York was now a wasteland.

She flew until mid-afternoon. They moved faster than she thought because she was in now Tennessee. She had read a broken sign proclaiming, "Tennessee Welcomes You." She couldn't have moved that fast, even on a train or car but maybe a jet. She was never good at geography and without a smartphone, she was going by her own instincts.

She flowed past grasslands, rolling hills and mountains. Nothing looked different or devastated until she flew by a small town, sleepy compared to New York and Los Angeles. Yet, as she moved closer, she saw most of the homes were ripped apart as if a tornado came through here and destroyed not just the vegetation and landscape but the homes and pavements.

Cindy was about to land and check if anybody needed help but her bird squawked, warning her. She saw dark creatures hidden underneath the shade of the trees. Red eyes glowed under the canopy. Luckily, she heeded her mount's warning. She moved far away from the city and decided to have lunch on top of a small mountain top. She could see for miles on top of the hill.

Cindy sat on the grass and ate her meal, consisting of beef jerky and water. She sensed the Leader and his movements. He was traveling away from Nevada, headed southeast. She felt his presence like a homing beacon and her bird was in-tune to her senses. She knew she would find them at Pyramid Peak in New Mexico. Cindy had never heard of the place, but it came out of her thoughts as if she already knew, as if this information was given to her. The destination felt right. It was where they should go and would finally meet.

She chewed on her food, happy to be alive, sitting on a beautiful mountain, waiting for the day to turn into night. Yet, a darkness passed over her. Something was coming and they didn't have enough time. And she was not sure what it was. She thought it was coming from the west and also from above, which didn't make sense to her.

When she was done, she didn't want to start traveling again. She loved being here. She wondered when she was done with whatever her destiny planned for her if she could finally settle down around this place. Cindy stood and brushed off the grass from her legs. The bird squawked and she knew a group of Grogs was coming their way.

"Yes, thank you."

She jumped on top of the bird and they took off into the skies.

LAZARUS AND MATTHEW approached the growing horde of spiders and flew closer to the man-creature. He snarled and scrambled toward them. Lazarus focused his magic and was about to unleash a spell on it, when the man-creature raised his hand and shot something at them. It happened so fast he didn't have time to react until the cobwebs entangled themselves over his and Matthew's body. He tried to break the web but it was as strong as steel. He swore. He should have known.

He and Matthew fell to the ground. struggling to free their bonds. Then pain lanced his body. Electricity ran up and down the webs. Lazarus and Matthew wriggled in anguish. He tried to focus, thinking at any moment the spiders would come and sink their poisonous fangs all over them. He could even feel their legs scrambling over his body. He almost screamed.

The man-creature started to pull them closer to him. The electricity lanced into them making them dance in an agony of pain. Lazarus looked over and saw the caravan of cars were safely away. He was happy they had bought them time to leave. He couldn't think. Every time he tried to conjure a spell more pain hit him. He was breathless.

A shadow fell over him. It was the man-creature. The hideous head looked down on him while a large insectile leg prodded him.

"Ah, my children, lunch will be served."

Lazarus tried to struggle in his bonds and pain struck at him again.

"No!" he said through clenched teeth.

Lazarus saw Matthew struggling. His face was almost covered by the gauzy web-like film. Then he thought about Grace's and Matthew's magic. They both had power related to an element. Grace was sand and earth and Matthew was fire. He wondered what his element was. Another bolt of electricity struck him, but Lazarus barely noticed. His bracelet became warm on his wrist. It started to burn through the cobweb. The spiders came scrabbling up to him as he freed himself with a snap of the last bonds.

The man-creature said, "No!"

Before the spiders could stop their movements, Lazarus realized he had powers, not in one element, but all of them. He stood and held up his hand. Fire sprouted from his hands, burning the first group of spiders coming to them. Matthew was also free of his bonds. The big man stood and conjured a large fireball. He chucked it like a baseball and the fireball hit the man-creature squarely on its chest. The creature screamed in terror.

Lazarus focused and they both soared upwards into the sky. He held up his hands to the air. Large boulders rained down, pummeling and obliterating the man-creature and the spiders.

They stood looking at the rocks piled up on top of the creatures. The boulders started to move and Matthew shot fire into the mound. A scream erupted and then it was silent.

Chapter 49

Lazarus flew with Matthew to Grace who was waiting for them behind the wheel of the jeep. Something had happened when Lazarus destroyed the man-beast spider. He felt stronger and understood that the last person of their group was coming toward them. He sensed the gathering of power when just this trio was together and wondered what would happen when the last person finally met them. Matthew didn't need his help to fly. He learned by himself to levitate and soar with him.

They stopped and descended toward the jeep. The heat of the sun burnt into his back and face. He would be happier inside the car while they traveled. They had decided not to use the air-conditioner inside the jeep to conserve gas. Grace hopped out of the car and Lazarus stepped closer to her. He felt the power between all of them and wondered why he didn't feel it before. He could tell she sensed it as well as Matthew. They were stronger, just being next to each other. But they didn't want to say it here or talk about it until the last person of their party was with them.

Matthew said, "You were going to tell us where we are going?"

"We are going to New Mexico. To a place called Pyramid Peak. Something is waiting for us there."

Matthew nodded. "Yes, that feels right."

"Are we ready?" Grace said.

"Yes, I don't want to see this place again. But I have to do something."

They looked at him in an expectant, and knowing way. They seemed to know what he was going to do. They all stood in a line facing the two casinos.

Lazarus said, "I am not sure this is going to work."

Grace was on his right and Matthew on his left. They didn't touch each other. They didn't have to. The connection was already there. Lazarus fed off their magic and made each more powerful.

He held up his hands and they all followed him. The ground started to rumble and their stones glowed as bright as the hot desert sun. A tornado appeared out of the horizon and moved toward Whisky Pete's casino. Sand, wind and debris were caught up in the maelstrom of the storm. Lazarus felt the tornado in his heart and body. He recalled the dead bodies inside Whisky Pete's casino and how the carcasses were ripped apart like broken eggshells with their guts and entrails falling on the ground. Lazarus hoped these people died before they were used as incubators for the mutant spiders, but he knew the people were still alive while their insides were being eaten.

Lightning sprouted from his fingertips, shot into the air and flew into the storm, combining with the tornado and creating a bigger tempest. The windstorm hit Whisky Pete's marquee, destroying it into little pieces, and then it hit the buildings. The walls and glass blew apart in a scattering of debris and disappeared into the twister. The wind pummeled the ground and the road. He had never felt such power. It grew with the windstorm gathering in him so that he wanted to fly up and become one with the storm, but he lowered his arms and let the tempest cease. He had destroyed all remnants of the casino and obliterated Whisky Pete's to the four winds.

Grace said, "Did you feel that? It was amazing. What happened?"

Matthew said, "It's the circle. I think it has something to do with the stones and us."

"Yes," Lazarus said, "I think you are right. We have to finish this quest. We have to find out the choice, or calling, that we have to make."

Grace said, "What are you talking about?"

"You can't feel it but we are meant to do something. Matthew, explain it to her."

The big man turned to her. "I have been on a quest for years, before the catastrophe and before the breaking of the seals."

"Yes, I understand we have to do something, but we should not be hasty. We don't understand what is happening," she said.

"I know," he said, "but time in running out. I can sense it. We have to find the pyramid or we will miss the time."

Grace looked at them for a second and then said, "We have a long journey. We can talk about it while we drive."

They stepped into the car and Grace started to drive south on the 15 freeway. The street was not broken or pitted. It seemed, Lazarus thought, that this part of Nevada didn't have storms or major catastrophes affecting it. If he hadn't come from Los Angeles and seen the craziness that transpired there, he would have thought they were traveling on vacation.

Grace was silent next to him. She didn't ask him anything. He thought she was trying to understand everything that had happened in the last few weeks. He was trying to grasp everything himself.

On the ride to the casino's they had tried to use the radio and all they got was static. Moving closer to the radio now, he almost turned it on but he stopped himself. The old world had gone, replaced by this brutal new world where death hid in every corner. He thought that if he didn't have these magical powers he would be dead twice over, maybe more, but he didn't want to dwell on those things.

The droning of the tires against the ground created a soft, relaxing sound. The landscape of the desert started to become fuzzy. He closed his eyes, thinking they knew where they were going. It was as if they had a destination calling for them, beckoning for them to come and enter, a homing beacon of magic and light. He could see the structure and something inside it and that thing was speaking to them. He thought it had been there for years waiting for a time like this.

He slept and recalled the past.

Part 3

Convergence

"The moon is dark, and the gods dance in the night; there is terror in the sky, for upon the moon hath sunk an eclipse foretold in no books of men or of earth's gods."

— H. P. Lovecraft, The Other Gods

"DEATH HAS A HUNDRED hands and walks by a thousand ways."

— T.S. Eliot, Murder in the Cathedral

Interlude 3: The Report

Notes:

When I started this project I didn't expect to know anything about the four Alphas. I knew their names: Lazarus, Matthew, Cindy and Grace. I have also read about and seen the movies about the Alphas. Combing through the large archive I have been researching there have been many eye-witness reports from all over the United State. They talked about their deeds and how they helped people survive. But this does not give a clear picture as to who these people were and I didn't want to become engrossed in the Alphas lives because I was focused on a written history during the Breaking of the Seals and thereafter. Except something happened last night and I am not sure if I can include it in this report.

Let me explain. After teaching my class on pre-history United States I was in my office and I found something on my desk. It was a small black book. When I opened it, the pages were blank. I was about to place the book back on my desk when words appeared. I couldn't read the script at first. It was written in some type of foreign language, but then it started to change into English. It was a handwritten account of an Alien race called the swarm, or the Magic eaters. I thought this was a joke, given to me by a gifted, fanciful, magical student. The book also refers to a group of people called the Atlanteans, who live in a magical city called Atlantis.

The book described the rising tensions between the Elves and the Atlanteans. I didn't have time to read the whole book and I fell asleep.

I had a dream, but I want to call it a vision. I was standing in the middle of a forgotten city. The buildings and pyramids were weathered down to the point of being unrecognizable and I had a fleeting notion that I was in the lost city of Atlantis.

The ground started to shake and a light as bright as the sun appeared on the far horizon. I looked up and I did not see open blue sky but a light green horizon.

I smelt the salty sea air and heard waves. I looked around but didn't see any water. Moving forward to the bright light, I thought this dream was more detailed than any I had before and felt a little trepidation as if I was trapped there and couldn't get home.

I felt the weight of ages past move through me in a span of seconds and I was breathless. I wished I had my notebook, paper and magical holo-recordings to note this and knew I could never find this place unless I had the key. The key the Alphas had.

I had wondered this through all the books and holo-movies written by the Alphas, why did we have all this information? The light became brighter the closer I got to the large pyramid at the end of this road. Then I realized the bright light was coming from the top of the structure.

As in all dreams, time flows in irrational ways. I was standing on the ground level and next I stood on top of the pyramid looking down to where I was standing a few seconds ago. I felt the magical tremors in my feet and in my bones. I don't have much arcane talent, but I can recognize raw power when it is laid out before me.

Suddenly, I felt people standing next to me. And I instantly recognized the four alphas: Matthew, the great, standing large and tall with a ruffle of dark brown hair; Grace, the sad, a short brunette with bright black eyes; Cindy, the beautiful, holding her arms around her waist as if she was cold, with her long blond hair flowing around and Lazarus, the Leader, a medium height man seeming neither young nor old. The sound of the ocean broke the mirage.

These people were not there. They were transparent and disappeared as soon as I saw them. I wanted to stare at them again and ask them questions about this place and what they did here because I knew this was the nexus, the goal where they had to repel the invaders. The bright light spilled from a round floating object. The object as far as I could tell didn't seem solid, but a force of nature.

"Professor Jacobs," the glowing object said.

The voice reverberated around me as if the voice was not in front of me but all around the valley.

"Yes," I said.

My mind reeled from the power before me. I had to place my hands over my ears.

"You have to prepare. They are coming."

"I don't understand. Who is coming?"

"You will need the help of the elves. They are still too far away. They have lost too much."

"I don't understand."

"I will tell you. Listen. You will have to fight the nothingness."

I AWOKE FROM MY SLUMBER and I don't know if all I experienced was real. Yet, I knew the swarm, the nothingness, was real and I have to tell somebody. The black book was in front of me and also a brown leather box.

My hand groped for the box and I opened it. Inside was a white glowing Crystal. This was the key.

Chapter 50

Lazarus saw himself floating in a maelstrom of magic. The energies around him sparkled with luminescence and brilliance. Something bright shot into his eyes and he couldn't see in front of him. His feet hit solid ground. Holding his arm up to shield the brightness coming at him he noticed his arm was small, tiny like a kid, then everything around him became normal. He was at the park. His mind felt fuzzy and odd. His mom held him in her arms and she was talking to the neighbor. He was sure about that, and the neighbor was holding a small girl in her arms. It was Cindy. They both sat on a park bench, chatting about their lives and the television.

Lazarus was scared. He could not move like he normally would and drool started to form in his mouth. His mom dabbed it with a napkin. Then he saw what he needed in this dream vision. Two tall people walked up to them dressed in gray suits and black ties. They both wore dark glasses and he realized one of the duo was a woman. Her black hair spilled out underneath her vintage 1950 fedora hat. Lazarus thought it was odd a woman would wear a hat like that.

The pair came up to his mom and the neighbor. His mom didn't even notice the two staring at him and at Cindy.

The tall woman in the fedora hat said, "These are the two."

Lazarus noticed the two tall people's eyes started to glow a phosphorescent light blue luster. Lazarus couldn't stare away from them. The tall man, who also wore a fedora, placed his finger on his head. He felt a slight stinging sensation and then a coolness. The other woman placed her hand on Cindy's forehead. He saw a mark showing an image of waves on Cindy's skin for a brief second and then it disappeared.

He wanted to reach for his head but his mom placed his hands and arms snug in a blanket. Lazarus tried to speak, but his words came out garbled.

Suddenly, a light struck his eyes and he couldn't see for a second. Everything blurred and a sound, a song came to him, a song which sounded familiar. It was a Depeche Mode song called, "Somebody."

Lazarus stood in a high school gymnasium. He was not a baby anymore but a teenager. Teenagers were slow dancing in front of him. Darkness hid their features. Strobe lights splashed along the crowd. A friend of his, named George, stood next to him. The song kept rhythm with his beating heart. He saw that the girl, Yvonne, who he had a crush on was dancing with her boyfriend.

George nudged him. Lazarus shook his head and looked away seeing another person. It was his friend, Cindy. She was all grown up and beautiful, with long blond hair and with her boyfriend slow dancing with her.

"Hey, Lazzy, let's get out of here. The dance is over. I have some more Jack Daniels and beer," George said.

Lazarus smiled. George had called him Lazzy and sometimes lazy, since Freshman year, when they met in English class. They both held a cup filled with coke and JD. They have been drinking most of the night. Lazarus chewed his gum, but he knew that even with the gum if a teacher came up to him the alcohol on his breath would have been obvious.

"Yes," he said.

This was the last dance of the year besides Prom and he was not going. He didn't get a date for Prom. He thought he would have asked Yvonne because she broke up with her boyfriend a week ago, but they got back together tonight. He had missed his chance. His heart was broken and he didn't know what to do. His mind was not wondering why he was back here in the past. All he felt was the pain of the past like it was new and sad.

They walked toward the high school's parking lot. George's dad owned several grocery stores. They were family owned for generations and would be bought up by the large grocery chains several years later. George always pilfered a few liquor bottles for his own medicinal use and kept them inside his bedroom.

Lazarus tried to remember something that happened tonight, something important or maybe something sad. He was not sure. They got to George's car. It was a top of the line BMW four-door sedan. George popped open the trunk and took out a large paper bag. Lazarus heard the clink of glass.

"Get inside. Let's blow this place."

"Ok."

They both got inside the car. Lazarus was feeling lousy. He grabbed a beer from the bag, popped it open and took a long drink. The beer was semi-cold and it tasted bittersweet and melancholy.

George took the bottle of Jack Daniels, unscrewed the top and took a swig.

"Hey, save some for me," Lazarus said.

George's eyes were red-rimmed and he screwed the top back on the top. "We have another pint in the bag. Don't worry. I don't backwash, Lazzy."

"Yuck," he said. Lazarus grabbed the bottle and took a drink. The taste burnt his throat and he almost gagged, but he held it down.

George pulled out of the parking lot and sped down the boulevard. They didn't have a destination and they rode around the outskirts of Santa Fe Springs and then up toward uptown Whittier. Lazarus knew where they headed. It was George's home in Friendly Hills. His parents owned a large house in the rich area of town where the homes were shaded by large foliage and had names like Williard Estates. That was George's last name, Williard. His room was in the back of the home, almost disconnected from the house. The room was created for George as a gift because he made it to his dad's alma mater, Whittier College, a private college that Richard Nixon had attended.

Lazarus had asked if Richard Nixon was a crook. George told him that Mr. Nixon was not a crook. He was pardoned, but according to George's dad, he was not a crook but a victim of circumstance. George drove past the venerable Whittier College. The school looked dead and melancholy on his right and he thought George was about to turn into the parking lot of the college, but he kept driving. Lazarus was feeling drunk. His vision seemed to tilt back and forth and before he knew it they were not driving towards George's house but toward Turnbull Canyon. They drove up a winding road. It had been rumored that Satanists lived in the surrounding hills and even an outcropping of ghosts were supposed to roam the lonely two-lane road.

The city was left behind as they drove toward the stretch of road. Their windows were down and the cool air flowed into the car. George was driving fast even when he took the impossible, crazy turns. The car's tires screeched and it swerved but Lazarus didn't care. He took another drink of his beer and then the Jack Daniels.

Lazarus didn't feel the sensation when the car left the street and plummeted down a steep embankment. He didn't hear the sound of glass breaking and metal screeching as the car careened into the trees. He also didn't feel his body as it flew through the glass window and shot out into the night air. He flopped a few times until he struck the ground and fell several times head over heels, smashing his arms, legs and chest.

He heard screaming and realized it was him shrieking. He stopped and tried to move, but the pain was so intense he yelled again. He couldn't feel his legs and arms. He lay on a slope with his body stretched out on the ground.

"Lazzy! Are you there? You got to help me."

Lazarus turned his head. The pain blurred his vision for a second and he yelped. He saw George and the remains of his car stuck in a tree, skewered by the branches and smashed by a boulder.

"George!" he croaked. "I can't move."

His friend was trapped. George could not get himself unstrapped from his seat belt. Lazarus smelt something. It was the bitter and sweet tang of gasoline. It made him light-headed and euphoric. Lazarus tried to help but he was paralyzed.

He said, "Can you get out of the car?"

George struggled to get out. Then Lazarus knew what was going to happen. It was inevitable. A fire erupted from within the car's engine.

George yelled as the flames engulfed the car. Lazarus couldn't do anything. The fire started to catch around the area of the crash.

Lazarus was in danger and he couldn't move. He watched as the flames caught all around the steep slope, coming closer to him. He was going to die. George was still screaming.

An explosion rocked the car and acrid smoke smothered his nostrils. He couldn't breathe and his sight was dimming. Struggling to keep awake, he tried to move his body to gasp for fresh air. He coughed violently which brought about another bout of intense pain.

The noxious fumes ceased. He smelt cool, clean air. And his pain became dull aches. Two people stood before him, silhouetted against the fire from the car. Lazarus couldn't see the features of the two people, but he knew who they were and he said, "Why did you save me? You should have saved George."

Suddenly, he was floating again in a maelstrom of magical energies. He saw his other body sleeping inside a jeep and the person next to him was shaking him.

"Lazarus, you have to wake up. Lazarus."

Chapter 51

Lazarus opened his eyes. "What's wrong?"

His body felt tight and cramped. The dream he had was a memory he wanted to forget. He hadn't thought about his good friend, George, since graduating high school. The pain and sadness rushed to him.

"Look," Grace said.

He realized the car had stopped moving. Lazarus couldn't believe what he saw in the middle of the road. It was a giant bird, a hawk maybe, and sitting on the bird's back was his friend, Cindy.

Lazarus opened the door and stepped out of the jeep. The wind blew around him and the sun felt warm on his skin. Cindy was smiling as she jumped off her mount. She looked radiant. Her blond hair seemed to glow in the afternoon light. Before he could say anything, she ran to him and gave him a fierce hug. She moved so fast that she was a blur and when they touched he felt a mild shock of electricity pass through them. They stopped hugging and he looked at her.

He said, "I knew you were the fourth person. I felt it."

Cindy looked at him and then at the other two coming out of the car behind him.

Matthew said, "So, you know this person?"

"Yes, we've been friends for years."

Cindy nodded to Matthew.

Grace said, "I like your giant bird."

"Thanks. I created it out of a water orb," Cindy replied.

He didn't know her powers would be so different to theirs. Cindy moved back to her mount and held up her hand. The large bird started to shimmer and become transparent. Lazarus shook his head. It was like watching a mirage. The bird got smaller and then morphed into itself. In a few seconds, it was gone, replaced by a round transparent water globe that hovered close to Cindy. Everybody was speechless. This was better than any of the magic tricks he saw on TV or even in the Vegas shows.

Grace said, "That was great! Can you make anything?"

"I'm not sure. I think all our powers are new and we are learning to use them."

Lazarus said, "Yes."

Cindy said, "What is this about the fourth member?"

"The circle is completed," Matthew said. "We can now finish this quest."

"Lazarus, who are these people and what is this quest?"

"Well, we need to talk." He looked around. "Where are we?"

Grace shrugged. "I think we are still in Nevada."

"Yes, we are," Cindy said. "I was going to meet you in New Mexico, but I decided to meet you here."

"Thanks for that," he said. "Should we start going? We can talk inside the car."

Cindy considered this. "Yes, we have until the new moon to find this pyramid."

Matthew said, "So you know what we seek?"

"Yes, but I don't understand."

"Well, I think we won't know everything until we get to our destination," Lazarus said.

Grace added, "It's a puzzle."

"I don't know about that," Matthew said. "I know we have to find this temple."

Cindy started walking back to them. "Ok, fine. Let's get going. But I think it would be faster on my bird."

"Yes," Lazarus said, "but inside a car, you don't have to worry about bugs getting into your mouth."

Cindy smiled at him. "You've got a point there."

They moved to the car. Grace took the driver's seat and Matthew took the front passenger side. Lazarus and Cindy sat in the back of the jeep.

"We might have to use your bird later," he said. "We are at a half a tank of gas."

Cindy nodded to him. She said, "Boy, Lazarus, if you wanted to get me in the back seat you could have asked."

"You are funny. Let's get out of here."

⚜

THEY DIDN'T TALK FOR a few hours. As soon as the car started, Cindy told him she was tired and wanted to take a nap. She closed her eyes and moved closer to him. The car jostled and moved along the lane. Cindy slumped next to him and her head hit his shoulder. He lifted his right arm and she snuggled against him. Her hair smelt like wind and sand.

After a few hours, they approached a city called Searchlight. It was a small town. Not really a city by any means. It was more a street with several homes and businesses. There was even a casino. They didn't see anybody walking or driving.

Lazarus said, "Do you see a gas station?"

"Yes," Grace answered. "It's over there."

She started to drive toward the area.

"Wait." Lazarus was not sure about it.

Matthew said, "Why?"

Grace stopped the car. "I feel it, too. Something is wrong here. It was the same feeling before I saw the Giant Worm at the State Line."

Matthew said, "We are almost out of gas."

"Yes, I know," Lazarus said. "I think I need to check it out first before we go any further."

Matthew said, "No, we should go together."

Cindy started to stir. She sat up and stretched, looking through the window. She yawned, "What are we doing?"

"I have an idea," Grace said.

They all turned to her. She continued, "When I was back at the State Line, I could see into the lair of the Giant Worm by touching the ground."

"Ok, let's try this," Lazarus said.

They all exited the car. The landscape had not changed in the last few hours. It was mostly sand dunes and hills on the horizon.

Grace went to the side of the street and knelt. Lazarus and the others walked close to her. He was wary, ready to unleash magic if somebody or something attacked them.

He watched Grace place her right palm onto the earth and close her eyes. Magical energies surged around her body and into the ground. After a few minutes, she shook her head and opened her eyes.

She said, "Well, I don't feel anything lurking underground. But I sense something and I don't know what it is."

Lazarus said, "Ok, we all should go, but I think we should fly over there using Cindy's bird or animal to help us."

He wished he had brought Sammy with him. He was a good guard dog and he could always sniff out the danger.

Chapter 52

Cindy flew on her bird while Lazarus and the others soared next to her. Lazarus thought he was being overly cautious, but in this new world, they had to be. The city, from this vantage point, looked abandoned and he didn't have any insight to anything lurking in the dead windows of the buildings and homes. The air smelt odd, like sulfur. They followed Cindy's lead as she circled several times around the town. Nothing moved or stirred.

Cindy started her descent to the gas station. The building was sagging on one side and the overhang over the gas pumps was gone, thrown to one side. The overhang jutted out of the general convenience store. It was as if a giant had torn the top off the overhangs and flung them aside.

This didn't look recent. Coming closer to the town, he noticed the other homes and building were also broken, either missing a wall or roof tops.

He said, "Grace, the sandstorm that hit Las Vegas. Could it have done this damage?"

"Yes, but it would have done more if it was as strong as the one that hit Vegas."

Lazarus noticed there was no evidence of large sand dunes or areas covered by debris and sediments.

"Do you smell that?"

They landed close to the gas station. Stepping on the cement, he waited for something to come out of the buildings.

Cindy was next to him. "Yes, it smells like rotten eggs."

Matthew lumbered next to him. He sniffed the air. "It smells worse than the dumpsters at home."

Lazarus looked at the big man. He had almost forgotten this person used to live in the streets.

"Yes, I don't like this. Keep a sharp eye out."

They started walking to the nearest gas pump, careful not to step on the debris on the ground. Lazarus saw movement from the small store at the gas station.

"Wait."

Something dark slinked inside, then the movement stopped and the figure was gone.

Cindy said, "Do you want my water globe to check it out?"

"What? Yes," Lazarus said.

His body was tensed and he felt at any moment a monster would fly out of the store. The giant bird flew toward the small building and started to change. It became a dog, which looked eerily like Sammy. The dog jumped inside the small room. It rumbled inside and make a big ruckus.

Cindy said, "There is nothing inside except a dead person."

The dog burst out wagging its tail. It was odd how it looked like Sammy, even down to the color of its fur.

"I saw a dog in my dreams and my water orb changed into it," Cindy said.

Lazarus smiled. "Was the dog called Sammy?"

"Yes, it was."

"That was my dog that I found in Los Angeles and he traveled here with me."

"I must have seen him in your mind."

Matthew said, "I think we need to get this over with. I think if we find some gasoline cans we can fill it up."

"We can just drive the car up here and fill it up," Grace said.

"Let's check if the pumps work, first," Lazarus said.

He walked over to the first fuel dispenser and grabbed the metal pump. He placed it toward the ground and tried the lever. Nothing came out.

"Great," he said.

Something shot out of the garage. It was a blur and it was headed toward him. He placed his hands upwards in a defensive posture. The creature hit an invisible barrier and bounced away. He shook his head. More creatures came out of the other buildings. The creatures looked like large mutated gorillas.

He said, "Get closer to me."

The creatures snarled and yelled, "Grog! Grog!"

Lazarus held up his hand and the invisible barrier came over them. The Grog gorillas pounded and hit the barrier.

He said, "Why didn't your dog find these creatures?"

"I don't know. Maybe he didn't look up or these creatures have a cloaking spell."

The creatures growled and pounded against the invisible field.

"We are leaving now!" Lazarus said.

They started to float upwards. They had to leave the car and he was not sure how long he could keep up this floating spell. He was already tiring. Sweat beaded his forehead and his body felt like lead.

They moved away from the small town of Searchlight. Grog creatures streamed through every structure and some beasts started to come out of the very ground. It looked like hundreds of monsters yelling at them.

"Do you need help?" Cindy asked.

He nodded, trying to focus on keeping them flying away. She touched his arm and he felt magic wash over him. They started to move toward their car, but he stopped.

Grog creatures were already streaming inside and out of the jeep.

"Damn!" he said. "Our supplies were in that car."

Grace said, "We have to leave. Look..."

Lazarus saw what she was looking at. More creatures started to pour outside and then he noticed some of the beasts were flying at them. Grace held up her hand and rocks and debris from the town flew up, hitting the soaring Grogs. Still, more monsters flew at them. "That's it," Matthew said.

The big man pointed at the nearest flying Grog and a wall of flames erupted between them and the monsters. Even with Cindy's help, he was soon tiring. She was also straining.

She said, "We'll ride on my animal."

"What?"

Before he knew what she was talking about he felt Cindy's magic coalescing and his force field disappear. They fell on top of a large half eagle and half lion. It was a mystical griffon. Cindy was in front of him and Grace and Matthew were behind. They all looked amazed.

The griffon squawked a loud piercing scream. The Grogs swarmed toward them. Lazarus was too tired to conjure any magic. Matthew pointed his right hand and green flames sprouted, killing the nearest line of creatures. The griffon flapped his large wings and flew away. The ground looked so far away that Lazarus felt dizzy holding Cindy in front of him. He didn't care how they escaped. He tried not to slump on Cindy's back but he couldn't help it.

They flew for several hours, following the road. The Grog creatures stopped following them as soon as the town of Searchlight disappeared from their view. They had lost all their supplies and even worse, they had lost their jeep. They wouldn't find another vehicle for miles, but he was fine traveling in the sky with Cindy in front of him.

Chapter 53

Royce stood in front of a crowd of minion followers. It was dusk and night was approaching. He was in front of his apartment in Barstow. He waited. They had told him it was almost time. Time for his reckoning. The Alphas had finally met and were going to the pyramid. The Thinners had come down from the sky and talked to him, except they looked different. The Thinners were not what he expected. They were tall as he seen before, but their bodies looked more insectile with skin that glowed an incandescent blue, and when they spoke they chittered. Yet he understood them.

They told him the Alphas needed to be destroyed but not before they showed them the ancient city. Royce didn't understand the reason why. He had told them he wanted to kill them now, but they told him to wait.

So, he waited outside his home, watching the Grogs come to him, massing in front. Every morning and night he commanded his Grogs to bring him food and they usually brought him a rabbit, dog and even a small horse. His appetite was huge, insatiable. The fresher the better.

Several large Grogs pushed through the crowd. They were holding a small goat and something else. It was a half eaten dog. He sniffed and the carcass of the dog was still fresh. The goat he might save for later.

Royce moved forward to the greet the Grogs but before he could start feasting a large creature came forward. He knew this was going to happen when the large apelike creature first came into his camp.

The large creature stood before him, with apelike comrades a few feet away.

The large ape creature said, "You cannot command me. I challenge your authority."

Royce liked this. He had been provoked several times by lesser Grog creatures and he always snarled at the poor creature, making it back away. But this time would be different. This ape openly defied him before his pack and Royce had to fight him.

He snarled, "So, what is your name?"

"My name does not matter," the ape Grog said.

Royce smiled with his long teeth jutting from his mouth. He said, "I'd like to know your name. So I can write it on your grave."

"My name is Victor. I shall destroy you."

Victor galloped at him using his long arms and legs as an ape would. The ape Grog raised his arms. Royce grinned and shot past him, using his long claws to swipe a long gash on Victor's shoulder. Blood started to flow. The Grog group growled in anger and in anticipation of violence.

Royce minion's felt his power and rage. They almost surged toward them. But Royce shot a dark stare at his minions and they moved backwards to give them more room to fight. The ape creature rushed at him, snarling and screaming. It grabbed him by his haunches and tried to pull him down. Royce bit deeply into Victor's wrist and turned his head. He heard the sound of breaking bones and skin. He spat out the remains of Victor's large hand.

The ape Grog howled into the air. He pounded at him. Royce swiftly moved out of the way and shot out with his claws to disembowel Victor. The smell of hot blood and intestines brought the blood lust. Royce growled and buried his jaws into Victor's throat, ripping his head clear off his body.

"Eat him and his group."

His minions moved to the nearest ape-like creature and killed it. The group turned to the rest of the ape Grogs and killed every one, feasting on the blood and entrails. Royce was sickened, but delighted. Nobody would dare challenge him again in front of his Grog pack. He sat on his haunches and dined on Victor's flesh.

⸎

THE MOON WAXED IN ITS cycle and Royce felt the urges of the cycle of the lunar phase affect him. He sensed the Alpha group was getting closer to the Pyramid. The crescent moon beckoned him to let loose his animalistic nature and join with his group. He had done this several times before. Royce joined with the women in his pack and felt his sexual urges sated. This was better than when he was human.

Except for tonight, he waited for the others to come to him. He had mistakenly called them Thinners and he felt such pain that he couldn't walk for hours. They wanted to be called the Vvong, the swarm. A bright light came out of the sky and dropped in front of him. The light was a round disk with a screen inside it like a TV. He saw the Vvong staring at him.

All he saw was the Vvong's face. Its insect-like face showed large mandibles and two large bulbous eyes. The eyes were multi-faceted, like a fly's. Royce looked away. Staring at the Vvong gave him the creeps.

The Vvong said, "Start moving tonight. The Alphas are getting close to their destination."

"What am I supposed to do?"

"We want the crystal and the entrance to the city. You have to wait until they are inside and then kill them and give us the crystal."

"I understand. But what do I get if I do your commands?"

The Vvong didn't say anything for a while. "You will have untold power and live among us in peace when we come to your planet."

Royce didn't know what the creature was talking about. "Where are you?"

"You cannot question us!"

He heard the noise of chittering and thought he saw more Vvongs in the background.

The Vvong said, "You need to leave tonight with your underlings."

The screen changed to a bright light and started to float upwards. Royce was ready to extract his revenge on the Alphas. They should never have invaded the army base and destroyed everything. It showed their contempt for authority. He would show them. He would show them.

Royce grinned. He was ready.

Chapter 54

Lazarus motioned for Cindy to land her great bird on a high bluff. It was night and the crescent moon shone in the sky. The stars were so bright they winked at them. Cindy jumped off the bird and they followed. Lazarus heard Matthew say he was hungry. He was hungry himself.

Cindy said, "Leave that to me."

She closed her eyes and the giant bird changed into a large wolf. The animal's yellow eyes flickered in the moonlight.

She said, "Get us some food."

Lazarus was amazed at her magic. He didn't think he could do that. The large wolf jumped down off the slope of the small hill and disappeared.

Lazarus said, "Let's build a fire. It's getting cold."

Searching the desert, he saw small plants and large clumps of grass and flowers and roses.

Grace said, "Those plants should not be here."

"Yes," he said. "I was thinking the same thing."

Off toward their right, Lazarus saw several groups of red trees sprouting upward to the sky. It looked like a forest was germinating.

Matthew said, "It's the magic. It's changed the area."

Cindy said, "Those roses are beautiful."

Lazarus noticed the rose petals glowed a light blue. Cindy moved toward it.

"Stop," he said. "We don't know if those roses are dangerous."

Grace said, "Yes, I believe he is right, Cindy. We cannot take anything at face value."

Matthew grabbed a stick and went closer to the rose bush. "Wait," he said.

Matthew crept closer and pointed the stick at the closest rose, that was glowing like a firefly. The plant instantly grabbed the stick and took a bite out of it. Matthew fell backwards onto the ground. None of them expected that would happen.

Cindy said, "Well, I guess I have to admire the rose from afar."

Lazarus smiled at the sentiment and then without warning he started to laugh. The statement was so perfect under these times. Things that looked so harmless before were now deadly. Matthew started to laugh as well as Grace. Cindy shook her head and then she also started to grin and then laugh, especially when she stared at the glowing rose.

Grace said, "Why are we laughing?"

"I don't know," Lazarus said and this made him chortle louder. He even fell to the ground and joined Matthew who was still lying on the dirt.

Cindy said, "I don't think it was that funny."

"Yes, I understand," he said while rolling on the ground. But he still laughed. "You don't think it is funny that we are stuck somewhere between Nevada and New Mexico going to a place we don't know. And besides, all that we have murderous creatures everywhere and the only beautiful thing we have found is also a murderous thing. I don't know what to call it."

Lazarus felt another round of giddiness come over him, but he stifled the laughter. He sucked in some air and relaxed, but when he saw Matthew sprawled next to him holding a half-bitten stick he started again, laughing like a loon.

Cindy turned away saying, "Boys!"

He kept on laughing until tears flowed down his cheeks. Matthew also laughed, moving back and forth on his back like a crab. This brought more peals of laughter. Grace chuckled.

She said, "I don't know why we are laughing so much."

Lazarus said, "I don't know myself."

Cindy came walking back to them. She had a bemused look on her face. "If you guys are done, I need to prepare our food and a fire."

Lazarus said, "All our supplies were in the car. How are we going to cook and eat the food?"

"Don't worry," Matthew said, "I always keep a switchblade on me. I can skin the animal and cook it over a fire with sticks. I learned to make do when I lived on the streets."

Lazarus and Matthew stood up. He stifled his chuckles and looked at Cindy who was petting her wolf. He watched as Matthew took the dead rabbits from Cindy's wolf and gutted the animals. Lazarus realized the big man didn't notice the disgust he saw on Cindy's and Grace's faces.

"Hey, let's get some firewood. But we need to stay together. Who knows what is out there?" Lazarus said. "Grace, do you want to stay here with Matthew?"

She said, "Sure."

Cindy nodded and her wolf followed. They moved down the slopes, edging their way toward a group of trees which seemed odd in this desert landscape.

Lazarus watched Cindy as she walked next to him. She was silent and her movements were graceful and strong.

He said, "What do you call your water familiar?"

"Familiar?" she said. Cindy bent down and grabbed a large wood stick.

"Yes, any wizard or witch has an animal spirit or guide that is under their command. Your water globe is your familiar."

"Oh, I didn't know that. Where did you learn that?"

"I read a lot of fantasy books. This all seems so..." He stopped talking. She grabbed his hand with her free hand and looked intently into his eyes. He met Cindy's blue eyes. They seem to glow.

She said, "Yes."

The bright stars of the night seemed to sing with the locusts and insects and he was not sure what he should do. She was close to him, closer than he had ever been to her. He smelt the sharp scent of the salty sea ocean. It came from her very pores.

He continued, "It seems like we are in a fairy tale and we cannot go back home."

She looked away from him and started to search for firewood. He felt the connection between them was stopped as if his chance for her touch was gone like the spring rain on a bright afternoon.

She said, "Tell me what you know."

Lazarus grabbed a few sticks and said, "I don't know much."

He scanned the sky. The stars looked so bright and close that he thought he could reach out and pluck them out of the air, one by one.

"I remember before all this happened. It was very hot in Los Angeles. It was late August." He paused. "Cindy, I don't even know what day it is."

"I know. Everything is different. We are not the same people as before the storms." She held several bundles of wood. "Is this enough?"

"Yes, it is."

Chapter 55

The next day the small group woke to the sound of thunder and crackling lightning. Lazarus slept on the small hamlet of grass and dirt. Next to him was the large wolf. It was breathing heavily and staring up at the sky. The beast's dark brown felt looked as if was in disarray. The thunder pealed and a flash of lightning shot in the clouds.

Cindy was sitting across from him, wide awake. She lifted her hand and the wolf changed into a round orb and then disappeared. Cindy was so comfortable using her powers. He wished he could be like that. The clouds gathered around the area, dark and pregnant with moisture. Cindy held up her hands.

She said, "I can feel the forces of nature gathering."

Lazarus sensed something but it was not the same feeling Cindy was sensing. "Is it going to rain?"

"No. Touch your opal on your wrist."

"What?"

Lazarus had forgotten about the bracelet and didn't even remember it was fastened onto his wrist. He looked at it. The opal glowed with an intense light. He looked at Cindy with wonder and noticed her necklace was also illuminated. Grace and Matthew were awake, staring up at the lightning and thunder. Their stones glowed in their rings.

Lazarus said, "What is this?"

"We need to get to Pyramid Peak today," Matthew said. "Tonight it will be the full moon. We don't have enough time."

"Time for what?" Lazarus said.

Grace looked at him with a silly look. "Lazarus, we were brought together to do something. We don't know what it is. But it is something important. I can feel it. Can't you?"

Lazarus felt foolish. He was supposed to be their Leader, yet he felt more like a follower.

He shook his head. "I don't like that we don't know what we are supposed to do. We need to plan."

Matthew said, "I don't mean disrespect, Leader, but we cannot plan. We don't know what we are doing. It just feels right."

Lazarus nodded his head. The big man was correct. They didn't know what they were doing. They had worked well so far, but how long could they keep moving forward without creating some deadly mistake?

"You're right, Matthew. I just don't like this one bit. I'm used to planning."

Cindy came close to him. "I understand. Before, in the normal world, we had guides and procedures. Here, right now, in this world, chaos rules and we are not prepared."

Lazarus said, "What do we do?"

"You lead us. I have a feeling you are the person who will show us the way. Even though you don't believe it," Cindy said.

She grabbed his hand and squeezed it.

"Alright," he said, "let's have some breakfast and then we'll go to Pyramid Peak."

AFTER A SMALL BREAKFAST, Lazarus and Matthew decided to fly next to Cindy's familiar while Grace and Cindy rode on top of the animal. They would travel for a while and switch places riding the great beast to conserve their energy.

Lazarus liked the feel of soaring in the air, hearing the sound of thunder and watching lightning sear the sky. He was not terrified. The feeling of raw power from nature's elements gave him a sense of power and destiny. He knew their time was coming and a choice had to be made.

They traveled for most of the day, passing through Nevada and into Arizona. They skirted along route 93, but decided not to venture toward the large cities. They passed Bullhead City and then Kingman without stopping nor looking back. Lazarus noticed a flock of birds on the far horizon moving south away from them. He sensed something. It was like a deep, dark wave had hit him, chilling his skin and bones. He motioned for Cindy to land.

They touched the ground. Cindy and Grace dismounted the giant falcon.

He said, "Did you see that flock of birds?"

"Yes, but you also felt something," Cindy said.

He nodded. "I don't know what it is. But I think I have felt this darkness before."

Matthew said, "Yes, something is coming for us. We have to hurry."

"If we all ride my falcon, we can reach there in less than an hour," Cindy said.

"Yes, but we might be spotted by unwanted creatures," Lazarus said.

Matthew said, "Leader, we have to get to Pyramid Peak before nightfall. We can outrun anything."

"I think we should all ride the falcon," Grace said. "It's a chance we have to take."

"So be it," Lazarus said. "But if we have to stop and fight then Matthew and I can fend them off."

Cindy said, "If you are scared my falcon cannot fight them off, I will change my familiar to something scarier."

"That's not what I meant. We just need to be more careful."

Cindy stalked away from him not looking back. She moved closer to her giant falcon and touched the animal's rump.

He walked toward her. "Cindy, you're not listening to me."

He was about to say something else, but stopped himself. Shaking his head, he remembered seeing her act like this before. Cindy was stubborn and when she was mad would not listen to reason. He felt her magic coalescing around her. It was powerful and strong. The large falcon started to change and morph. The head of the bird changed into an eagle and the body transformed into a lion. It was the griffin again. The beast roared and it sounded like an eagle with the voice of the lion.

She turned to him. "Are you ready?"

The griffin looked at him with a quizzical look.

"Ok. You're right. The time is short."

They all mounted the beast and with a flap of the creature's large wings they flew into the heavens.

Chapter 56

Cindy steered the griffin toward the outskirts of Phoenix. Lazarus told her to go around the city. He sensed something was odd and he didn't want to enter the area, but Cindy told him it should be fine. He agreed because they were tired and thirsty and they needed to find some water.

"We should find the nearest market and then land. This should take less than five minutes," he said.

Cindy nodded and moved her griffin toward the first group of buildings they encountered, but when they flew toward the city of Phoenix they saw that the streets and stores were overrun by vegetation. It was as if the town was swallowed up by nature and had stood abandoned for eons.

Matthew said, "This cannot be."

Grace said, "What happened here?"

Nobody said a word. Everything looked old. The walls of the homes were covered with dirt and dark black stains. Some of the roofs had caved in as if the weight of ages caused it. Then Lazarus saw something along the street and Cindy pointed downwards.

There were statues with plants and ivy overgrown over them. The statues looked so lifelike and were in different poses of horror. Something came to him. He sensed a deep darkness and fear.

"Wait," he said.

"There is nothing," Matthew said and nodded to a large creature in the middle of the statues. The creature was also petrified in stone and it was dead. Yet the magic overlaid over the whole place.

He said, "Ok, let's find a store."

"I already found one. My familiar spied it a few seconds ago," Cindy said.

"Ok, let's go, but we have to be careful. I sense something not right around here."

"We might not find anything at the store."

Grace said, "But we should try. I'm thirsty."

Lazarus nodded. He was thirsty himself and they had only a few hours left before nightfall. They were more than halfway to their destination and they needed to get some supplies if they were going to be stranded somewhere. Lazarus hated not knowing what they were supposed to do and find when they got to Pyramid Peak. Yet still, this felt right.

The griffin landed at a large broad area of the street with creeping plants coming from the ground. The beast touched the ground but they didn't dismount for a few seconds, sensing something was about to attack them. But nothing came forth from the dark shade of the dead buildings and structures. In front of them was a building called the "Grocery Super Store." It was large and cavernous. The glass front of the store looked furtive and black.

They jumped off the creature one by one. Lazarus surveyed the street and buildings.

He said, "We need some light."

"Let me," Matthew said.

He held up his hand and a ball of fire appeared. Their voices sounded muffled as if the very stones and buildings created a buffering effect. The large man, Matthew, led the way toward the store. In the parking lot were several cars, all overgrown with plants and vines. Their paint looked rusted and stained by time.

They moved through the lot, crunching over the plants and vines. Lazarus felt his body was on high alert and that if anything came at them he would blast it with magic. He saw the large griffin morph into a wolf and pad close to Cindy. Lazarus was amazed that he didn't feel Cindy used her magic. Matthew gained the front entrance of the store, grabbed the door and tried to open it but the entry wouldn't budge.

"Forget this." Matthew held up his hand and blasted the glass entranceway.

Lazarus wanted to tell the big man to not destroy the front but it was already done before he could say anything. The glass and steel crumpled from the intense heat of Matthew's spell. The opening shot inwards creating a vortex of sound.

Lazarus turned to Matthew and said, "Next time you destroy anything, we need to talk about it."

"What?" Matthew said, "There's nobody here. The city is dead."

Lazarus shook his head. "Look at the statues. Those things used to be people. Something caused that. And we have to be cautious."

Matthew's eyes seemed to glass over as if he didn't hear him. "Yes, Leader, I will be more careful."

"Ok."

Matthew entered the building. His magical fireball went in front of him and illuminated the interior. The first thing Lazarus saw was aisles of cash registers with numbers on top of them. More lifelike statues stood in the front. They were all looking out the front windows and seemed to be caught unawares by the magic that bound them into stone.

Matthew went toward the nearest statue and peered at it. The stone sculpture was a large man with a round belly. He wore a vest with a name tag. The man's name was Joe.

Grace said, "Let me try to check."

They watched her move a few feet away from them and kneel on the linoleum ground, touching it with her fingers. She closed her eyes and then jolted upright as if she had been shot with lightning. She made an "Ah" noise and then came back.

"Are you ok?"

She said in a whisper, "These people were attacked, not by a creature, but by the winds."

"The winds?"

Grace said, "We need to leave the store and get out of here."

Lazarus stared at the aisles filled with grocery items and cans on the shelves.

Cindy said, "Let's find the bottled waters and then we can go."

Matthew led them past the cash registers and into the first aisle. Most of the food besides the canned goods looked spoilt, oozing with black mold and bacteria. A noxious smell was emanating from the shelves.

Cindy said, "I don't think we can find anything here. Everything is in ruin and smells of rot. The water is probably the same."

"Yes, you're right."

Matthew said, "Over here."

The big man was standing by one of the empty cash registers. He was opening one of the small fridges on the endcap and peered inside. They all moved toward Matthew. The big man was pointing at the bottles inside the container. There were the usual sodas and bottles of water. But the water was all milky white.

"Yuck!" Grace said.

"Let's go. We won't find anything here."

A noise started to come from outside. It was a whining noise cascading into a loud scream.

Cindy's wolf started to growl.

Chapter 57

Lazarus and his group ran to the front of the grocery store. Outside, a whirling tornado picked up plants, debris and parts of the building. The shrieking sound came again and he saw a face appear inside the maelstrom of wind. It was a magical creature created by the vortex of the tornado.

Cindy said, "What should we do?"

"We will fight!" Matthew said. Twin globes of fire appeared before the big man. His face looked fierce.

"No, not yet. We need some type of distraction. So we can leave," Lazarus said.

"Yes, I have an idea," Cindy said. "I will use my familiar to distract that thing outside and we can fly away."

Matthew said, "We should fight it. That creature killed people and we will avenge those people."

"Matthew, you are not a knight on a quest. This is for real. We can die."

"I'm not going to let this creature live," Matthew said. He trembled with anger and his fire globes burned higher.

The creature outside was getting closer to the store. Lazarus knew they didn't have much time to decide what to do.

He said, "We can have the familiar go outside and distract it and then we attack. But we should be careful. I want Grace and Cindy to come behind me as soon as the creature is looking at the familiar."

They all nodded. But the sound of the creature came from behind them.

Lazarus turned around and said, "Run! The creature is behind us."

He glanced behind him. The wind buffeted and struck them. He was almost flung off his feet. He grabbed Grace and pulled her toward the entranceway. Matthew didn't follow but faced the beast.

Lazarus said, "No!"

But his cry was not heard over the sound of the wind's screaming. Lazarus rushed out on the street. Grace was breathing hard and sucking in air. Her eyes had a darting, fearful look.

She said, "What? I don't know what to do."

The large windows of the grocery store exploded outwards. He jumped and pushed Grace out of the way, but the glass shards still pelted them. Then the glass stopped hitting them and he realized he held his hands up in a defensive posture and a light blue haze surrounded them, stopping the falling glass from hitting them.

Grace was about to say something when Matthew and Cindy ran out of the building. Behind them, her large wolf jumped to the street. The wind creature burst out of the building in a rush of hurricane and noise and a face appeared in the middle of the gale. It examined the large running wolf and blew a breeze at the animal. Instantly, the wolf changed into stone.

"Hurry, let's go," Lazarus said.

They stood and started running. The blue haze surrounding them disappeared. Matthew turned toward the creature. The big man smiled and held up both of his hands. Fire erupted from his hands.

He snarled, "Come and get me."

Flames shot from Matthew as he attacked the wind creature. Lazarus knew the spell was not going to reach the wind elemental. The creature blew a mighty gust and struck the flames, changing them into rock.

"No!" Lazarus said.

Matthew's hands started to change into stone. Lazarus focused and lightning came forth from his body, striking the wind elemental creature in a loud burst of sound. The creature suddenly came at him.

Cindy, at the far corner of the street, shot a blast of water at it, knocking the elemental to the side. She yelled in a fury he never knew she possessed.

The creature moved so fast he didn't see it cluster around her. She changed into a rock statue. He looked at Matthew who was also a stone figure. Grace grabbed his arm.

She said, "We need to leave. We can't help them until we know what we're dealing with."

Grace flew up and he followed. Lazarus felt that he betrayed his friends by leaving, but he had no choice. The elemental creature didn't follow them like he thought it would but stayed on the ground spinning in a whirling mass of wind.

They flew toward the distant mountains. He landed on the ground but couldn't see because his eyes misted with tears and he couldn't go any further. The sun was fading on the horizon. They didn't have much time left.

They landed at the nearest open spaced on the ground far away from the city. He held up his hands in supplication.

"What are going to do? We need them."

She came up to him and gave him a hug. "I know. But we have to think."

He moved away from her. "We don't have enough time."

She looked around the area. "I wonder why the creature didn't come after us."

"That thing is an elemental creature of wind and it takes its power from some type of source."

"How do you know that?" Grace said.

"I can feel it." He closed his eyes. "The reason why you couldn't feel the creature is because it was hiding its essence."

"But that's impossible."

"No, magic has certain laws that we are just learning. What do we know about this creature?"

"It is a being made of wind and it makes humans into stone."

"Yes, but does it think and know."

"What are you saying?"

"Somebody created that thing, like Cindy's familiar. And this person is also controlling it."

"So, if we find this person we can control the creature?"

"Yes. This person is near."

"What if you're wrong?"

He studied the city. "I've been trying to be too safe. But the time to be careful is over. Follow my lead but don't fight the creature until I tell you to."

Grace nodded.

He said, "Your magic talent derives from earth magic."

"What? I do?"

"Yes, you can control dirt, sand and stone. I want you to use your magic to throw pieces of concrete and cement around the homes and buildings surrounding the grocery store. But stay close to me. We will concentrate our efforts around Matthew and Cindy."

He flew upwards, going directly to the location of his friends. He didn't slow but raced forward.

Chapter 58

Lazarus flew around the grocery store and saw his friends petrified on the street. The elemental creature was roaming the area. He recalled the creature didn't show until they entered the structure. He knew as soon as Grace destroyed the homes and buildings on the ground the creature would come forth.

He said, "I am going to distract the creature. You have to find the person controlling it."

"Wait," she said.

Lazarus hovered over the street.

"I don't know what to look for," Grace said.

He felt the breeze start to pick up and push against them. The creature screeched and came at them.

"Go now," he said.

Grace soared away. The elemental creature saw Grace leave. Lazarus focused and sent a lightning bolt at it. The spell bounced harmlessly through the beast. It turned toward him and charged. Lazarus anticipated this and swooped far away, circling the area. Behind him, he heard the sounds of buildings and walls crashing.

Dusk settled in and it was getting dark along the street. The creature blew a blast of wind and he steered away from the spell. It barely missed him and he felt a tingling sensation pass close to him. He checked his body. None of his limbs were stone. He darted up higher. The creature followed, but then stopped.

He quickly scanned the buildings looking for somebody who could be controlling this creature, but all he saw was abandoned homes and offices. Deciding on a course of action he looked where Grace was flying. She was several feet away from him. Using her magic, she flung pieces of earth, stone and building walls all over creating a large explosion of noise. The creature, alerted to the sounds and havoc, rushed toward her.

"No, you will not."

Lazarus's anger swelled. His body burned with desperation. He would not have another one of his friends become stone. Magic coalesced. He felt more powerful. Placing his hands before him, Lazarus shot a water funnel tornado out of his hands. The spell came out of him like a roaring lion. It pounded down, spraying the air elemental. It pushed the creature backwards as if it was solid. He concentrated and long, sharp icicles fell upon the air beast, hitting it in multiple places.

The creature roared in pain and turned toward him. Lazarus rushed backwards. The beast spewed another lethal spray of its breath. Luckily, he moved away before it hit him. He flew upwards into the sky. The creature didn't stay on the ground but soared up to him. Lazarus smiled. He had anticipated this. He realized the creature, like all animals, had a vulnerability. The creature became weakened when struck by water magic. He wondered why he didn't see this before. Cindy, before she was turned into stone, hit the creature with a water spell which caused it to stagger. He shook his head. The time for reflection was not now. The creature was gaining momentum, pushing up towards him.

Lazarus kept flying up, almost reaching the highest strata but stopped. He was not sure he could do this and everything counted on it. He would not have another shot. Summoning his magic, he sought power he had never used to its full potential. Clouds gathered around him, dark and fluffy things that moved in unison, surrounding him in such a frenzy he thought the clouds were alive.

The creature, not understanding or noticing its predicament came after him, intent on destroying. It didn't merely look like a tornado but it sprouted hands with razor claws six feet long. Thunder rolled and lightning sparked along the surface of the nebulous fog. Rain poured forth.

The creature still came at him, until the water pummeled the elemental. Before his eyes, Lazarus saw the wind creature shrink and change into a man. This person still had rage in his eyes, but stripped of his monster garb he looked harmless. The man was older than him with glowing white hair. His face had the countenance of pure hate. It almost stopped Lazarus from defending himself. He lifted his hands and lightning split the air from the clouds and struck the man repeatedly.

The spell pierced the man and lit him up like fireworks, then he fell to the ground. Lazarus should have known the person controlling the creature was inside it. He couldn't let the man fall, even though he was probably dead.

Lazarus focused his magic and the rain stopped. He flew down and caught the man by grabbing him from behind, but the ground rushed too close to him. He focused and an invisible shield surrounded them before they hit the roof of a large warehouse. They bounced when they touched the ground. The sound of explosions and booming came from the walls and cement they hit. The man's body flopped to the side and then struck Lazarus. They bounced back and forth until they finally stopped moving after a few minutes. He had been on a roller coaster before but this was worse. He knew the man next to him was dead. Lazarus could tell by his burnt skin and slackened facial features, as if he was sleeping. This was in marked contrast to the diabolical hatred he displayed when attacking. Lazarus stood after a few minutes. The world spun.

He focused and the magical barrier disappeared. Looking around, he saw they were inside an old dilapidated warehouse. The smell of rot and mold assailed his senses. The sun shone from the hole he created in the rooftop. He moved away, walking into the empty interior.

"You will die."

Lazarus turned and looked at the man. His eyes were open but bloodshot. Lazarus held up his hand, anticipating an attack.

"Who are you?" he asked.

"Nobody. He sent me to kill you."

"That didn't happen."

"I know. But he will find you."

The man started to cough up blood. His eyes glazed over and he fell to his side. Lazarus shook his head. He wondered who this man was talking about.

"Lazarus!"

He turned to see Grace running inside the building with Cindy and Matthew following close behind.

"What?"

Grace said, "I don't have time to explain. Something is coming and we have to leave now!"

They all rushed out of the warehouse. Outside, he saw large Grog wolves waiting for them. The beasts growled and moved to attack.

"Go!" he said and launched himself into the air.

Before they left the city, Lazarus saw the biggest Grog saunter out of the crowd of beasts. It looked at him and smiled a wicked grin.

Chapter 59

The full moon shone in the sky. The wind was cool against his skin. Even though they were tired and hungry they forged onward. He felt their quest was now at an end. On the way to their destination, Grace told Lazarus that after she saw him fall into the warehouse all the people who were turned to stone started to change. Except they didn't stay human, they morphed into hideous creatures. Luckily, Cindy and Matthew changed back to themselves.

Lazarus asked, "Cindy, Matthew, are you ok?"

The big man spoke first. "I don't remember anything after I was turned into a statue. I feel normal."

"So do I," Cindy said.

The winds buffeted them as they flew away from the city. They flew as fast as they could and suddenly they saw lights in the far distance. The lights were faint as if coming from a cave or somewhere underground.

Lazarus said, "We need to fly faster."

He sensed the closeness of their magic. He concentrated and let his magic overflow and envelop theirs. A commingling of all their powers made them stronger and more powerful.

Lazarus said, "Are you ready?"

They all nodded. He focused this newfound power and stretched it to encompass their flying. Suddenly, they shot forward faster than they had traveled before. Everything before them was a blur. Still, he knew they could go faster. He concentrated and focused his power with theirs. Another burst of speed shot them forward. They were quickly approaching their destination. He slowed their movement until they saw the tops of the hillside of Pyramid Peak.

He thought he would find a pyramid or even some type of natural formation but what he saw astounded him. It was a hilltop but it was open or merely burst out. It was as if a huge explosion from underground caused the earth to explode upwards creating a large crater, and inside this hole was the light. He also saw something else.

In front of the crater and in silhouette a mob of flying creatures waited. He stopped them. The full moon had enough light to discern the monsters. He saw large flying bats with big jutting teeth and below on the ground were thousands of Grog creatures of all types, from large canines wolves to gorilla-like monsters, and in the midst of them was a creature he knew was the leader. The other creature he saw back at the Phoenix was not the leader but maybe a doppelgänger. He was not sure if this was correct, but he said, "We need to get to this pyramid."

Matthew said, "We will get there. I will make a path."

"We will all do this together."

The leader of the Grogs walked out of the crowd and moved close to them. They didn't dare move closer. Lazarus and the others floated in the sky.

The creature from below said, "Alphas, you need to give me the keys and let me into the lost city. And I shall let you leave."

"No, and we don't have the keys."

"You have the keys. Give them to me."

Matthew said, "Come and try!"

Matthew started to move forward.

"Stop!" Lazarus said. He floated forward. "We will do this together."

Lazarus studied his friends. They all looked determined and ready. He turned to the large Grog on the ground.

"Come and get us!"

They moved as one toward the open crater. The flying bats attacked in a wave of fangs and long taloned wings.

"Wait until they get closer! Now!"

Lazarus held up his hands. Lighting sprouted from his fingertips. The noise of creatures screeching and the scent of burning flesh filled the air.

He said, "Matthew, I want you to shoot an arc of fire upwards and then downwards when I tell you."

He stopped and let loose another barrage of lightning at the creatures. The spell moved in wicked trajectories, hitting into the first line of creatures. The sounds of screams filled the air. The charred smell of roasting meat was in his nostrils and he almost gagged.

He said, "Cindy after Matthew is finishing with his spell, I want you and Grace to combine your spells to create a path into the caverns. Are you ready?"

They nodded.

"Follow me." He moved closer toward the entrance to the underground chamber. "Matthew, now!"

The big man moved next to him. A wave of blistering flame hit the large bats in an arc downwards hitting the Grogs on the ground. The flames dispersed leaving destruction and death in its wake. Cindy and Grace came forward. A large tsunami flew out of Cindy and hit the remaining large bats, creating a hole, and Grace placed her hands downwards and large fissures opened up in the ground, swallowing groups of Grogs.

"Follow me inside."

They darted into the cavern. He didn't realize there would be more Grogs waiting for them inside, standing along the structure. It was a pyramid embedded inside the chamber a hundred feet below, and the structure was glowing.

Lazarus said, "Cindy, clear the area."

They descended. Cindy unleashed a spell. A giant wave flowed down onto the glowing pyramid, washing away the Grogs waiting for them. After a few minutes, the structure was clear. They landed on the topmost area of the pyramid. His eyes were almost blinded by the light emitted from the very stones.

Grace said, "What do we do now?"

He was about to say something when he noticed all their stones glowed just as brightly as the pyramid. He said, "Take off your jewelry and give it to me."

Lazarus grabbed for his bracelet but noticed it was not on his wrist. Before them, floating in a bright brilliance, each of the items of jewelry spun next to each other.

Cindy said, "Look."

Each of the stones from the two rings, his bracelet and Cindy's necklace merged together and formed a round crystal. And behind the floating crystal was a doorway to another place, but it was dark and no light shone inside.

The growling noise of the Grogs was coming from the sides of the pyramid.

Cindy said, "We need to enter."

He hesitated for a second and then ran inside the portal.

Chapter 60

Instantly, everything around him turned gray, but not just dusky and dark but perpetually silvery and somber. The horizon was an inky blackness which spread out in front of him and he was not sure who was next to him or if the others had run inside. Yet he felt their presence and felt the others who were waiting for them. He turned but could not see his friends at first until they appeared out of the gray, almost touching him.

"Where are we?" Matthew asked.

"You tell me. You've been having visions for years."

"I have never seen this in my visions. This place is barren."

Stars appeared in the background, bright and fierce. Suddenly, all around them were bright pinpricks of lights. It was as if they walked into the universe and they were gods. A light formed before them and two figures started to appear. It was a man and a woman. Each wore a blue leather uniform with insignia on the top right. The insignia was not something he had seen before. Both of them were tall and skinny and had almond shaped eyes and milky white skin.

Lazarus said, "Elves."

The man said, "Yes, we are the elves. We don't have much time. Our ship was attacked and we were late to purge the magic from Earth. We are sorry that the world as you know it has been destroyed."

Matthew bowed to these newcomers. "We are here to fulfill our quest."

The elf continued, "My name is Captain Romo and this is my first mate, Lieutenant Lara. The Swarm is coming and you have to stop them."

"The swarm?" Lazarus asked.

"Yes, you have to construct the weapon and insert the key."

"How do we do that?"

"You already have the key. But you have to make the choice. We called you because you have the means to repel the Swarm. But you have to choose how your race will survive."

"I don't understand."

"You will also need help from the Professor from the Future."

Lazarus was stunned. There was too much information and it didn't make sense to him.

Captain Romo said, "You have to choose and it is up to you, The Leader, to come to the decision."

"What decision?"

"You have to understand. We, the elves, were selfish. We knew if the Swarm got to Gaia or Earth, we would all perish. So we hid Earth's magic with the aid of the Atlanteans. But they also had a weapon that could repel the Swarm for several hundred years."

Captain Romo looked at him and the others.

Lazarus said, "Tell me the choice."

"You have to decide if you want everything back to the way it was before - the world without magic and the earth dying by your pollution and destructive ways."

Lazarus didn't like the sound of that. He said, "Is the earth dying? How long do we have?"

"The earth will be dead in fifty earth years."

Grace said, "Can you help us? You must know a way to help."

"Yes, there is another way. You have to choose to have magic all over the world. It is the natural lifeblood of Earth or Gaia."

Lazarus said, "It cannot be that easy."

"No, it is not, Lazarus. If you choose to have the magic back to your land the Swarm will return. They are the eaters of magic and this is the reason we hid the power in the Bastions."

"So," Lazarus said, "both choices are bad. You said there is a way to repel the Swarm."

Lazarus noticed both of the elves had eyes that were dark but flecked with gold, making their pupils look luminous.

Captain Romo said, "Yes. You have to get to the first Bastion and use the key. Then you will be transported to the city of Atlantis. There is a weapon there which can only be used once and it will repel the Swarm."

"It will not destroy them. They are too powerful for that, but will give you, hopefully, enough time to gather your forces."

"How long do we have to choose?"

"Look beyond the stars and you shall see."

The elves disappeared and before them was a picture of earth and all the other planets in the solar system. He saw Mercury, Jupiter and all the other planets. A chorus of stars were all around them. He thought they were swimming in the night, drunk in the shining bright lights.

At the far reaches of their galaxy, Lazarus saw something. It was flashes of dark crimson light and it was coming toward them.

Captain Romo said, "The Swarm is not yet here, but they have their agents talking to a man named Royce. He is sent to stop you."

"Why?"

"We don't understand human emotions. But he will try to stop you and no matter which path you take nothing is guaranteed. We have given you all we can to aid you on your journey. But we have a slight problem."

Lazarus said, "Besides everything you told me. What is it?"

The elves appeared to them, floating along the stars, standing in front of them.

Captain Romo said, "When you make your decision and place the key in the main Bastion, you will not have all your powers."

"Great," Lazarus said.

"Please make your decision. You don't have much time."

"How long do we have?" he asked.

"A few minutes at best. Just call out to us when you have decided."

The two elves slowly disappeared into the grayness of the background.

Lazarus turned to his small group. He didn't like this. It was unfair to have him and his friends decide the fate of the world in just a few minutes. He suspected he knew what he wanted to do, but he needed to know how the others felt.

"Well, what do you think? I want to hear all your thoughts, because frankly I really don't know what to do."

Cindy said, "I think everybody here wants everything back the way it was, but if the earth will die in fifty years it's not worth that choice."

"But what if we find a way to fix the problem," Grace said. Her youthful face looked tense and hopeful.

Matthew said, "If everything is back to normal the people, I mean the leaders, will not believe you."

Grace said, "We will make them believe."

Lazarus said, "How will we do that? If we have everything back to the way it was there will be no magic in the world. The cops will probably throw us in jail and call for the insane asylum doctors to come and pick us up."

Matthew said, "I don't want to go back to the old world. I lived on the streets and starved most of the time."

Lazarus nodded. He recalled that when he first saw the big man coming to him he thought Matthew would beg him for food or money. He was living with the dregs of society.

"So, you vote to keep magic in the world and use the mysterious weapon to repel these invaders?"

"Yes," Matthew said. "Magic should be in this world. It is natural and should not be hidden away. We can do this together."

"Cindy, what do you say?"

"I don't know."

"We have to agree on something."

Grace said, "What do you think?"

"Before I tell you what I think, I want you to know that I loved my old life. It was comfortable and I had no problems. But living that way I would have died alone without doing anything significant in my life. Now I know why I was chosen to be your Leader. I was meant to do more, as well as all of you."

Grace said, "What are you saying?"

"We need to think about more than ourselves. We need to think about humanity and every animal on this earth."

Interlude 4: Journal Entry 1

I'm departing from my usual writings because this new development made me, unfortunately, a main proponent in this secret report. Of course, this portion of the report will never see the light of day if I don't succeed. I just need some record of my travel and hopefully success.

The day after my vision I held the glowing crystal in my hands and knew I needed to go to the secret archives and use this magical object to find the catalyst for the vast weapon. I was not sure why I had to find this object because the past is past and can never be experienced again, but I was wrong. The invaders, the Swarm, the Vvong, will be coming soon, maybe by the end of the lunar year and I need to tell my Government about these creatures. I will help the Alphas in the past to help the present and the future.

I had clearance to the ancient archives far away from my apartment on campus and I was not sure how I was supposed to get it and steal it away from the many guards stationed at that area. I had my morning breakfast as always and called the Dean of the Magical Studies in New California. I told him that I had an emergency and that I had to leave as soon as possible. The Dean was a young man and pure bureaucrat. He knew I had pull with the head of the magical order and let me have a short vacation without a clear explanation of my emergency.

"Yes," the Dean of the College said, "I have somebody who can take over your classes. You teach history."

"Yes, I do. Thanks, that would be great. I should be back in a few days..."

"Don't worry. I'll take care of everything. Take as long as you need."

"Thank you."

I closed the magical receiver. I wished they had wireless phones like they had back in the past. These magical receivers were clunky and I didn't like to use them. Of course, powerful magic-users could use a magical listening globe. I am not gifted in this area and had to use the old methods.

I walked out of my large apartment and went to my automobile. The car was not the newest model but ran on magical dilithium crystals. I drove out of my complex and noticed a black car start to follow me. I was getting paranoid, I told myself. Nobody could have known my vision last night and knew my destination today. I have been to the archives several times to do research and so it would be considered, in my opinion, routine to go there.

It would take me most of the day to reach the archives and I knew where the area was that this catalyst should be. The crystal was safely tucked away in my sack. I thought about the vision and realized the elves talked to me. Real elves. I was astounded at this development. Then I wondered why the elves didn't come to help them. It was a valid question and I would ask them when I contacted them again. I laughed. All this must be a dream and I was doing this because I was still in this vivid delusion.

I drove my car up the causeway and onto the long freeway. The secret archives were located due south from the college and in a remote area. Most of the region of California was under water and considered unlivable, mostly because of warring Grogs still living there. I had protection with me, but I knew with the treaty between the humans and Grogs I should be safe passing certain places.

I drove down the long, almost empty lane (most people transported with the aid of teleportation spells or flew with mages). I didn't want to rely on magic to move this special object. I was not sure exactly where this object was located but knew what it looked like. Also, I rarely use magic in my normal routines and hoped nobody was following me. I looked at the rear view mirror the fiftieth time and didn't see anybody. But I could feel somebody watching me. I felt it in my mind and bones.

There are no signs in the causeway and I wondered why, after the Great War, we didn't decide to create signals where we tarry. But in this world where magic holds sway people don't need signs to know where they are going. They use sigils and cast spells to move from one place to another.

I drove most of the day and only stopped at a small roadside café for an hour, to eat. I was in a hurry to get to the place. The waitress knew me from the time before I came here when I did research at the archives a few months ago.

There was a Grog teenager at the restaurant while I ate. He had his fur combed and fashioned in the style of the day. It was odd thinking these Grogs used to hate us so much. The teenager even flirted with the waitress. I shook my head. I held my notepad before me and wrote, brainstorming some type of plan.

After, I started driving again on the freeway. I noticed a black jeep far away in the thoroughfare. I thought I had seen this car before when I left my apartment back on campus, but I was not sure. I drove a few miles and took an off ramp down to a small city called Bakersfield. I stopped at a small market and waited. The black jeep didn't follow me. I was being paranoid again.

The next few hours I spent driving to the large underground area. The sand and dirt were all over the car while I drove into the complex. The building was a large black warehouse looking impressive and bleak at the same time. Several guards manned the front, but security was slack. Nobody wanted any of these old relics and books, just professors or students, and only a few people had security clearance.

The guard waved me through the security checkpoint. They knew me by sight. I parked my car by the front entrance and was surprised that another car was in the parking stall.

I walked toward the door and showed the guard at the small office my badge from the Office of Magical Studies.

"Ah, professor," the soldier said, "you are back for more research."

"Yes." I nodded and wanted to get away from the soldier's station.

"Aye, another visitor is with us today," the other soldier said from behind the desk. "It's getting crowded." The soldier chuckled.

"Ok, I have a lot of work to do. I should only take an hour."

"Ok, Professor."

I walked away from them and wondered if they noticed how nervous I was. Walking down the stairs to the first landing, I hoped the other person visiting here wouldn't want to talk. My forehead was moist with sweat and I dabbed it with my handkerchief. The temperature was climate controlled and I knew my trepidation and nervousness were getting the best of me. I almost stopped myself and walked away.

The next corridor was brightly lit and showed closed doors on both sides. My destination was a door at the end. The archives I was looking for were located in the inner bowels of this structure. Facing me was a large elevator. I pressed the button and heard the hum of the motors moving. The doors opened and a man was inside.

He said, "Hello, Professor Jacobs."

Chapter 61

"We are ready," Lazarus said into the dark gray void with the pinpricks of stars floating around. The two elves materialized before them.

Captain Romo said, "We don't have to know of your decision. We will know when you have turned the key."

"Tell me what to do," Lazarus said.

"We will transport you to the Bastions. When you get there you have to get to the Main Bastion and place the key in the lock. Now, this is important. If you turn the key toward the left the world will be without magic and the earth will die. If you turn the key toward the right, magic stays in the world and you will be transported to Atlantis."

"I understand. But we want to know why you are not here to help us."

"Ah, we are trapped somewhere. You cannot help us. It is a trap of our own doing. At another time, we will tell you of our problems, but for now, you have to leave." Captain Romo hesitated. "Are you ready?"

"Yes, we are."

"So be it."

The fuzzy grayness of the horizon and stars started to change into a dark underground chamber. Lazarus felt the key appear in his hands. It was warm to the touch. He held the key closer to him and placed it in his pocket. Before them, large cylindrical objects appeared. The chamber was well lit with bright lights situated on the ground and the ceiling.

Grace said, "Where is the main Bastion?"

Lazarus didn't see it, but felt it. He pointed toward a general area. Before he could say anything a noise shot through the area. The alarm was deafening to their ears.

Lazarus said, "Hurry."

They darted forward, moving very fast as if the wings of Mercury bore them aloft, heading to the far doors marked with green lighted signs stating exit. Lazarus heard the loud sounds of gunfire and bullets striking around them.

Matthew stood still and stretched his hand outward. Nothing came forth. No fire or magic. A soldier bore down on him. He raised his rifle and aimed it at Matthew. Lazarus shot forward and barreled into the startled soldier.

"Everybody, we don't have magic here. Come with me," he said.

A soldier came after them. They ran deeper into the huge chamber that seemed to go for miles underground. Lazarus was headed toward the Main Bastion but it was still too far away.

In frustration, Matthew ran and hit several of the soldiers trying to attack them. One soldier was moving behind Matthew, and Grace kicked at the soldier, knocking him unconscious.

Cindy said, "Watch out!"

They jumped to the side and the sounds of ricocheting bullets hitting metal filled their ears.

Lazarus said, "Hurry!"

Matthew grabbed a handgun and started to shoot back at the soldiers. He missed them but it sent them scurrying away. Matthew grabbed a large rifle.

"Don't kill them," Lazarus said.

The large man stayed behind, holding onto the gun and pointing it back and forth.

"Get to the lock. I'll hold them off."

Several soldiers attacked him. Matthew ran and cut them down. Blood and the scent of death peppered Lazarus's nose. He was getting sick.

Cindy said, "You heard him."

She flew and attacked several of the soldiers, smashing them against the large Bastions. The sound of cracking skulls and broken bones became like musical tones. Lazarus ran and found the keyhole. This Bastion was different. It was huge and it was square shaped with a small altar-like shape near the bottom. Matthew and his group of friends followed close behind. He reached the small altar and was about to place the crystal into the keyhole when he sensed something odd.

A soldier came toward them, but he was different. He seemed marked as if a light came forth from him. Two creatures appeared that were not elves but part of the swarm. Lazarus felt it in his magical senses. He felt the stirrings of magic. The soldier, before the two swarm creatures, changed into a large Grog wolf.

"Matthew! Get away!"

But he was too late. Matthew was speared by the Grog wolf's claws and disemboweled. Both of the girls screamed.

At that moment he became paralyzed. Matthew was dead and would not come back. He had to make a decision and he was not sure if it was the correct one. Cindy grabbed him.

She said, "Do it now. Or all of this was for nothing."

He grabbed the key and placed it in the hollow. The crystal slid inside with ease, but still Lazarus hesitated. The large wolf Grog stalked them, moving toward Grace. He almost called out to her, but Grace ran toward an adjacent corridor.

Lazarus took a deep breath and turned the key toward the right. A bright hot light blasted him and all the cylindrical Bastions lit up with a brilliance. He fell backwards and Cindy grabbed him. She looked at him with a questioning expression but he couldn't see her because the light was so brilliant.

He turned and saw the large Wolf Grog was gone.

"We need to go," Cindy said.

The ground of the chamber shook violently. They fell on top of each other. Suddenly, he heard the sweet twinkling of the music he heard before. Cindy heard it also and pointed. Next to the altar was a doorway toward a place with a light green horizon.

"Grace!" he said.

She was suddenly next to them. The ceiling debris started to rain over them. Grace held up her hand and created a magical barrier.

"Run!" Lazarus said.

They all pushed through the small gateway. Grace and Cindy fell on top of him and entangled themselves. Grace laughed as well as Cindy and himself. Their laughter was hysterical and was an emotional release after seeing their friend slaughtered in front of them.

"I can't believe what happened," Grace said. Her eyes studied the buildings.

Cindy said, "I know. Poor Matthew. I hope he didn't suffer much."

"Yes. If I knew by opening the Bastions we would get back our magical powers I would have done it sooner."

Grace said, "It's not your fault. We were not prepared for the attack."

Cindy brushed the dirt and grass from her clothes and looked around.

"Lazarus, you chose to have magic in the world," she said. She said this so softly he almost didn't hear her.

"Yes. It is the best choice."

Cindy turned to him with tears in her eyes. "I wish Matthew could have lived to see this."

Chapter 62

Lazarus walked forward and looked around the landscape. They were not in New Mexico or anywhere he could recognize. In front of them was a jungle peppered with ancient buildings built with stones. The architecture was neither Mayan nor Aztec, but a combination of all styles from Greek, Roman, Byzantine to Egyptian. The buildings were all styles and no styles. He recalled this from his college courses in art history, a subject he particularly liked. It came to him as if his memory was enhanced by the magic of the ancient city before them.

Everything in the landscape and structures had an air of abandonment as if eons had passed and nobody dwelt or visited here. He looked up at the sky but there was no horizon, only a light green glowing mass which stretched beyond his sight.

Grace said, "Where are we?"

He knew. "This is the lost city of Atlantis."

Cindy stood close to him and nodded. "Yes, I can feel it."

She pointed toward a large building that rose higher than the others. It was a pyramid, almost looking both Egyptian and Mayan at the same time. On the top of this structure was a shimmer of light barely noticeable from their perspective. It was like a tendril of smoke escaping upwards. But as he looked up toward the pyramid he knew that this was their destination. It just felt right, like the magic he possessed and the power of this city. He was about to step forward when a noise alerted him.

Grace said, "We have company."

The large wolf Grog walked out of the cover of the jungle from their right while other Grogs came out of the buildings from around them. He noticed the assortment of creatures, some walking and some staggering forth in odd gaits.

Lazarus said, "You shouldn't be here. You know you don't have to do this. Even though you killed my friend, you can redeem yourself and let us through."

Grace grabbed his arm and Cindy gave him a disapproving look. He didn't turn to them. Discussion time was over and the Swarm was getting closer. His magical senses felt the delegation of alien forces gathering closer and moving at a fast speed.

The tall Grog said, "You don't know the power of the Swarm. When you opened the portal, they help transport us here." The Grog grinned. Lazarus saw the rows of razor sharp teeth in the Grog's snout. "You are like those people who think they are above everything."

Lazarus shook his head. He was not sure what this creature was talking about. "We are just like you. We are both human." He said this without even thinking about it, but the large wolf Grog growled.

"I am not human anymore. You did this to us."

"No, I didn't do this. It was the Swarm. They want to take over our world and magic. They want us all dead."

"That is not true. I have talked to them. They say you want to be better than us. You are human."

The wolf Grog spoke incomprehensible words. He snarled and flexed his large muscles.

Lazarus said turned to Cindy and Grace, "Get ready. We will fly."

Lazarus bent lower and was ready to jump to the horizon when a noise like thunder rocked the area and a lightning bolt shot at them. Lazarus held up his hands and erected a barrier, but it was not strong enough. They were propelled backwards and hit a tree. He shielded some of the blast, but he had the wind knocked out of him. They lay on the ground.

Royce smiled. "The swarm upgraded my powers." The large Grog smiled, showing his wicked teeth. "Get them!"

The creatures rushed them. Lazarus felt his power curl around him. Focusing, he stood and held his arms up. Fire erupted, hitting the foremost Grog creatures. The smell of charred flesh and fur hit them.

"Hurry!"

Lazarus moved upwards. Grace and Cindy followed. Flying up, he saw several of the Grogs taking flight and moving toward them. *Oh no,* he thought. *The creatures can fly.*

He said, "Keep moving to the pyramid. And wait for the others."

Cindy looked at him with an uncomprehending look. Lazarus turned toward the Grogs.

"No!" she said.

He said, "Keep going."

He wanted to shake her but the Grogs were gaining speed. "We don't have enough time. You can feel it. The Swarm is getting closer."

He focused his magic and shot a lightning bolt at the enemies. The creatures looked like giant bats. Lazarus struck some of the bats but missed most of them. Some of the pack of creatures followed Cindy and Grace. He suddenly took off and aimed a blast of flames. The spell engulfed the bats and the dead bodies fell to the ground.

He turned but a sharp pain hit him on the back and then a searing burn on his side. A Grog bat was next to him clawing and beating him with its long claws. Lazarus opened his palm and acid flowed out. A sizzling sound came, followed by the stench of burnt flesh and the creature fell, flashing past him. Another creature raked its claws against his legs and Lazarus erected a magical barrier. He floated away, staring at the Grog bats with the nimbus of his field surrounding him, but one of the creatures burst through his magical field.

He flew backwards holding his arms in defense. Fire erupted and he killed the creature. He was shocked the creature could pass through his barrier, but before he could think about this new development more bats attacked. A beast struck him on the back and then on the front. He tried to fly up but he was swamped with pain. He held up his hands and lightning shot out, hitting the creatures.

Lazarus was free. He flew away. The creatures followed him instead of going after Cindy and Grace. Then he saw the spell before he moved forward. It was a fireball and it came from the ground. The heat singed his pants. When he stopped flying, the Grog bats struck him in several places. He flew in a circle trying to understand if he was upright or upside down. He was not sure. Then something hit him hard on his back of his head.

Before he knew it, he was falling. The rush of air flowed over his body, but he couldn't move or think. It was as if his mind and body were not connected. But an animal instinct told him to create a spell, a magical barrier. Instantly, the nimbus of magic surrounded him and he plunged to the ground, hitting the tall trees first and then a stone building. He was protected by his magic, but the breath was knocked out of him as he bounced from each building and foliage.

Interlude 5: Journal entry 2

I thought it was odd how the events unfolded before me. Sitting in my office, recollecting the events I didn't think the struggle I became embroiled in was actually true. I thought I was in a dream, but in reality, I could have died. Yet, the events were unclear as if my actions were not mine but somebody else altogether. So when I ventured into the elevator and saw the man standing before me I naturally propelled myself backwards trying to get away, because the man was not human. I moved into the corridor.

"Hello, Professor Jacobs," the creature snarled.

I noticed it was not a Grog or anything I could recognize from my research, but something else entirely. The face was at first human and then morphed into large multifaceted eyes and large mandibles. It, as I call it, looked like a large locust creature but with harsher features.

I didn't have any weapons and stood frozen in fear for several seconds.

The creature said, "Why should we fear you? You don't have any armor or claws. This will be easy."

"You are part of the Swarm."

The creature laughed a throaty sound. "Yes. We will take your planet and your magic. There will be nothing left but the ashes of your dead."

"Why do you do this?"

I groped for anything and tried to recall any spell or incantation to fend off this beast, but to no avail. My earlier magical training was in medical healing and I didn't have any offensive power. My terror was strong.

"Why?" the creature screamed. "Your kind are always looking for answers where there are none. There are no answers in the darkness of space, only resources and magic. We are the nothingness."

From behind the creature, I saw a large stinger. It rose up ready to strike at me. I tried to get to the guards posted at the front. I knew the door to the guard station was securely locked and soundproofed from the outside. But I ran all the same.

Something struck me hard on my leg and I fell to the ground, banging my knee and my hands. I turned to see the monstrous creature tower above me, its large stinger poised to strike at me. I didn't have anything on me to protect myself. I raised my hand up knowing at any time death was awaiting me.

The creature smiled at me with a mouth filled with large sharp teeth and then suddenly moved backwards, making a gurgling noise. The corridor started to smell of ash and something alien. A hole appeared on the creature's chest and it fell to the floor. I was stunned and stared at the smoking carcass.

"Hello, Professor. Sorry, we're late."

Looking behind the smoking insect, I saw a group of people. It was a trio of two elves and a shorter fellow, a dwarf. I was confounded and confused. I had never seen an elf or even a dwarf, but I knew one when I saw one.

"Professor," the dwarf said. "We have to hurry. Only you have access to open the relic and you don't have much time."

I heard a rasping noise coming from the door at the far end of the corridor. A soldier came into the large passageway. I didn't know what to do and was thinking of some type of plausible excuse but came up with nothing. Suddenly, the elves, dwarf and the stinking carcass vanished. My eyes must have looked surprised.

"Hello, Professor, sorry to startle you. We thought we heard something." The soldier's face changed to show repugnance. "Wow, what is that smell?"

"I don't know. Maybe a rat died in here."

"Yes," the soldier said. "We will check on it."

"Can you wait until I finish? I won't be long."

"Sure, Professor."

The soldier closed the door. The elves, the dwarf and the dead creature appeared again. I was shocked. None of the mages at the University had such power.

The dwarf said, "We will dispose of the body but you do not have much time. Della will escort you. Once you have the catalyst, she will transport you back."

I wanted to ask more questions. I wanted to know all the hidden mysteries but I complied. I walked to the elevator with Della walking next to me. I pressed a button and the elevator started moving down. Being this close to an actual elf thrilled me. She was tall and slim in build. She wore a dark blue leather uniform with an insignia on the right front of her chest. I couldn't recognize it.

"Professor, I know you have many questions, but you have to focus. Only you can unlock the catalyst. You have the necessary codes?"

I nodded. "It's in my pocket and I memorized it."

"Good, I'll be close by."

This facility was not enhanced like the other government buildings with magical holo cameras and force fields. Nobody came here. But they had to be careful, magic or no magic. A powerful mage or sensitive, if there was one here, would have sensed the elves' or dwarf's magic.

I said, "Are you all magic users?"

"Yes, but the dwarf is a cleric."

I did not understand the reference. The elevator stopped at the bottom floor and the doors opened. An acrid scent permeated the long corridor.

"Wait," Della said. The elf walked forward. A scratching came from the far corner and several large insectile creatures attacked Della. The elf stood there not moving and then she held up her hand. I sensed magic. I am a sensitive but with mild powers and I felt her magic gathering inside her. A bright light appeared in her hands. It was sabers made of pure magic. She moved so fast I only saw a blur when she attacked. The creatures all fell with eviscerated stomachs, guts and intestines splattered along the walls and ground. The doors of the elevator started to close. I pushed through and entered the massacre.

The elf waited for me at the other end. The magical sabers were gone. She nodded for me to move to her and I gingerly walked around the guts and gore, shaking my head.

I reached the far corner and opened the adjoining door. The next room was a vast chamber with many shelves where the device with the catalyst was located. Each shelf contained an item or book. I moved through the labyrinth, picking my way along a trail I have walked several times before.

I came to the area where I knew the suitcase would be. Looking behind me, I saw Della following, moving silently in the bright lights of the archives. Her eyes scanned the area. I turned back to the shelf and saw it was empty. I froze.

"It should be here."

"It's fine," the elf said. She waved her hand and the leather suitcase appeared

Della said, "A day before we scouted the area and placed an invisible barrier over it."

"Why didn't you take the case?"

"Only a human with the specific code can do that."

I nodded. This suitcase was not a mere container. It was called a nuclear football. All the leaders of the free world had such device close to them. It usually had a device that can authorize the leader to attack with nuclear weapons. But I knew this satchel was not the case for nuclear attack but for something special. It was made out of black leather with a strap for a man to be strapped in.

I had to be very careful. I was not sure if the device would still work. I grabbed the top hand strap and moved it toward me. Unzipping the top, I heard the noise of something entering the room.

Della said, "Take this."

She gave me a round white crystal. "When you get the catalyst, touch the top of the stone then you will be transported back. Here, take it."

I grabbed it and before I could speak she left. I placed the stone in my pants pocket. The bag was heavier than I thought and it flopped to the side with a heavy thump. I jumped back when I heard a loud scream. It sounded inhuman and I looked up to see Della facing a large beast, bigger than the other Swarm creatures I saw before. I wanted to help her but I needed to get the catalyst to the Alphas.

Grabbing the top of the bag, I unclasped it and peered inside. I could not see anything at first. Then a box inside started to glow a bright green from a square display panel. On the display was several numbers. I placed my hands around the box and took it out. The sickening sound of a body being cut in pieces sounded very loud in my ears. I didn't look up. I started to enter the numbers. I had to make sure the code was entered in the correct order and before the time limit of three minutes or I would have to start again and if I didn't enter it correctly the third time the box would explode.

I punched in the code and then something hit me, sending me sprawling. I could hear a clicking and growling noise. I saw a small insect creature looking at me. Its mouth had hundreds of razor sharp teeth. It growled again at me.

The creature was about to attack me when its face exploded in a spray of gore and blood. I shielded my face as I was showered with gore.

"Sorry," Della said. She stood close to me, holding a weapon in her hand.

"Hurry, before they come back."

I tried to brush some of the blood and gore off my face as I stood, seeing the box with an opened lid. The device inside was made of round clear glass. It rolled out on the shelf and then stopped.

"What is that thing?" I asked.

The glass started to change. In the center of orbs pinpricks of light appeared like a small star. It started to glow so brightly it hurt my eyes.

"Are you ready, professor?"

"What?"

"Are you ready?"

"Yes."

The orb spoke to me. I said, "Della, do you hear that?"

"Yes," the elf said. "Get the crystal and leave."

Another creature came slithering into the room.

"Go," the elf urged. She ran toward the creature.

I took the crystal out of my pocket. I was not a mage and didn't know what to do. Instantly, the crystal grew warm in my hands. And then the world spun and I fell down a chasm and found myself standing on a pyramid with the biggest Grog wolf I have ever seen. Its glowing eyes bore into mine.

Chapter 63

Lazarus stared upwards. His back and sides burned with pain. Several Grog wolves ran toward him. He quickly stood and held his hands up. A wall of fire erupted, stopping the creatures. He needed to get to the top of the pyramid. Lazarus hoped Cindy and Grace had made it. Something struck him on his side, sending him sprawling forward and smacking on the ground. A bat screeched at him.

Lazarus pointed and a lightning bolt blew apart the creature. His fire wall was ebbing out. He jumped up and flew into the sky. When he moved, a sharp pain lanced his ribs. He saw large claw marks ripping into his shirt and penetrating into his skin. A flock of Grog creatures that looked more like large monkeys with wings attacked him. He shot several spells in succession, destroying a dozen of the creatures.

He flew toward the pyramid and created a tornado. It engulfed the remaining creatures blocking his way, but it greatly weakened him. He almost fell to the ground, but he pushed forward, flying toward a bright light.

He heard something in his head. It was Cindy. "Be careful. We are here, but Royce is here waiting for us."

He shot upwards toward the structure. He could see Cindy standing with the large Grog named Royce. And there was another person there. A man who was covered in blood and holding a bright object. And around them were groups of wolf Grogs. They were all looking at him. He felt cold fear moved through his body. He didn't know what to do. Then he saw Grace lying next to them, not moving.

A sharp pain of sadness struck him so hard he felt it was physical and he was struck a blow to his midsection. He moved forward and landed on the top of the pyramid. The top was a broad surface of stone with tufts of grass growing along the ground.

Lazarus moved a few yards from Royce. Cindy and the other man, who was holding the glowing object in his hands, were surrounded by several beasts. He waited, watching Royce and Cindy. The stranger next to Cindy had a very wide-eyed surprised look on his face. He still held the object in his hands. It glowed with an odd rhythmic fashion like a beating heart.

Lazarus said, "What do you want?"

Royce started to cough, but Lazarus realized it wasn't coughing he heard but laughter. It sounded odd coming from a large wolf Grog.

"I want you to apologize for what you did to me for starters," Royce said.

Lazarus stared at Cindy. Her eyes were not terrified. She looked at him as if he was her savior. He didn't feel like a savior.

"I have nothing to apologize for. We didn't do anything to you."

"You did this to me. Look at me. I am not a human. I am a beast."

"We didn't make you change into this. It was the Swarm. They made you into this creature."

"No, if you hadn't opened the Bastions then I wouldn't be like this. It was you and your friends who did this. All I want is for everything to go back to normal."

Lazarus said, "You don't understand. The Swarm is not your friends. They don't care about you."

"You're wrong."

The ground started to shake. Lazarus heard a large noise like the sound of rushing water and everybody looked around. He saw sunlight coming from the top and the green sky being replaced by blue. It was like watching Moses part the Red Sea.

Cindy yelled. The man holding the strange globe moved forward and threw the glowing object upwards into the maelstrom of the churning waters. Royce looked at the shiny object floating upwards.

Lazarus yelled, "Duck."

Cindy and the stranger fell to the ground. Lazarus pointed his hand at Royce and the Grog creatures. Lightning sprouted from his fingertips, hitting the creatures around them. He missed Royce. The giant Grog jumped backwards and fell off the top of the Pyramid.

Cindy and the man stood and ran toward him. She gave him a hug.

Lazarus said, "Is Grace ok?"

"I don't know. She's lost a lot of blood."

He turned toward the stranger. "My name is Lazarus." He shook his hand.

"I'm Professor Jacobs."

The ground shook again and he felt them rising upwards into the churning waters. A wind started to flow around them.

He said, "So, Professor Jacobs, how do we use this weapon?"

The stranger looked at them with a quizzical stare. "I thought you knew. I don't know. I only brought the catalyst."

Lazarus nodded. He focused and used his magic to bring the glowing round object closer to him.

It said, "Hello, Lazarus."

He jumped back. "Did you hear that?"

Cindy said, "Yes, but you have to hurry. They're coming back."

She was peering down. He knew the Grogs were climbing back up the sides of the pyramid. He didn't kill all of them.

The noise and the wind got louder and stronger.

He said, "Professor, are you a magic-user or have any weapons?"

"No, I have limited magic."

Lazarus said, "You should go back from where you came."

"I'll stay and help you with the weapon."

The glowing round object floated lower and moved next to the Professor. The ground shook and he stumbled to the ground.

"Please help us," Lazarus implored to the glowing object.

"It is simple. You have to use your magic and you will know."

Cindy held up her hands and sent a barrage of razor sharp icicles at the monsters below. Her eyes were fixed on them. The Professor joined her, picking up stones from the ground, throwing the rocks down. Lazarus shook his head.

He scanned the round glowing object. It looked like it was made of glass and the inside held a pinprick of light. He held his hand toward it and the object instantly flew to him. Around them, the sea churned and flowed against a magical barrier. He recalled a time when he went to an amusement park and saw the water part before them and they drove safely through. He was barely a kid and he was amazed, but only the first time. He saw the trick for what it was. It was only an illusion. Yet, this magic was no illusion. They were standing on top of an ancient city moving up to the surface. The ocean had parted for them and it was real magic.

In the sky it was night. The stars glowed like the object in his hands. Then he saw them. He knew that what he saw in the sky was the Swarm.

"Lazarus, hurry. I can't keep them from coming," Cindy screamed. The giant Grog, Royce, towered over her and pushed her to the ground.

Royce said, "You're too late. They are here."

The sky was filled with large ships the size of small cities. Their hulls glowed with angry red lights. The lights detached themselves and flew straight at them.

"No!" Lazarus said.

Chapter 64

Professor Jacobs was suddenly next to him. The Professor grabbed the glowing ball and broke it on the ground and as it broke the bright light inside the ball exploded upwards. Lazarus's body jerked a few times and his hands moved up. Without his knowing his magic combined with the bright light coming from the broken globe.

Lazarus knew the light was a seed, the seed of a star and it needed his power to generate the magic. He focused his whole will onto the seed, seeing Royce rushing toward him. The Professor moved in front of the large Grog and tried to stop him but was knocked away like a leaf blown in a wind. Lazarus couldn't focus on both the large Grog and on the magical seed.

The Grog ran toward him with his claws and razor sharp teeth extended. Lazarus couldn't protect himself. He felt his body swept up in the power of the magic of the star. It pummeled him and took his power. He was being drained of his life force. Sensing he was going to die, Lazarus redoubled his efforts into the magic of the seed. His body shook. He felt he was going to break apart. He suddenly flew up before Royce reached him, toward the bright star seed now floating several feet above him. He was in the middle of the turbulent waters and then he was in the sky floating up to the enemy ships. Royce was still standing on the top of the pyramid screaming unintelligible words at him.

"I am not the catalyst," the star said in his mind. "You are the catalyst."

Red lights flew around him. It was the Swarm attacking him. Insectile creatures the size of large trucks flew around his position and tried to attack him with their giant claws. He stopped shaking. He felt more powerful than he had ever felt before. Lazarus held up his hands and killed scores of insectile creatures.

"You need to repulse the creatures."

Lazarus heard the star seed speak to him.

"What do you want me to do?"

"You know. These creatures need to be sent far away. But be warned, this power can destroy you."

Lazarus knew what he had to do. It was simple but with his new found power could he conjure such a spell.

"I will do it. I am the catalyst. I will take the change."

The Swarm creatures flew back to their ships. He sensed they were gathering their combined power to attack him. The seed star flew and entered his body. Pain course through him. It felt like thousands of needles hit every inch of his skin.

"Summon the vortex."

Lazarus focused on the sky. A swirling black hole appeared. Its forces pulled the Swarm into its maw and all the ships were gone. It happened so suddenly that he didn't notice the earth starting to move toward the back hole. The black hole beckoned the earth away from its orbit. He had to do something, but he was exhausted and could not cast another spell.

The power of the star embedded in his body was almost gone. Lazarus had to do something. He screamed an inhuman shout into the heavens and focused all his will and strength on closing the vortex. Nothing happened.

He had an idea. Lazarus concentrated his remaining power and cast the star out of his body. The pain was unimaginable. The light shot out of him. It floated a few feet away. Lazarus added all his magic into the star seed and then propelled it toward the swirling vortex.

Once the star seed struck the black hole his magic and the star seed exploded. He screamed another inhuman cry. And he fell.

CINDY WATCHED FROM the top of the pyramid. Her body hurt all over. The large Grog had shredded parts of her arm and shoulder. When she saw Royce attack the Professor and then attack Lazarus, she was powerless to stop him. She was being attacked by several creatures. And then Lazarus flew into the sky and created the vortex that swallowed the Swarm ships. When the Swarm was gone, Royce and his group fled.

She would have yelled in triumph but she saw Lazarus falling. She conjured a large falcon and the bird snatched Lazarus before he fell to the ground.

"Nice catch."

She forgot. The Professor was still here on the top of the pyramid. He was on the ground close to Grace.

She looked up and saw the black hole was gone from the sky. This island they all stood on was now on the surface. The morning sun shone above.

"Professor, are you ok?"

"Yes. But I'm not sure about your friend."

Her large falcon flew to her position and deposited Lazarus on the ground before her. He was breathing. She ran to him and knelt.

"Lazarus, do you hear me?"

He nodded and opened his eyes. "Did we do it?"

"Yes. You did."

Lazarus stared at the orb of the sun on the horizon and heard somebody moan. It was Grace. They moved close to her. Lazarus's body was so weak he stayed where he was and watched from afar. Grace turned to Cindy.

"What happened?" Grace said.

Cindy said, "We defeated the Grogs and the Swarm. We will tell you all later."

Lazarus smiled, feeling the warmth of the new day's sun on his body.

Interlude 6: Journal Entry 3

I cannot believe the events which transpired and that I, Professor Jacobs, was instrumental in fighting the Grogs. It all seemed like a dream and yet I was cognizant of my actions. It's difficult to put into words as I watched the miracle. The Alphas thwarted an imminent attack with my help by creating a black hole and sucking the enemies into it. The magnitude of arcane power used to create such a vortex was immense. I felt the growing power coming from the Alpha named Lazarus who created this spell.

After the Swarm was gone the Grogs fled the scene and disappeared away from the island where we stood. This ancient city was a wonder to believe and I will try to find it when I get back home to my own time.

I stayed with the Alphas for several hours. They were in bad shape and I, since I was skilled in magical healing, helped bandage them and heal some of their light wounds. They talked about the day when the Bastions were opened and how in the preceding days before this they all met to decide the fate of the world.

When the shadows started to lengthen and I realized Lazarus, Cindy and Grace were going to be fine, I took out the white crystal. I waved them a goodbye and wished I would see them again. I held it close to me and activated the stone. I was instantly transported back to the secret archives. The first thing I noticed was that the shelves and archives were clean. I almost thought the battle with the elf and the Swarm were just a mirage and that it never happened but I knew that was not the case.

"It did happen, Professor."

I saw the elf, Della, come out from behind a group of shelves and items.

"We cleaned everything. You shall not have any problems leaving. But we need you to understand. The Swarm is coming back and you will need help. We will be coming. You have to talk to your leaders."

"Can you help me now? My leaders will not listen to me alone."

"No, we are late. We have been waiting for you for several days."

"I don't know if I can talk my leaders into believing me."

"You will find a way."

I left the secret archives without any problems. While I was driving back to the University, I pondered how I was supposed to get anybody to listen. I didn't get any ideas but I will. I touched the time travel stone and realized I had something.

Chapter 65

The days had been growing longer and the shadows came later. Lazarus didn't know if it was summer or fall. This island had an abundance of wildlife and food. He wondered where the Grogs went to but knew his answer. In the far horizon, he had seen several times since they stayed here the outline of a land mass. It was far away but not too far away for a creature to swim toward and stay. He had so many unanswered questions and didn't know their future.

Cindy had joked that they could stay here on this island forever. He would like to, but he knew he had to find other survivors and help rebuild the fragile society. Grace wanted to go back home and find Lawrence, the small boy who befriended her back at Las Vegas.

They gathered wood for their breakfast. The morning dew peppered all the plants. Cindy sat next to him, close to the roaring fire. Grace was staring into the ocean. He thought that tonight he would build pyres for his fallen friend, Matthew.

They watched as the golden orb of the sun rose on the horizon.

ROYCE SAT, WITH HIS minions of Grogs next to him. They fled when they saw the Swarm, their saviors, disappear into the black hole. He decided they could fight again another day. They swam to the land far away from the island. He didn't want to see that pyramid and island again. He saw the Alpha's fire from where he sat. The Alphas were too powerful right now. He would find more of his kind and have his revenge.

Get E. M. Aguilar's Free Book

Building a relationship with my readers is the best thing about being a writer. You will get free books and details on new releases, if you sign up to my mailing list. Also you will get my debut novel, The Darkness Within, for signing up.

You can get the novel by clicking the link below:

http://eepurl.com/b-2Qov

About the Author

ERIC AGUILAR (1970 to present) was born in Los Angeles, California. He started writing when he was in high school. He received a Fine Arts Degree in painting and drawing from CSULB and attended Otis Art Institute. Eric is a Filipino American writer of Fantasy, Horror, and Sci-fi. He lives in southern California.

If you like Eric's writings, check out his website at http://cyrusman183.wix.com/eric-aguilar-1

You can connect with Eric on Facebook at https://www.facebook.com/emaguilar283

Don't miss out!

Click the button below and you can sign up to receive emails whenever E. M. Aguilar publishes a new book. There's no charge and no obligation.

https://books2read.com/r/B-A-ONGB-MLKS

BOOKS 2 READ

Connecting independent readers to independent writers.

Printed in Great Britain
by Amazon

60171563R00173